FINAL SHOWDOWN

A Crime Action Thriller

Robert Goluba

ISBN (Paperback): 979-8-9906197-3-9

ISBN (eBook): 979-8-9906197-2-2

Edited by Lisa Davis and Red Adage Editing

Cover Design by Miblart

CONTENTS

Chapter 1

Jason Mulder shifted his weight on the stoop of a two-story brownstone, his eyes locked on the man striding toward him. The upscale Washington, DC, neighborhood pressed in around him with rows of tightly packed homes with ornate trim, sloped roofs, and bay windows that glinted in the weak winter sun. Dormant golden grass blanketed the small front yard, with a narrow brick path slicing through it toward the steps. Behind him, the muffled roar of traffic echoed off the canyon of brick and glass, but Mulder tuned it out. His focus was on the approaching figure.

Clad in a long black wool trench coat, Senator Conrad stepped onto the sidewalk and gave Jason an acknowledging smile. As a member of the US Senator's private security detail, Jason was responsible for ensuring his principal's safety until he was secure inside his home. His eyes scanned the street and sidewalk, alert to potential threats that could harm the senator. An eruption of barking disrupted the peaceful street and caught Jason's attention. He turned to see a rambunctious Jack Russell terrier barking excessively at a disinterested rottweiler three houses down the block. It took the owners several attempts to separate the canines and continue their walks.

When Jason turned back to welcome the senator home, motion in his peripheral vision swung his attention to the three men who appeared from nowhere and surrounded Senator Conrad. Before he could react and unholster his weapon, they whisked the senator down the stairs and forced him into a waiting black van parked across the sidewalk. Jason leaped over piles of snow and rushed into the street after the windowless van speeding away. He pursued on foot for half a block until the vehicle turned left and drove out of view at the next corner.

"I have a 134! I repeat, I have a 134. Duke was just forced into a van!" Jason shouted into his comms microphone.

"Copy. Do you have a description of the abductors and vehicle?" Clay Landry, Jason's supervisor, asked over the radio.

Jason tried to replay the scene in his head.

Was it three men, or could it have been four? Was it a navy-blue van, or was it black?

"Um, three men in, ah... a black van took him."

"What were they wearing?"

"They were all dressed in black. I think they may have had masks on."

"Make and model of the van? License plate number?" Jason heard the irritation in Clay's voice with each question.

Jason wasn't sure. He remembered the high-pitched squeal of the tires as the van turned the corner, the shadows of the barren trees dancing across the roof, and the smoky gray exhaust billowing out into the frigid late afternoon air. Nothing that could help Conrad's PSD team or law enforcement find the principal he swore to protect.

"I... I didn't get either one."

"Dammit!"

"Okay, hold on, guys. Let's take a minute." A new voice had entered the conversation.

A man exited a parallel-parked vehicle two houses down and approached Jason in his police uniform. It was Sergeant Ashby from the Capitol Police Crisis Negotiation Unit.

"Hey, Mulder, get off the street and join me on the sidewalk," Ashby said in a Philly accent.

Jason ambled to the sidewalk then shook his head as he stood before the Sergeant, streaks of gray mingling with his black hair.

"I told you the training, especially this exercise, would be intense. Did you feel your body tense up when you saw the officer playing the senator get shoved into the van?"

Jason nodded.

"Remember what we talked about in the classroom yesterday? Your first priority is to stop the abduction, but that's rarely possible, so what's your second priority?"

"Be a good witness," Jason replied confidently.

"Exactly! Take in all the important details that will help the rest of the team capture the bad guys and save the principal. Pay attention to the people and what they're wearing, how they move, and especially how they talk if you're fortunate enough to hear a conversation. You must get the make, model, color, and approximate year if a vehicle is involved. Once you relay all that information moments after an abduction, the odds of a happy ending increase dramatically. Make sense?"

"It does, but I should have stopped them before they got the senator in the van," Jason chirped.

"Did you just hear a word I said?" Ashby asked.

The muscles in Jason's jaw clenched and relaxed as he glared at the Capitol Police officer.

"The chances of you stopping an abduction in progress are slim to none, and slim just left town, so get those thoughts out of your head," Ashby barked. "Your goal is to bring the senator home safely and catch the bad guys, right?"

"Yeah."

"Do what I tell you, and heaven forbid Senator Conrad ever gets abducted, your story can have a happy ending."

His bruised ego still stung, but Jason sighed and pushed aside his emotions. "Okay. I get it. Since I didn't get a good description, what's next?"

"We move to the investigation phase and gather as much evidence as possible while it's still fresh in the mind of any witnesses. In a real kidnapping, after we get a call, a couple of officers immediately canvass the area of the abduction and even the last two or three places he or she visited for potential witnesses. Other members of the Crisis Negotiation Team conduct forensic analysis, identify surveillance footage, and scan for any physical evidence. All of that will be processed at our command center one block north of the Hart Senate Office Building. Let's head over and link up with the rest of your team."

Jason followed Sergeant Ashby into the seven-story sandy-brown brick-and-mortar headquarters of the Capitol Police. They passed the bustling front counter and the rows of desks buzzing with activity. Ruben "Zee" Zambrano was the first one to greet Jason when he entered the conference room.

"That will teach you to sleep on the job," Zee said with a snort.

Jason shot him a glare with the force of a slap, causing Zee to recoil. "See how well you do when it's your turn."

Clay was more subtle. He stood beside him and whispered, "What the hell happened back there?"

"I don't know. I watched the fake Senator Conrad walk toward the steps, and before he got there, the abduction team snatched him. Watching it unfold was like a bad dream where I couldn't move or yell."

"I would have thought your reaction speed would be faster with all your pararescue, PSD, and DEA training."

Jason was not thrilled with his friend and supervisor's rebuke but was also surprised that he was slow to react to an obvious threat. "Me too."

"Everyone take a seat around the table," Ashby commanded.

"We're moving to the second phase of the exercise—evidence analysis."

The four members of Senator Conrad's PSD team watched as men and women from the Capitol Police Investigations Division and Intelligence Division arrived and presented their evidence and insights. They were all participating in the mock kidnapping drill that the Capitol Police offered to every PSD team on Capitol Hill. The exercise was authentic, giving all involved parties much-needed practice if the unimaginable scenario of an abduction of a member of Congress occurred. The last presenter transitioned the training from an investigation to a recovery.

"We have security footage of a black van parked near the Union Market in the old warehouse district with four men dragging someone in a hood through the back door of a building. Our records show it's an abandoned textile manufacturer, so that's our target for a hostage recovery."

Although it was just a simulation, moving to the next phase evoked a visceral reaction in Jason. His knees bounced restlessly under the table, and his chest tightened with anticipation. This was the moment he'd been waiting for since the van sped away with the acting senator in it.

Ashby stood at the end of the table. "Normally, we'd contact the FBI Hostage Response Team to assist with the recovery. They don't participate with us in these drills, but we have several volunteers from our Containment and Emergency Response Team who have experience with HRT to give you guys the full hostage-recovery experience. Suit up, and let's go."

As Ashby instructed, Clay parked the GMC Yukon two blocks from the target. Jason, Clay, Zee, and the fourth member of the PSD team, Ian "Central" Park, met the Capitol Police CERT team at the rally point.

"Have your men join each of our squads—two on Alpha and two with the Bravo team," the CERT leader told Clay.

Conrad's PSD team split up, and Jason joined Zee on the Bravo team. They all donned black tactical uniforms, camouflaging the entire squad under the cover of darkness while they skirted the right side of the alley. Bravo waited for Alpha to catch up on the opposite side of the alley when the rear door of the former textile warehouse came into view under the flickering streetlight.

Alpha leader held up five fingers, and the CERT team raised their unloaded rifles to the ready. Once his hand chopped toward the target, both teams moved through the door with surgical precision and stormed the interior with guns drawn. Jason followed the CERT member ahead of him and instinctively scanned the area for the abducted principal. His desire to find the man posing as Senator Conrad was as strong as if he were actually kidnapped.

The aggressive shouts of "drop your weapons" by the CERT team were quickly replaced by laughter and pats on the back as the Capitol Police members understood the simulation was over. Jason continued to charge ahead at full speed and ripped the acting senator from the grasp of a confused officer posing as the abductor. The motion yanked the officer off balance, and he nearly fell.

"Chill out, bro. It's over," the officer said. He added a push that sent Jason back several steps until he crashed into a wall.

Jason responded with a two-handed push on his chest, but the larger man stepped back with one foot and recovered. He responded with a quick right hook to Jason's chin that knocked the PSD member to the concrete floor.

"Control your man," Ashby yelled to Clay. "CERT, fall out and regroup in the alley."

Clay rushed over to Jason as he wobbled to his feet and grabbed him by the collar. "What the hell are you doing, Mulder?"

Jason rubbed his jaw without a response.

"That's twice today. Go home and get your mind right. We'll do the after-action without you."

"I'm fine. I just got a little caught up in everything."

"No, you're not. You've been on edge for weeks, and your head hasn't been in the game for the last few days. What is it? Are you homesick or something?

Jason locked eyes with Clay. "I know I'm new on this team, and I'm trying to contribute as much as possible."

"You haven't been home since you started working here full-time two months ago. I said you'd regret staying here over Christmas and the New Year, and I was right. Pack a bag and go home for a few days. Make sure we get the old Jason Mulder when you return."

Jason had no way to refute Clay. He was right. Jason missed his wife and son, and a few days back home could reset everything. He nodded, checked his watch, and left the building.

It was only four p.m. in Arizona, so if he hurried to the airport, he could catch the last direct flight and be home before midnight. He called Shanna to tell her he was coming home, and the call went directly to voicemail, so he texted her and left for the airport.

Jason arrived at Reagan International Airport and reached the gate before the final passengers boarded. He leaned his head back once they were airborne and tried to sleep, but the failed mission early that day was still running continuously through his mind. The member of Senator Conrad's private security detail was trained to react to all threats to his principal, but the abduction threw him off his game. Jason was prepared to protect the senator against any danger, though he secretly hoped he'd never have to confront an actual kidnapping attempt.

Chapter 2

Jason was wide-awake for five seemingly endless hours in the dark cabin of the narrow-body commercial airliner during his flight from Washington, DC, to Phoenix, Arizona. All the passengers around Jason slept while he stared out the window and squeezed his armrests. He watched the streetlights and illuminated buildings drift below his plane like stationary fireflies between intermittent clouds. Jason perked up at the site of the sprawling metropolis in the Sonoran Desert growing larger and brighter with each passing minute.

The principal-abduction training with the Capitol Police felt like it happened days ago. The tongue-lashing from Clay was painful to hear then, but Jason felt no lingering sting. His mind had shifted to Shanna and JJ.

Jason checked his phone once he deplaned at Phoenix Sky Harbor Airport. He received a text from his wife.

Sorry I missed your calls and texts. I dropped JJ off at your parents' house while I went to the shooting range.

He scrolled to the following text and picked up his pace through the terminal.

JJ and I miss you and can't wait to see you when you get home.

Jason entered his house quietly through the back door to ensure he didn't wake up JJ. As soon as the door shut behind him, Shanna turned the corner and ran into Jason's waiting arms. He kissed her deeply and held her tight.

"I missed you so much. That was too long," Shanna said.

"I agree. I won't ever be away for that long again."

Shanna remained pressed against his chest until Jason backed away. "I read that you went to the shooting range. How long have you been doing that?"

"For a while now. I've been waiting to surprise you."

"That was a nice surprise. How are you doing?"

"I think I'm doing pretty good. I want to go to the range with you and kick your butt."

"Is that right?" Jason asked in feigned anger.

Shanna stood ramrod straight and bumped her chest into Jason's. "Yeah, that's right."

He scooped up Shanna and carried her like a bride on her wedding night toward the bedroom. "Enough talk. I missed you."

Shanna's raven hair cascaded over Jason's chest as they lay together in bed.

"We should have another baby," Shanna said.

Jason's fingers stopped caressing her arm. "Um, shouldn't we have discussed that before—"

Shanna slapped Jason playfully. "I'm not talking about right now. JJ is fifteen months now, and I think a two-year age gap between siblings is perfect."

Jason scooted up and leaned against the headboard. "Maybe, but what's not perfect is my job on the other side of the country. I just missed Christmas, which still pisses me off every time I think about it. Plus, I won't leave you with two babies in diapers without me around to help."

Shanna kissed Jason. "Well, I've been thinking about that. Maybe you can look for something around here. It may take some time, but since you're working full-time, you can be picky and hold out for the best job."

Jason pulled his arms behind his head to support his neck as he gazed into the darkness.

I love the idea of working closer to home. Finding something close to home will take a while, so I should start looking soon.

"I think it's a good idea, but I have one condition," Jason said. "I don't want to relocate anywhere, even down to Phoenix. I want to raise our kids here."

"Me too, but are you talking about just for a new job, or is having another baby also a good idea?"

"Both."

Shanna kissed Jason hard. "I think we need more practice."

The next morning, the bedroom basked in dim gray light coming through the window instead of the usual golden sunlight from the rising sun. Jason rose from bed and pushed aside the partially open curtains. The clouds he'd bounced over on his descent into Phoenix the previous night had deposited seven inches of fresh snow overnight.

Jason found Shanna placing cut-up bananas and cereal in front of JJ at the dining room table. When JJ saw his father, he raised his arms high and wiggled in his booster chair. Jason snatched him up, and JJ clung to him like a python on its prey.

"I missed you," Jason said to JJ. He followed it up with a kiss on his cheek that evoked a toothless grin from his son. "I think we should take JJ sledding today."

"Sledding? I don't know if he has clothes for that."

"His normal winter clothes are fine. I'll just pull him around the yard. He'll love it."

After breakfast, the sun broke through the clouds and sparkled off the fresh snow. Jason shoveled the snow off the patio and steps before tying a rope to the bright-blue plastic saucerlike sled. The back door opened, and Shanna emerged on the patio with JJ. In his multiple layers of winter attire, he looked like a tiny sausage inside a thick, fluffy pastry.

"You didn't mention earlier that you're taking JJ to the South Pole," Jason yelled from the backyard.

"Ha ha, Jason. I don't want him to catch a cold."

Jason laughed out loud at his son waddling across the patio like a penguin. "My poor boy. He can't even move."

"Instead of laughing, help him down the steps," Shanna ordered, seemingly tired of the jokes about JJ's winter clothes.

Jason carried his son to the sled and showed him how to hang on to the handles. JJ curled his hands around the flexible nylon, and Jason dragged him around the yard. Shanna took pictures of her son smiling wide at every bump, curve, and straightaway until Jason dropped the rope and bent over, panting.

"That's harder than it looks," he said between breaths.

"Come on, Jason. Mush! Pull JJ around the yard some more," Shanna shouted, her sly grin widening above her scarf.

"Mush?" Jason asked. "Did I just hear you right?"

"Come on, get going."

Jason bent down and grabbed a handful of snow. Seconds later, he formed it into a perfect snowball and raised it for Shanna to see.

"You better not," Shanna warned.

Jason reared back and tossed a fastball that would make a major-league baseball pitcher envious. The snowball exploded into a million pieces on the back of Shanna's puffy coat. She quickly formed a snowball and chucked it at Jason. He wasn't expecting the velocity or the accuracy of Shanna's return fire, so he didn't react in time before catching the bundle of ice crystals above his right ear.

"Okay, you may have the high ground, but I'm taking you down," Jason yelled in his best battlefield voice.

Shanna launched two more snowballs before Jason's kill shot missed low and exploded across the patio railing.

A high-pitched squeal came from behind Jason. He turned around and saw JJ's toothless grin as he clapped with his mittens. JJ seemed to love watching his parents pelt each other with snowballs.

"You want to try?" Jason asked.

He placed a snowball on JJ's lap. The toddler examined the icy sphere as if it held special powers and then tossed it at Jason. His father pretended to duck a dangerous object coming at him at high speed, sending JJ into a laughing fit. Once JJ stopped laughing, Jason snagged his son and moved to the patio next to Shanna. She kissed her husband.

"I'm so glad you came home."

Jason packed slowly as visions of the three days he spent with Shanna and JJ flashed across his mind. They took JJ back to the zoo in Phoenix and his first movie on the big screen. Jason also spent some quiet time with his son tossing rocks into the river trickling behind their home. It was harder to leave than he expected.

If I had a local job, I wouldn't be leaving today.

Jason finished packing and dropped his bag near the back door.

"My dad just pulled up to take me to the airport," Jason shouted.

Shanna emerged from JJ's nursery, wiped her hands on her pants, and wrapped her arms around Jason.

"Don't wait so long to come back to visit next time," Shanna said and kissed her husband.

"I'll come back soon so we can do this again. I promise."

It was a promise Jason couldn't keep.

CHAPTER 3

Washington, DC

Jason entered the Dirksen Senate Office Building in Washington, DC, before the streetlights along Constitution Avenue yielded to the rising sun. The seven-story building featured tall strips of dark glass interspersed between white marble and limestone facades to form a faux colonnade. It sat across First Street from the Russell Senate Office Building, next to the Hart Senate Office Building, and the fortunate senators with corner offices were treated to a view of the adjacent US Capitol building.

Once inside the small lobby with floors and walls finished with marble, Jason moved to the rear of the line, waiting to go through security. The building contained forty office suites and twelve committee rooms, so airport-style screening was required to enter. Jason always tried to arrive early to pass through security before the crowds of staff and tourists arrived. It was bustling after the setting of the 119th Congress two weeks earlier and the inauguration of a new president looming in less than a week.

Jason looked at his watch several times as he moved closer to the metal detectors. He wanted to be in the office early enough to speak with Clay before the other staff arrived.

"At least the line is moving fast," Jason whispered.

He spoke too soon because two people ahead of him, a woman with designer sunglasses perched on top of her perfectly arranged auburn hair sauntered to the security checkpoint. She let her expensive, overflowing handbag fall to the table as if she couldn't bear the weight any longer.

"Can I go through now?" Designer Woman asked.

The security personnel responded in a courteous and professional tone. "All jewelry and electronics must also go through the metal detector."

"Are you serious?"

The security guard stared back with indifference until she made a production of taking off all her bracelets and rings and set them in the bin beside her two cell phones.

Buzz.

The metal detector went off as she attempted to hurry through.

"I'm sorry, ma'am. You'll have to remove your belt and sunglasses."

Designer Woman rolled her eyes and huffed as she stomped back to the beginning of the security checkpoint. Jason could hear every word of her high-pitched ranting despite her facing away from him.

"This is ridiculous. I'm here to see Senator Pederson. The new senator from Rhode Island."

Jason shook his head and muttered, "This is my new life."

After a short staring standoff, she put her belt and glasses into a new bin, but the rant continued. "Nobody ahead of me had to go through all this. Why are you all harassing me?"

The patient security guard stepped toward the woman and looped his thumbs through his bulletproof vest. "Ma'am, I don't care if you're here to see the King of the Galaxy. Everyone has to put their jewelry and electronics in the bin to be scanned."

Jason laughed so loud it echoed throughout the lobby, causing Designer Woman to turn around and glare at him with disdain.

Finally, Designer Woman made it through security, and Jason reached the fourth floor twenty minutes later than he'd hoped. He found Clay meeting with Jasmine Mitchell, deputy chief of staff, in a conference room. Jason poured himself a cup of coffee and lingered nearby until he saw Clay leave the room. He jogged to catch up with the head of the PSD.

"Thanks for forcing me to go back home—I needed it more than I thought," Jason shared once he caught up with Clay.

"I'm glad it worked out. When did you get back?"

"Last night."

"Wife and kids good?"

"Yeah, they're doing great."

"Are you refreshed and ready to go now?"

"I'm ready for action," Jason said as they breezed by several offices.

"It's good to see you back to your old self, because we're skipping the frying pan and going right into the fire tonight."

"Tonight?" Jason asked. "I thought the schedule said Senator Conrad was speaking at a Meet the New Congress event with the local and national media. I assumed that would be back-slapping, handshakes, and softball questions."

"It usually is, but Crenshaw warned me that Conrad is hell-bent on using his time in front of the press to push another controversial new bill. He believes the passage of the POLAR Act last summer mandated that he lead new efforts to solve America's biggest problems."

Jason abruptly stopped walking. "Are you serious?"

Clay also halted and nodded.

"How big are we talking? Infrastructure? Healthcare? Social Security?"

"Bigger."

"What could be bigger than that?" Jason asked.

"He wouldn't give her any specifics. I guess we'll have to tune in tonight with the rest of the country to find out."

"What does Crenshaw think about this?"

"She's shitting bricks. Crenshaw tried to talk him out of it, but she said it got heated, and Conrad wouldn't budge. He wants to steal the spotlight before the new president is sworn in and the media turns their focus to monitoring every detail about his first hundred days."

Clay looked at his watch. "I've got to run, but get with Zee and Central so they can fill you in on all the details."

Jason watched Clay disappear around the corner, much like his long-term chances of staying on Senator Conrad's security detail. The prospect of spending another year in a pressure cooker protecting a principal with a target on his back was overwhelming. Jason inhaled and then exhaled slowly. He had to focus on getting through tonight, and then he could worry about his future.

Senator Conrad strode on stage to enthusiastic applause and waved to his supporters and friendly media members in the audience. Jason stood at the end of the platform to Conrad's left and faced the crowd. He had a clear view of Crenshaw standing on the opposite end of the stage.

She looks like she may vomit at any time.

Jason saw his three PSD teammates in the other corners of the room, ready to act on anything or anyone that threatened the senator.

The applause ended, and Senator Conrad stepped up to the microphone, coiled like a cobra on the podium. "Ladies, gentlemen, and esteemed members of the media, thank you for your honest coverage of me, my platform, and most importantly, the POLAR Act. As a returning member of the United States Senate in the 119th Congress, I have spent considerable time considering what I can do differently this term and in this session. The fight for the POLAR Act last year was fierce and, at times, bloody, but the bill I cosponsored is now law. The water supply in the Colorado River is more secure now than it has been in five decades, and the country is better because of it."

The senator paused and leaned closer to the microphone. "I've been a fighter my entire life. I fought to put food on the table as a citrus and cotton farmer in Arizona, an Infantry Officer in the US Army, and a US Senator. This session, I want to tackle one of the biggest threats to our country, and I expect it to be the biggest fight of my life."

Conrad paused and took a drink from the water bottle on the podium. Jason saw Crenshaw swallow hard and cross her arms.

"Here it comes," Clay shared through Jason's discreet earpiece for their comms.

"The national debt is now twenty-five percent more than our total annual GDP for the last year and fifty percent more than all the private liquid funds in US savings accounts. We're adding a trillion dollars to the national debt every hundred days, and the interest payments alone on the debt exceed all other federal government expenditures, including Social Security, Medicare, and even defense spending. Those interest payments will soon be over one trillion dollars a year, and that won't pay down a penny of our crippling national debt."

Jason felt the mood in the room shift from hope and excitement to apprehension in seconds. It was like the debate in Tempe, Arizona, during the campaign where the audience turned raucous halfway through and the night ended in riots on the street. Jason didn't think the media would start a riot, but nothing would surprise him after the last campaign season.

"To fight this insatiable debt monster, I will work with fellow West Point graduate and incoming Congressman Andrew Kane from New York on new legislation to tackle another problem that has plagued our nation for decades with nobody in Congress willing to act. Also, I'm excited to work with both parties on—"

"What's your plan?" a reporter in the front row from a New York–based newspaper yelled.

Senator Conrad paused and smiled. "Thank you for your interest. Congressman Kane and I will share more details about our plan soon."

"You must have some draft of a plan, or you wouldn't have mentioned it to over a hundred members of the press and Congress. My readers would like to know what you have in mind."

The smile on Conrad's face vanished, and Jason saw the muscles in his neck twitch and tense up. He saw Crenshaw wagging her head, willing the senator not to take the bait.

"Of course, the fine details of my plan require many more drafts and committee meetings before they are final, but the general mechanism is to hold Congress accountable for fixing the problem. We must stop our hemorrhaging debt and balance the budget each year. Once we accomplish that, we can do much more for the American people without raising taxes."

"Are you planning to withhold the paychecks of members of Congress until a balanced budget is signed? That's a popular meme on the Internet, but it will never work," the reporter replied.

Senator Conrad cleared his throat and flashed a quick smile. "I agree, and that's why I'm proposing a bill that will restrict and reallocate campaign funds from every member of Congress if a balanced budget is not passed each year. I'm enforcing the Congressional Fiscal Obligation we all took to get here, so it's called the CFO Act.

A wave of murmurs came from the audience filled with new members of Congress. Conrad leaned closer to the microphone on the podium. "Billions of dollars are raised every year by incumbent candidates seeking to keep their jobs, but I contend that we're not doing our jobs if we can't balance the budget. We'd all be fired if we were in the private sector and we accepted losing money every year like we do in Congress. I know the CFO Act will not be popular with this crowd, so I intend to make my case to the American people."

The volume of voices in the crowd grew louder, and random shouts echoed throughout the room like mini volcano eruptions.

"Is this because you don't take any PAC money?"

"This is antidemocratic!"

"It will never pass!"

Jason stood on his tiptoes to see everyone in the crowd. He recognized genuine anger, but nobody had raised his suspicion as a threat to Conrad's safety—yet.

Come on, Crenshaw. Get the MC to pull him before this gets out of hand.

Almost as soon as Jason thought it, the MC walked to the podium with a wide smile. "Thank you for coming, Senator Conrad. We look forward to hearing more about you and your plans in the coming session. Next, we'll hear from the senator from—"

Jason stopped listening as soon as Senator Conrad left the platform, and he turned his attention to the nearest members of the audience.

"Duke is leaving the hall," Clay radioed the team.

The crowd's shouts went from a boil to a simmer, and the temperature in the room seemed to fall ten degrees.

"Duke is secure."

Clay left the banquet center, shaking his head.

"I didn't think this session could be worse than last year's campaign."

The elevator was still broken, so Jason climbed the stairs to his third-floor apartment. He entered his family room, caught his breath, and grabbed a beer. Jason ambled to his couch and opened his laptop. Once the screen loaded, Jason's cursor hovered over several shortcuts he often visited. He guided the cursor over emails, stock prices, and the video-call icon to connect him with Shanna. Jason clicked when the curser landed on a job-search website.

He loved working with the best PSD team in the Capitol, but a virtual giant magnet was at play. One side repelled him from Washington, DC, while the other pulled him home to his wife and son in Whispering Pines, Arizona. The ultimate outcome seemed inevitable, but actively searching for a new job was more challenging than Jason imagined.

Can I really leave Clay and the team when they need me the most?

CHAPTER 4

Whispering Pines, Arizona

Shanna's eyes fluttered open, and she blinked quickly, trying to adjust to the sunlight streaming into her room. She was grateful for the solid eight hours of uninterrupted sleep after being awakened by JJ's cries shortly after midnight. Shanna knew her son missed his daddy because he'd woken up crying at least once every night since Jason returned to Washington, DC.

She rolled over in bed and snagged her phone off the nightstand. The wood-burning stove that heated their home had extinguished hours ago, so Shanna pulled the thick comforter up to her chin after she propped herself up with a couple of pillows. She went straight for her text messages. Shanna was looking for the early-morning texts Jason had sent her daily since he had taken the full-time job with Senator Conrad's security detail.

Her straight lips curved upward when she read the text.

`I can't wait to add to our family with you.`

Shanna reread the text a dozen times and stared at it until she heard a thud outside the bedroom window of their Whispering Pines home. Her eyebrows pinched tight above her nose as she tossed off the covers and scampered to the window.

She peered outside, moving her head left and right, and didn't see anyone or anything that may have caused the sound. Her eyes dropped to the snow that had almost melted, and she noticed footprints. Shanna backed away from the window and noted all the other footprints left behind by Jason while he was home.

"Jason must have been doing something around the house," Shanna said aloud to reassure herself.

She hurried to the bedroom across the hall and opened the door to see JJ awake but playing quietly with his blanket. Her heart swelled with a mixture of relief and love for her little boy.

Shanna and JJ spent the day playing and eating until it was time for his afternoon nap. Still on a high from the text, she wanted to do something special for Jason to show her appreciation. Shanna loaded the magazine for her Glock 19 and called Jason's mom, Celeste, to see if she could watch JJ. Once his grandma confirmed her availability, she bundled up her son for a short trip to Payson.

While driving on the mostly deserted road into town, she noticed a black SUV trailing close behind her. Shanna slowed to see if she recognized the driver, but the person, wearing a hat pulled low, concealed their face before turning onto a side street. Pick-up trucks, SUVs, and hat-wearing residents were as common as mosquitoes in the summer, but something about this one seemed suspicious. She made a pit stop at the grocery store to pick up more diapers, baby wipes, cereal, and bananas, and she thought she may have seen the same SUV in the grocery store parking lot but couldn't be sure.

Shanna arrived at her in-laws' and carried JJ inside to his doting grandparents.

"He hasn't had his nap yet for the afternoon, but he's too wound up to go down now. Please put him down for a nap after you play while I'm at the range," Shanna said.

"Sure. We'll play for a while and then put him down for a nap. We'll take good care of him," Celeste said.

Shanna drove to the range and waited for an open lane. She slid on her protective eyewear, pulled over earmuffs, and sighted the front post over the manlike target. Shanna squeezed the trigger fifteen times and put all the rounds center mass at eight yards, her personal best. She was having so much fun after the first one hundred rounds that she went to the front counter and purchased another hundred rounds to put through a new target. After she finished sending the next hundred rounds into her faux attacker, she folded the targets and put them in her gun case. Shanna stepped into the parking lot with a contented grin and sang aloud to the music blasting over the speakers as she drove back to her in-laws' to pick up JJ.

Shanna entered Jason's childhood home from the back patio without knocking. Celeste insisted Shanna enter their home like family, not a guest. Celeste was unloading the dishwasher while Phillip chopped vegetables on the counter.

"Sorry I'm late," Shanna said. "There was a line for the lanes at the range, and I'd hoped to get here before it got too dark."

"No problem. You can always leave JJ here as long as you like," Celeste replied with a genuine smile.

"How long has he been down for his nap?"

Celeste turned to the clock above the kitchen table. "It's been about ninety minutes. We played for a while, and then he got cranky, so I knew he was tired."

"Thank you. I want to wake him and get back home to keep him on schedule. Where is he?"

"I put him in Jason's old room."

Shanna strode down the hallway she had traversed dozens of times while dating Jason. She opened the door and let the hallway light illuminate the dark room. Shanna expected to see JJ hugging his favorite teddy bear between the bedrails on both sides of the bed. Instead, the bed was empty.

Creases formed across Shanna's forehead as her eyes darted around the room. She flipped on the overhead light and rushed to the other side of the bed to see if JJ had somehow fallen out of bed.

I wonder if Celeste got the rooms mixed up.

Shanna walked back to the kitchen and found Celeste helping Phillip prepare dinner.

"Are you sure you put JJ down in Jason's old room?" Shanna asked.

"I'm positive. I checked on him several times, and he was sound asleep thirty minutes ago. Why?"

"He's not in there."

Celeste tossed the towel in her hands onto the counter and rushed to Jason's old bedroom. Once Shanna caught up, she was on the floor looking under the bed.

"He was here a half hour ago," Celeste said with concern in her voice.

Celeste marched into the hallway. "Phillip, did you move JJ into a different room?"

"What?" Phillip yelled back from the kitchen.

"Come here! JJ is not in Jason's room."

Seconds later, Phillip appeared in the doorway. "Did you look under the bed and in the closet?"

"I already did that," Celeste barked, her voice cracking.

"Could Uncle Noah have taken him?" Shanna asked, searching for a positive solution.

"He left right after you did," Phillip said.

"He has to be around here somewhere. Everyone, look around the house," Celeste commanded.

Shanna's pulse quickened, and her eyes widened in shock. She tried to speak, but no words escaped her trembling lips. The realization that JJ was gone began to hit her.

Celeste and Phillip rushed into the hallway and turned in opposite directions. Shanna heard doors opening and cabinets slamming while she stared at the empty bed. Her mind searched for answers in dark places, but she shook her head to stave off the possibility that her worst nightmare might be coming true. Her eyes fell to the worn tan carpet as she tried to imagine how a fifteen-month-old could escape a bedroom.

Could JJ be hiding as a joke?

Shanna concluded those days were coming but knew he couldn't hide so well that nobody could find him. She scanned the room again and noticed a brown stain on the carpet near the bedroom window. The appearance of a stain in Celeste's house felt out of place, so Shanna approached it slowly as if it were a dangerous serpent. As she drew nearer, a partial brown boot print became visible.

A rush of adrenaline hit her stomach, and Shanna quickly covered her mouth, worried she might throw up all over Jason's old room. She knelt and gently touched the stain with her index finger. Turning her finger over, she noticed that the cherrywood-colored soil had transferred onto her skin. Rubbing her thumb and finger together, the soil smeared across both fingers.

"This is fresh," Shanna muttered.

Her chest tightened. Shanna could feel every beat of her heart pump blood through her neck. She turned toward the window and noticed another stain on the sill, the same color as the one on the carpet. The window opened vertically, so she looked up to see the bottom pane a few millimeters higher than the stationary pane. The window was unlocked.

Shanna leaped to her feet and rushed to the empty bed.

"JJ's favorite teddy bear is also missing," Shanna said shakily.

This can't be happening.

Shanna wanted Phillip and Celeste to wake her from her horrible dream. She had to wake up and hold her son, but like a nightmare, she couldn't summon enough breath to yell.

"He's been taken," Shanna said, barely above a whisper.

When nobody came to the room, the reality of the situation hit the terrified mother like a rogue wave, and with it came a secondary surge of adrenaline mixed with fear and resolve. Her voice caught, and a piercing scream emerged that echoed through Jason's old home.

"Someone took JJ!"

CHAPTER 5

Washington, DC

Jason stepped into the dark interior of his Washington, DC, apartment and flipped the switch that illuminated the lamp on the end table. He closed the door to shut out the traffic noise and bad memories from the workday. Jason kicked off his shoes, untucked his shirt, and made a beeline for the couch but not before he grabbed a cold beer. He collapsed onto the soft cushions of his rented sofa with a groan and gazed at the dark television for a few moments.

"What a day."

The repercussions of Senator Conrad's statements at the Meet the New Congress event the previous night were swift. The impact on Jason and the PSD team wouldn't be felt until his next event, but Crenshaw's entire staff received relentless backlash from friends and foes the moment they started their day. Jason couldn't wait to leave the negativity spreading through the office like a cold in a kindergarten class.

He turned on the TV and snagged his laptop from the couch cushion beside him. Once the next episode of the Netflix series started, he moved his eyes back and forth between screens. Jason browsed the usual news sites, job boards, and emails. After opening one email, he leaned closer for a better look. It was from an article consolidation service that monitored the web and sent links to websites, articles, and news stories based on keywords.

Arizona search-and-rescue jobs were the keywords that sparked the email, so Jason opened the link to the article from the Flagstaff, Arizona, newspaper, the *Arizona Daily Sun*. The headline said: "`Forest Service Beefs Up Staff`." He skimmed the first two paragraphs until he reached the part about the hiring agency.

The US Department of Agriculture Forest Service Law Enforcement and Investigations Staff is charged with protecting the public, employees, and natural resources throughout 192 million acres of National Forest System lands. With an increasing number of visitors to the national forests and grasslands, the need for law enforcement personnel continues to grow, and to keep up with demand, the agency is adding to the 650 existing law enforcement officers nationwide.

Jason clicked on the link to the law enforcement officer position mentioned in the article and found an open position based in Flagstaff. His finger moved swiftly to click on the link, and he read the position details aloud.

"Uniformed law enforcement officers enforce Federal laws and regulations governing National Forest System lands and resources. They establish a regular and recurring presence on vast amounts of public land, roads, and campgrounds, taking appropriate action when illegal activity is discovered."

Jason took a draw of his beer and scrolled further down the page.

"In addition, uniformed law enforcement officers enforce controlled substance laws, assist outside agencies with search-and-rescue missions on National Forest System lands, and assist special agents in conducting investigations."

Jason pumped his fist. "This is perfect!"

He checked his watch. It was nearly 6 p.m. in Arizona, so he'd give Shanna another half hour to feed JJ and then call her with the news. A return to Arizona with a good job finally seemed possible.

Jason returned to his laptop to reread the details of his future career when his phone buzzed. He noticed it was Shanna and led with his news.

"Hey, honey, I have good news. I found—"

"JJ is missing!"

Shanna's words were clear but were so unexpected that his mind struggled to comprehend the shocking statement. "What?"

"JJ is missing. We don't know where he is," Shanna said shakily.

This time, the impact of Shanna's statement struck Jason like a gut punch. The street noise outside his apartment disappeared as he tried to process the situation.

"Okay, tell me exactly what happened."

"I-I dropped JJ off with Celeste and Phillip while I went to the range. Your mom put him down for a nap around four o'clock, and when I got here around a little after five thirty, he wasn't in his room."

Shanna paused, and Jason heard sniffles and soft sobbing.

"And then what happened?" Jason whispered. He was eager to gather information on the whereabouts of his son but was careful not to push Shanna too hard.

"We looked all over for him, and he's nowhere to be found."

"Did Noah take him somewhere? He likes to play with his nephew."

Jason's state of shock allowed him to maintain hope that a simple resolution might be possible. It was like some calls he'd received to scramble as an Air Force pararescueman in Afghanistan. His team received reports of unimaginable carnage, and intellectually, he understood the gravity of the situation, but he always hoped that he could help everyone once he arrived. Jason understood this was his way of coping with major trauma, a mentality adopted by most PJs he knew. In this case, hope wouldn't last long.

"We already checked. He's not with Noah."

The line grew silent as a million scenarios played out in Jason's head.

Where could JJ be? Could they all be mistaken? I need to get back to see what's going on.

"Jason, I think somebody took JJ," Shanna said.

"Why do you think someone took him?"

The idea that someone may have taken JJ had crossed Jason's mind, but he pushed it away. Shanna's mention of it made him face reality and acknowledge that it was a real possibility.

"JJ was sleeping in your old room, and I found mud on the floor and the windowsill. I looked closer, and it looked like a boot print. The window was unlocked and still a little open. Somebody came through the window and took JJ while he slept."

A vision of JJ's face with a toothless smile flashed in Jason's mind. The unbearable thought of never seeing JJ again shocked his body like a bolt of lightning. He shook his head to rid his mind of the terrible thought as his jaw clenched and his free hand turned into a fist.

I have to find my son and bring him home. Focus on finding JJ and nothing else.

"Shanna, are my parents near you?"

"Yes."

"Put the phone on speaker so I can talk to everyone."

Jason paced around his apartment as he formed a plan. A second later, his mom's voice boomed over the speaker. "I'm so sorry, Jason. He was sleeping the last time I checked on him."

"Mom, this isn't anyone's fault. I need everyone to listen closely because if someone took JJ, our next steps are critical to finding him. Is everyone listening?"

"Yes," his dad responded.

"I know this is hard, but all of you need to get out of the bedroom, and nobody goes outside to look for JJ."

"Why?" Shanna asked, choking back her tears.

"After we hang up, call the police and preserve all the evidence until they arrive. The kidnapper had to leave footprints, fibers, and maybe even fingerprints, but the more you look for him, the harder it is for investigators to sort through all the evidence. Speed is essential to finding JJ, and any searching you do around the house will only slow the investigation down."

Nobody spoke, but Jason heard sniffles and someone blowing their nose.

"Do you understand why you can't keep looking for him?" Jason asked as he moved into the bedroom in his apartment.

"Yeah," Shanna whispered.

He sounded calm and confident on the phone, and in reality, he was. Jason's brain shifted from a crisis that could eternally devastate his family to problem resolution. It was another temporary coping mechanism that Jason had developed after suffering so many sudden losses. However, he also knew reality was lurking around the next corner, and once it appeared, the gravity of someone kidnapping JJ would hit him like a sucker punch to the chin. Until that happened, he had to move.

Jason checked his watch. He knew that if he could catch the last flight out of Reagan International Airport, he could get a connection to Phoenix tonight. Jason tossed a handful of clothes into his carry-on and zipped it up.

"I have one last question before I head to the airport. Did you bring JJ's teddy bear to my parents' house?"

"Yes, he was sleeping with it the last time I checked on him," Celeste answered.

"Is it still in the room?"

"No, it's gone too," Shanna answered.

"Okay, I have to go to catch the next flight. Call 911, don't taint the evidence, and I'll see you in a few hours."

In a conversation filled with soul-crushing news, the missing stuffed bear was the only source of hope for Jason to cling to during his cross-country flight to Arizona.

CHAPTER 6

Payson, Arizona

Headlights slashed across Shanna's face, highlighting new tears cascading down her cheeks. She stood by the front window in the dark family room of her in-laws' home and watched a Gila County Sheriff's Office vehicle idle down the gravel driveway and park. A half minute later, a second GCSO SUV pulled behind the first one, and the two deputies met in the middle to talk.

After a brief conversation, the first deputy opened his trunk, removed a roll of yellow police caution tape, and tied it to a nearby tree trunk. The other officer adjusted his wide-brimmed campaign hat bearing the Gila County Sheriff's Office logo and strode toward the front door. Shanna opened it before he knocked.

"Thank you for coming so fast," Shanna choked out.

"Are you Shanna Mulder?"

"Yes, my son is missing. He was taken from his bedroom."

The deputy's eyes narrowed. "Do you know who took him?"

"No! He was taking a nap and was gone when I went back to wake him up. We looked everywhere, and I found a muddy boot print that wasn't there before his nap."

The deputy nodded slowly. "Are you the only one in this home?"

"No, my in-laws are just down the hall."

"Can you please ask them to come out here? I want to speak to everyone at the same time about your missing son."

Shanna disappeared down the dark hallway and returned a minute later with Phillip and Celeste behind her. Phillip held his wife tight as she continued to sob.

"Is this everyone?" the deputy asked.

Shanna nodded.

He cleared his throat and began. "I'm sorry for this horrible situation you are all in, but I want to let you all know what to expect. Please have a seat," the deputy said, pointing to the nearby couch.

Everyone sat, and the deputy continued. "The FBI is on the way from Phoenix, so they should get here in about an hour. When they arrive, they'll want to talk to all of you separately, so no more discussing what happened until the FBI special agents arrive. Also, we don't want to disturb any evidence a potential abductor may have left at the scene, so nobody outside or in the room where the boy was taken."

"We know. My husband already told us to stay away from any potential evidence," Shanna said.

"Where is your husband?"

Shanna wondered if sharing that Jason worked for a US Senator would speed up or slow down the intensity of the investigation. She quickly concluded that mentioning Senator Conrad could move the focus away from JJ.

"He works out of town. He's flying home now."

The deputy jotted something down in a small notepad. "Missus Mulder, do you and your husband live here with your in-laws?"

"No, we have our own house up in Whispering Pines. They were babysitting JJ here when it happened," Shanna said, her voice cracking. "Aren't you going to look for the person who took my son?"

The deputy looked over his notepad. "The FBI has people who specialize in kidnapping and crimes against children, so they'll start the investigation when they arrive. I know it's hard to answer all these questions right now, but they'll help speed up the investigation."

Shanna nodded while Celeste leaned into Phillip's chest. She'd stopped crying, and both looked to be in shock.

"Does anybody else live here?"

This time, Phillip answered. "Yes, my adult son, Noah, lives here. He's over at his girlfriend's house right now."

"Can I make some tea?" Celeste squeaked.

"Yes, that is all for now," the deputy said. "Remember, do not discuss what happened, and stay in the kitchen or this room."

Phillip held Celeste's and Shanna's hands as they silently sipped their tea at the kitchen table. Seventy-five minutes after the GCSO deputies arrived, Shanna heard unfamiliar voices in the family room. She rose and found four individuals in navy-blue jackets with "FBI" emblazoned on the back speaking with the deputies. One of them noticed Shanna and excused herself to talk with her.

"Hi, I'm Special Agent Priya Reddy from the FBI. I'm here to get your little boy back," she said with a slight Telugu accent from India.

"I'm Shanna Mulder, JJ's mom."

"I'm sure you're overwhelmed and have questions for me, but before we talk, I want to get everyone moving on the investigation, so can you give me a few minutes?"

Shanna nodded.

Special Agent Reddy returned to the group of men in FBI attire. Moments later, two FBI agents with stocking hats, gloves, and flashlights exited the front door.

"In which room was he last seen?" Reddy asked Shanna.

"Down the hallway. Last room on the right."

The other FBI agent strutted down the hallway and entered Jason's old bedroom. "I'll join you as soon as I'm done with the family," Reddy yelled down the hall.

Special Agent Reddy stood before Shanna and lowered her voice to almost a whisper. She waved to the nearby couch. "Please sit down so we can talk."

Shanna sat, moved a pillow over her lap, and squeezed it. Reddy sat beside her and turned to face Shanna.

"The deputies briefed me during my drive up here. They told me you believe a stranger took your son. Can you explain why you think a stranger would take JJ?"

Shanna inhaled deeply and hugged the pillow tighter. "I didn't know what to think at first, but when we couldn't find JJ anywhere, I thought somebody could have taken him. I know Celeste and Phillip didn't take him, so I wondered if Noah came home without knowing it and took JJ to play with him."

Shanna paused. "JJ loves his uncle, so I hoped Noah had him, but then I learned he's at his girlfriend's house. Then I—"

"Tell me more about Noah," Reddy interrupted. "Does Noah like to play alone with JJ? Has he shown an interest in JJ that makes you feel uncomfortable?"

Shanna's cheeks grew hot, and she leaned back from Reddy as if the FBI special agent was on fire.

"No! Never! It's not like that. This family loves JJ as much as my husband and I."

"Speaking of your husband, I understand he works out of town. That can't be easy," Reddy countered.

"It's not."

"How are things between you and your husband? Is there any reason he may come home without your knowledge and take JJ?"

Shanna jumped to her feet. Her face flushed red as she stared down at Special Agent Reddy. "I can't believe my son was taken from his room by a stranger ninety minutes ago and you're sitting here asking me if it could be a family member. Hell no, it wasn't a family member! It wasn't Noah, Phillip, Celeste, or my husband, Jason. It wasn't my brother, an ex-boyfriend, or some long-lost cousin. It was a stranger, and now he's further away with my son while we discuss this utter bullshit!"

Reddy did not show any hint of emotion during Shanna's tirade. She stood and pulled on her jacket to straighten it out. "Ma'am, I'm sorry I upset you. We have three people already investigating your son's kidnapping, and I'm just covering all the bases. I hope you understand that."

Shanna continued to glare at Reddy.

"I have one last question before I help process the bedroom. Does your family have any enemies you believe would take your son?"

The fury swirling inside Shanna slowed when she considered the long list of people who had tried to harm her or Jason and could conceivably take JJ.

"Um," Shanna stammered. "It could be a pretty long list."

Reddy raised one eyebrow and removed a notepad and pen from her coat pocket. "Oh really? Please explain."

Shanna sat back down on the couch, and Reddy followed.

"My husband is responsible for putting a lot of people in jail. A cartel, a former sheriff, and a crooked DEA agent are all currently in jail because of Jason."

"Is he in law enforcement?" Reddy asked as she scooted closer to Shanna.

"He was a DEA special agent for about a year, but now he's on private security detail."

The FBI special agent wrote furiously in her notepad. "Has he crossed anyone in private security that may want to hurt your family to get back at your husband or his principal?"

Shanna looked down at her hands folded on her lap and cleared her throat. "Someone tried to kill our entire family last year when they planted a bomb in our truck because they were mad about Senator Conrad's Colorado River water bill."

"Is your husband on Senator Conrad's security team?"

Shanna nodded.

"Did he work with FBI Special Agent Archie Woods on the case?"

"Yes," Shanna whispered.

Reddy stood, took several steps toward the hallway, and stopped.

"I'm going to help process the evidence. We're going to get your son back as soon as possible."

"Please hurry," Shanna said with tears of hope welling up in her eyes. "I'm sure JJ is scared and upset. We need to find his kidnapper before he vanishes with my boy."

Chapter 7

Near Payson, Arizona

Jason pressed harder on the accelerator of his rental car to chew up the last stretch of deserted highway outside Payson, Arizona. He was shrouded in darkness except for the blue glow of the speedometer, highlighting his intense expression. The only sound inside the sedan was the white noise from the road and the whine of the engine while climbing the undulating hills between Phoenix and Payson. For the past ninety minutes of the usual two-hour drive from the airport, he ran countless scenarios through his mind.

The shock of the initial call had worn off, and now dread coursed through his veins. He understood JJ was missing, but a part of him still hoped to see the smile that always melted his heart when he walked through the door.

Jason turned into his driveway and skidded to a stop at the police tape blocking further passage to his old house. He ducked under the plastic yellow ribbon tied to a nearby tree and sprinted toward the open front door.

"Hey, you can't go in there," a voice yelled out from the nearby GCSO vehicles.

Jason didn't turn to acknowledge the command or break his stride. He crossed the threshold into the living room and found his parents on the couch. His mother was sleeping on his father's lap.

"I'd get up, but she just passed out from exhaustion," Phillip whispered. "I'm going to let her sleep a little before I tell her you're home."

"That's okay, let her sleep. Where's Shanna?"

"She's in the kitchen."

Shanna must've heard her husband's voice because she met Jason the instant he stepped into the kitchen. She threw her arms around him and buried her face into his chest.

"He's gone!" Shanna sobbed.

Jason pulled her close. Her body shook with each breath. After a minute, Jason pulled away and looked into his wife's wet eyes.

"Have they found anything?"

Shanna sniffed and dried her cheeks. "Not yet. They've been in the bedroom and the backyard and just started checking the woods around the house."

"Who's in charge?"

"Her name is Special Agent Reddy. She walked out back a few minutes before you got home."

Jason looked through the kitchen window and observed a woman of average height wearing an FBI jacket with black hair pulled into a ponytail talking on the phone on the back patio.

"I'm going to help look for JJ."

He hustled down the hall and stopped like he'd hit a brick wall when he entered his old bedroom. During his short time in the DEA, he attended classes on evidence collection and immediately noticed the ash-gray fingerprint powder on and around the windowsill. Jason did not move as his eyes took in the scene. He recognized the signs of silicone casting residue on the window glass and the discarded wrapper on the floor for the gelatin lifter sheet that must have been used to pull shoe prints from the carpet. The comforter on his old bed was missing and surely bagged in evidence to look for hairs and fibers under a microscope in the forensics lab.

The thought of an intruder breaking into his room and snatching his sleeping son from the bed made Jason feel queasy. For a moment, he thought he'd have to bolt to the bathroom to throw up, but he took several quick breaths to calm his stomach.

Don't go there. Be strong for JJ and keep searching until you find him.

Jason turned to his old dresser and pulled out the bottom drawer. It contained neatly folded tactical pants and cold-weather shirts from when he lived at home. He moved to his closet and yanked a warm tactical fleece hoodie jacket off the hanger and his black microfleece watch cap with matching gloves from the bin on the floor.

He returned to the kitchen and found Shanna looking out the window with her arms crossed as if hugging herself. She had the thousand-yard stare he'd seen on men and women in Afghanistan countless times. He had an idea of the scenes playing in her mind like a recurring nightmare since he was also fighting them. He'd do anything to find his son and eliminate her pain.

Jason removed a flashlight from a drawer in the kitchen and slowly approached Shanna.

"Honey, I'm going out to look for JJ. I have my cell phone, so call me if you learn anything new."

Shanna nodded but did not reply.

Jason patted his waist and realized he didn't have a weapon. He'd left his SIG Sauer P226 in Washington, DC, to catch the last flight to Phoenix without checking his luggage.

"Shanna, do you have your Glock?"

Her nose pinched as she locked eyes with Jason. "Why?"

"If somebody was brazen enough to take our son, I don't know what they'd do if I find them. I don't want to take any chances."

A flicker of hope flashed across her face. "Yeah, okay. The gun case is in my diaper bag."

Two minutes later, Jason tucked the fully loaded Glock in his waistband at the small of his back. Layers of warm weather gear covered it so nobody would notice.

He kissed her on the forehead and turned to exit, but he heard his name before turning the door handle.

"Jason, you're home," his mom called out.

Celeste stood in the kitchen with slumped shoulders and red-rimmed eyes. Jason crossed the room and gave his mom the hug he knew she desperately needed.

"Are you leaving?" she asked.

"I'm going to help search the woods for JJ."

Celeste's chin quivered. "I'm so sorry, Jason. JJ was asleep the last time I checked on him, and I never—"

Jason put his hands on her shoulders to stop her. "You didn't do anything wrong, Mom, so you don't have to apologize. Some sick asshole broke in and took JJ, and now we all need to focus on finding him."

"Okay," Celeste responded with a forced smile. "Be careful."

Jason exited the kitchen and moved next to Special Agent Reddy on the back patio. She was still on the phone, but when Jason appeared beside her, she quickly ended the call.

"Mr. Mulder, I'm so glad you made it. I'm Special Agent Reddy with the FBI. I'm leading this investigation and have several questions for you. Is there somewhere warm we can go talk?"

"Have you found any actionable evidence yet?"

"Can we go inside and talk?"

"I'm not going inside," Jason replied.

The back patio was silent for several beats until Reddy spoke. "We found boot prints in the mud outside the bedroom window and a potential hair on the comforter. We haven't found any fingerprints or tracks leading away from the house, but my team is in the woods now looking for more."

"I'm going to help them look."

"That's not how this works," Reddy chirped. "If you really want to help with this investigation, we'll go inside and you'll answer my questions."

"Do you know who I work for?"

"Yes, I know you're part of the private security detail for Senator Conrad, and I have several questions about your role on his security team."

Jason took a step closer to the FBI special agent. "That's exactly why I'm not talking to you. I'll tell you everything after we find my son, but right now, we don't have time to explore every threat and piece of hate mail my principal has received. I know that's where you'll go with your questions, and we can't waste valuable time going down that rabbit hole right now."

Reddy turned to the flashlight beams darting through the trees behind the house and sighed. "How can you be sure this isn't related to Senator Conrad? It happened before with the car bomb under your truck."

"That's why I know this isn't related. The Saudi brothers wanted to kill Senator Conrad and everyone associated with him, so my family was collateral damage. This is personal. Shanna told me she saw a suspicious black SUV when she was driving JJ over here. They must have broken into my old bedroom and taken my son. This person is targeting me or my wife, not Senator Conrad."

Reddy stared at Jason for several seconds and looked away as if she were contemplating the validity of his answer. Jason assumed the conversation was over and started toward the stairs.

"You know I can have the deputies detain you until I get some answers."

Jason turned, crossed his arms, and widened his stance.

"That would be a very bad idea."

Reddy swallowed hard and took another approach.

"I can't have you out in the woods interfering with my investigation. I already have three agents scouring the area for your son."

Jason felt the heat building up in his chest and his jaw tightening as Reddy wasted time they didn't have.

"I know every boulder, game trail, and tree in that forest from behind our property to the main highway. I won't interfere with your precious investigation, and nobody is going to comb every inch of the woods like I will," Jason growled.

"You shouldn't go out there if you're angry and upset," Reddy warned.

"My son is missing, Special Agent Reddy. Somebody took him while he slept in my old bed. Angry and upset don't even come close to describing how I feel."

Jason was done talking, so he stepped off the patio and strode toward the dark, dense forest.

Reddy jumped off the patio to catch up and handed Jason her business card. "Call if you find anything."

Jason slid the card into his pants pocket without looking at it and continued across the backyard until he disappeared into the dark shadows of the forest. The former pararescueman was determined to hunt down JJ's abductor and rescue his son.

CHAPTER 8

The full January moon cast Jason Mulder's silent shadow on the forest floor as he skirted past the FBI agents undetected. He continued his stealthy insertion into the woods behind his boyhood home until he was far enough to avoid detection. Jason didn't want the FBI agents in the woods focused on anything but finding JJ.

Once all the lights from his parents' house and FBI searchers were lost behind the stand of trees, Jason paused to gather his bearings. He knelt and grabbed a fistful of pine needles and damp dirt with his gloved hand while he scanned his surroundings. Jason pinpointed his location on a game trail two hundred yards from the house and just over a mile from a small day-use park just off the highway. He knew the park was a prime location to sneak to and from his old house in order to drive away with JJ undetected.

Jason checked his watch and looked at the sky. He noted it was 6:07 in the morning and that a line of clouds was moving in with a cold front behind it. JJ had been missing for over twelve hours, and with temperatures dropping into the high teens overnight, Jason had to find his son soon if he was still in the woods.

Hang in there, son. I'm coming for you.

Jason flipped on his flashlight and followed the game trail toward the park. His eyes, trained from years of pararescue missions, scanned the path for any sign of disturbance—a broken branch, a scrap of cloth, anything that might lead him to JJ.

Ten minutes into his search, Jason noticed a twig dangling beside a narrow section of the game trail. Jason checked the soft earth for signs of shoe prints before his eyes rose from the ground to the broken branch. The fibrous split in the twig was still green.

"This is new," Jason said aloud. His heart raced at the realization that someone had recently been in the area, and it was most likely the kidnapper. Jason continued on the path, but halted abruptly when the beam of his flashlight highlighted something out of place for the game trail. He approached slowly, but the source of the red, white, and green pattern on a flexible material under the light became clear. A small two-inch-by-one-inch section of JJ's forest-animal blanket he always slept with clung to the dry grass next to the trail.

JJ's blanket must have been caught on the jagged branch.

Jason scanned the trail in all directions with his flashlight. He held the light over disturbed earth several feet past the piece of JJ's blanket.

He ran through here, so he must have been nervous. Maybe he's still hiding nearby.

Jason noted the coordinates on his GPS watch and increased his pace. A flood of emotions accompanied the confirmation that JJ was here. It was a reminder that the nightmare that Jason, Shanna, and his family were living was real, but it also brought a glimmer of hope that he was on a path that could lead him to JJ and his kidnapper.

The crisp night air carried the scent of sap and earth, punctuated by the occasional coyote yip as Jason resumed his journey. His powerful one-thousand-lumen flashlight swayed back and forth, illuminating the trunks of the tall ponderosa pines. The shifting light created shadows that seemed alive, encouraging Jason to continue his charge to rescue JJ. His heart pounded, not from exertion but from the urgency of his task. He knew he was near the park and probably his best chance to find his son and the person who abducted him. Jason pressed on, his determination to return JJ to his mother growing with each step.

He stopped on the trail and listened for any sound out of place in the Arizona wilderness. He considered calling out for his son but didn't want his abductor to hear him and flee deeper into the remote forest with JJ.

The sound of a diesel engine and the whoosh of a truck driving past his location at high speeds confirmed he was close to the park and highway. The game trail turned to follow the contours of the forest, but Jason continued through the underbrush toward a clearing past the tree line. Feet from the clearing, Jason swept the beam of his flashlight across the park. Something flashed in his direction, and he dove to the ground.

Jason waited for the crickets to resume their nightly chorus before he lifted his head above the tall grass and ferns surrounding him. The sole streetlight at the park's entrance along an otherwise desolate highway cutting through the pine forest cast dim light on the outline of a vehicle. His flashlight had illuminated the rear reflectors on the truck. Although Jason was thirty yards away, he could see it was a pickup truck with a topper that looked to have spent many seasons enduring the relentless Arizona sun.

Why is a vehicle still in a day-use-only park at six forty-five in the morning? Could that be the person who took JJ? Could my son be in that truck?

His mind raced with potential next steps. Jason checked his phone and considered calling Special Agent Reddy to help secure the site while they inspected the vehicle.

Thud.

A dull sound came from the direction of the vehicle.

Is that JJ trying to get out of the truck?

Jason couldn't wait for Reddy. He had to clear the vehicle as soon as possible if his son was inside and struggling to escape.

He inched inside the tree line until he was twenty yards from the vehicle. The emerging twilight made it easier to make out more details, and Jason observed it was a Ford truck and that the windows in the topper were fogged up.

Somebody is inside the bed of that truck!

Jason removed the Glock 19 from the small of his back and verified it had a round in the chamber. He rose slowly from his crouched position and pressed himself against a massive pine tree. The foggy windows didn't allow Jason to see inside, but they also prevented the vehicle's occupants from seeing Jason approach—at least while it was still dark. The sky was a brilliant blue, and he only had minutes before the first rays of sun peeked over the mountains in the east. A backlit Jason could be easily seen from inside the vehicle, so he brought his weapon to the ready and crept in a combat crouch toward the tailgate of the truck. He aimed the stubby metal sight post at the twist handle on the camper shell in case someone saw him coming and jumped out with a weapon. When Jason was within ten feet of his target, the truck shook from someone moving inside, so he froze. A minute later, the first rays of sun kissed the mountain peaks behind him, so Jason moved to the rear of the truck.

He moved his left hand to the T-handle of the bed topper while he kept his gun trained on the glass door. He twisted slowly then jerked the door up and pulled the tailgate down.

The muzzle of the Glock was first to enter the vehicle, followed by Jason's flashlight. He expected to see a kidnapper inside the camper shell attempting to flee or shoot at him, but what he saw caught him by surprise. His flashlight highlighted two naked bodies covered by a single blanket.

"Oh my gosh," a female voice shrieked. She pulled the blanket off the man to cover her bare chest.

The young man sat up and raised his hands.

"Don't shoot," the man said shakily. "Take whatever you want."

Jason was so sure he'd see JJ and his abductor inside the vehicle that it took him a millisecond to process the situation. He lowered his pistol and turned off his flashlight as the park was flooded with sunlight.

"What are you two doing here?" Jason asked.

"We meant to leave at dark but accidentally fell asleep."

Now that the sun was up, Jason noticed that the man and woman were both very young, so he turned his head.

"Both of you, get dressed."

Moments later, Jason leaned into the camper shell and scanned it for any sign of JJ or his belongings. He saw a blow-up mattress and two open condom wrappers but no sign of JJ.

"Are you two in high school?" Jason asked.

"No, sir," the boy responded. "We both go to Gila Community College in Payson."

"Did you go to Payson High School?"

The boy nodded.

"Did either of you know Josh Mulder?"

"Isn't he the boy who—"

The girl started to ask a question but stopped. Jason knew she was going to ask if Josh was the boy who was killed by the cartel. Everyone in the small town knew.

"Yeah. He's my little brother."

"He was a sophomore when I was a senior," the boy said. "He was cool."

Jason turned the conversation from small talk to business. "Did either of you see any other people or vehicles when you arrived?"

"A car pulled up a little bit after we moved under the topper, but I didn't see any people," the boy said.

"Did you see what kind of car it was or if the person had a little kid with him?"

"No. We didn't want anyone to know we were back here, so we stayed low and kept quiet, especially because he pulled up with the headlights off."

"The car pulled up with no headlights on after dark?" Jason asked.

"Yeah. I thought it was a cop, but then I never heard anything again."

"When did the car leave?"

"Um," the boy stammered. "I'm not sure."

Jason realized the boy and girl were probably messing around when the man came back and wouldn't be much help.

"Are we in trouble?" the boy asked.

"You're not in trouble with me," Jason assured them. "But in a few minutes, a bunch of cops will be here, so unless you want to explain why you were illegally camping here overnight, I'd leave now."

The boy and girl scrambled from under the camper shell and into the front cab. The Ford truck roared to life, and the two kids quickly departed. Jason ambled from the truck to a nearby picnic table and sat down. He buried his face in his hands and exhaled loudly. Jason removed his cell phone from his pocket, along with Reddy's business card, and dialed.

"Special Agent Reddy," the voice on the other end answered.

"It's Jason Mulder."

"Where are you?"

"I'm in a park just off Granite Dells Road. Bring your team. I have something you need to see."

Chapter 9

Jason sat at the picnic table with his eyes closed and let the morning sun warm his face. It was the first time he'd stopped moving since he arrived in Payson, and he welcomed the quiet solitude in a deserted park surrounded by pine forest. His measured breathing increased as vivid images of JJ's toothless smile with his chubby dimples flashed in his mind like a movie reel. Bile swelled in his stomach as his mind took him to darker places that Jason had tried to avoid, but his tactical brain insisted on processing potential outcomes without his permission. Jason's eyes remained shut until JJ was replaced by Josh's battered and bruised face.

"No!" Jason yelled into the empty park, causing roosting birds to flee nearby trees. The memory of his little brother's death at the hands of the La Palma cartel three years ago still felt like a fresh cut from a razor-sharp blade.

Jason opened his eyes to destroy the haunting image, and that's when drops dotted the worn wood planks on the picnic table. The tears came like the start of a torrential rainstorm that stopped before the ground was wet. He wiped the salty wetness from his cheeks and jumped to his feet. Jason paced near the picnic table for a minute and exhaled loudly as his eyes lifted to the blue sky.

JJ, I'm sorry I wasn't there to protect you and bring you back home last night. I won't stop searching for you until you are safe and back home. I'm coming for you.

Jason waved for the lead black SUV to pull toward him and for the second SUV to park behind the first. Four people exited the vehicles and huddled together near the front bumper of the first SUV. Reddy whispered instructions to the three men and then walked over to Jason sitting at the picnic table.

"Did you find anything back at the house?" Jason asked.

"We have a lot to process back at the lab in Phoenix but nothing conclusive on a suspect yet. What about you?"

Jason pointed to the tree line. "That broken branch marks where I exited the forest. Go straight back about half a mile along the game trail, and that's where I found a patch of my son's blanket. It was near some jagged branches and disturbed soil, so the kidnapper must've caught it while he bought JJ here. I didn't touch or walk near it, so one of your guys may get a shoe print or something in the area that's not mine."

Reddy put her hands on her hips and scanned the small park. "So, our abductor parked here, snuck through the forest to your house to take your son, and then drove away undetected."

"That's why I waved your SUVs over to this side. When I arrived, two young kids were sleeping in the back of a pickup truck. They didn't see any people but heard a vehicle pull up, and it parked on the other side of the parking lot," Jason said of the patch of gravel that could accommodate up to four vehicles.

"Two kids?"

"Yeah, a boy and girl, probably around nineteen or twenty years old. They were messing around under the truck topper.

"They didn't see anything? No make or model of the vehicle?"

"No, but I stuck my head under the camper shell to look for signs of JJ. I didn't see anything, but I did get a picture of the license plate if you want to track down the kids and question them yourself."

"Send me the picture."

Reddy took several steps, stopped, and returned to Jason at the picnic table.

"How are you holding up, Mr. Mulder?"

"I'm fine. Just worried about my son and Shanna."

Reddy sat next to Jason on the picnic table and turned toward him.

"I get it. That's a common attitude for someone in your position, but you must also take care of yourself. This is every parent's nightmare, and you'll drive yourself crazy if you aren't careful."

Jason looked up from the ground and into Special Agent Reddy's eyes. "What are the chances we'll find my son?"

"We're going to find JJ."

"But what if his kidnapper is already in another state?" Jason's voice cracked.

"We will find him," Reddy responded in a resolute voice. "Stay positive and never give up until he's home."

Jason nodded and returned his focus to the patchy grass below the picnic table.

Reddy stood and waved for Jason to follow her. "You look exhausted. Let me take you home so you can rest while we process everything here."

Jason's instinct was to decline the offer, but she was right. He was exhausted and could also check on Shanna back at the house.

"Okay, I'll take that ride home."

Jason entered his parents' home through the back door and found his mother sitting at the kitchen table in her bathrobe. She looked up when Jason entered, and he could see the deep, dark circles under her eyes, showing she also hadn't slept. She placed her palms on the table, pushed herself to her feet, and shuffled to her son.

"Did you find anything?" Celeste asked.

Jason didn't want to put his mom through any more emotional roller coasters, so he withheld that he found a piece of JJ's blanket and the likely parking spot for the kidnapper.

"The FBI is looking for evidence at a new location, so maybe they'll find something." Noah had also risen from his seat at the kitchen table and moved beside his older brother. He placed his hand on Jason's shoulder. "I'm so sorry, Jason. I feel horrible for poor little JJ. Let me know if there's anything I can do."

"Thank you," Jason said to Noah and returned to his mom. "Where's Shanna?"

"She was up most of the night but finally went to bed in Kevin's old room a few hours ago."

Jason nodded to Celeste and Noah and then left the kitchen. He plodded down the hallway to check on Shanna but stopped before he got to the bedroom door. He returned to the kitchen, where Celeste and Noah stood by the back door.

"Noah, do you still have a drone with those good IR and 4K cameras?"

Noah straightened and crossed the room until he stood in front of Jason. He was a senior software engineer at a company specializing in commercial-grade unmanned aerial vehicles. Noah and Clay played a crucial role in tracking down Josh's killers with their high-tech drones and advanced UAV piloting abilities.

"Yeah, I still have the quadcopter from last season with the forty-five-minute flight time, three-mile range, and 4K visible-light camera. I'm also testing the latest model for this season with even more range. What are you thinking?"

"I know it's a long shot, but I know the last location where we know the kidnapper had JJ. I'd like to see if he may be holed up nearby."

"We can cover a lot of ground pretty quick," Noah said. "Give me a few minutes, and I'll pack both drones. Meet me at my Jeep."

Noah pulled onto the highway with Jason in the passenger seat as the sun crested the White Mountains.

"Where should we look first?" Noah asked.

Jason pursed his lips. "I don't think the kidnapper would risk driving through town, so that eliminates north and west. South to Phoenix is highly likely, while east has endless places to hide in the National Forest. Let's go east a few miles and see if we can find something."

Noah pulled off the highway into a clearing on a ridge. He unpacked the two drones from their case and handed Jason a controller. "Alright, I've got both birds ready to fly. Do you know how to operate a UAV?"

Jason shrugged. "How hard can it be?"

"Jason, these aren't cheap toys. They are professional-grade search-and-rescue drones, so take it slow until you get the feel of it. The infrared cameras won't help as much now that the sun is up, but the 4K cameras will give us a crystal-clear view of the terrain."

Jason nodded, his eyes scanning the tree line. "Let's start at the forest road off the highway and work our way out in a grid pattern."

"Got it," Noah replied, powering up the first drone.

The propellers whirred to life, creating a small whirlwind of pine needles at their feet. "I'll take the eastern side of the forest road, and you can search the western side."

"Sounds good," Jason said. His drone bounced up and down and tilted back and forth until he got more familiar with the controls. "Remember, we're looking for any sign of disturbance—broken branches, fresh tire tracks, anything that looks out of place."

The two drones soared twenty to thirty feet above treetops in opposite directions. Jason and Noah's eyes were glued to their respective screens, methodically scanning the forest below.

After about twenty minutes of silent concentration, Noah spoke. "I may have something."

"What is it?"

"A white-hot heat signature. IR camera's picking it up about a half mile northeast of here. Looks like a stove or a fire. I'll be overhead in ninety seconds."

Jason recalled his nearby drone and shuffled to Noah's side, his boots crunching against dry pine needles. He leaned in to see the screen. "That's a GP Small," he said, narrowing his eyes.

"A what?"

"Military surplus tent. General Purpose Small, with space for maybe a couple guys—and that heat source means they're using a stove."

Noah's fingers danced over the controller, directing the drone into a careful circle above the target. "It's nearly invisible out here under the canopy. If not for the infrared, I'd never have spotted it."

"Why the hell would someone be camping out here in that tent?" Jason muttered, his gut churning with anxious anticipation. His mind leaped to one possibility, adrenaline surging down his spine like a forest fire.

"Grab the coordinates," Jason snapped, stepping back. "We're heading out."

They reached the site quickly, skidding to a stop about twenty feet from the tent. The earthy scent of damp soil and decaying leaves hung heavy in the air, the forest eerily quiet except for the faint crackle of something burning inside the canvas. Jason could feel his pulse pounding in his ears, eager to know what was inside the tent.

Noah approached the tent's entrance, his eagerness overriding Jason's signal to wait. The canvas flap exploded outward as a large man burst through, shoving Noah aside like a rag doll.

"Noah!" Jason shouted, instinctively lunging forward.

The man didn't look back. He tore into the forest, crashing through the undergrowth with surprising speed for his size, his wild hair and shoulders blending into the shadows. Jason checked that Noah was on his feet then locked onto the retreating figure.

"Go!" Noah shouted, waving him off. Jason was already moving.

Years of training took over. Jason sprinted after the man, ducking under low-hanging branches and leaping over fallen logs. The suspect plowed ahead with reckless abandon, leaving a trail of snapped twigs and trampled leaves in his wake.

They reached a dry wash where recent rains had carved jagged channels into the sandy soil. The man stumbled on loose gravel and faltered, giving Jason the opening he needed. Jason surged forward, launching himself into the man's midsection. They tumbled down the embankment, trading blows as they rolled.

The stench hit Jason first—wood smoke, sweat, and body odor. The man's beard, filthy and knotted, bristled as he swung wildly, catching Jason in the jaw with an elbow.

Jason twisted, using leverage and muscle memory to lock the man's arm behind his back, driving him face-first into the ground. Seconds after the scuffle began, he had the man pinned, his knee pressed firmly between the shoulder blades.

"Don't move!" Jason commanded.

Noah arrived seconds later, panting and wide-eyed. "You caught him!"

The man squirmed, prompting Jason to dig his knee deeper into his back until he went limp.

Noah squinted at the man's face. "I think you caught somebody wanted by the Gila County Sheriff's Office. I remember seeing his face in the paper."

"You know him?"

"I believe his name is Marcus Wheeler," Noah replied. "He's been evading the police in these woods for months. Sheriff's office wants him for assault and other charges."

Jason felt hope leave his body like a deflating balloon. He pulled out his phone, keeping pressure on Wheeler's back, and called Agent Reddy.

Thirty minutes later, flashing red and blue lights washed over the forest. Deputies swarmed the campsite as Agent Reddy dug through the scattered contents of the tent. Jason leaned against Noah's Jeep in silence, his temporary surge of adrenaline replaced by bone-deep exhaustion.

Reddy finally approached, wiping a hand across her brow. "We found evidence linking Wheeler to a string of burglaries," she said grimly. "But nothing about your son. Sorry, Jason."

Jason nodded, his jaw tight. More precious time was lost while his son was alone out there somewhere.

"Hey," Noah said softly beside him. "We'll find him."

"Yeah." Jason pushed off from the Jeep, already planning his next move. Wheeler wasn't their kidnapper, but JJ was still out there. And Jason wouldn't stop until he brought his boy home.

He climbed into the Jeep with Noah and stared out at the dark, endless forest for a moment longer. He couldn't afford dead ends. His son needed him. Somewhere out there, someone knew where JJ was.

And Jason would tear apart every corner of the earth until he found him.

Chapter 10

Whispering Pines, Arizona

Jason gazed into the blackness, oblivious that the coffee in his cup had turned lukewarm. His mind raced with possibilities, considering every potential location where he may find JJ. It was like a never-ending horror movie playing on repeat since his son disappeared fifty-nine hours earlier.

He'd returned home to Whispering Pines with Shanna once they exhausted all possibilities of finding JJ near his parents' house. Shanna struggled to get out of bed, so Jason did the only thing that prevented him from slipping into the abyss of depression and madness. He continued searching for JJ even though he was ninety-nine percent sure that neither the kidnapper nor JJ was in the area. The one percent possibility that his son was still somewhere nearby was enough to drive Jason to physical exhaustion each day.

Jason dumped the remaining coffee into the sink and padded into his bedroom to grab his gear for another day of searching.

He passed his phone charging on the nightstand when it buzzed. Jason dove to answer the call like every other one the past three days. He'd hoped it was good news from FBI Special Agent Reddy, but it was Clay Landry.

"Hey man, anything new today?" Clay asked after Jason answered. He'd called every day since JJ went missing, and Jason appreciated hearing from his friend and boss on Senator Conrad's PSD team.

"No, nothing new. I'm getting ready to go out again to search for JJ."

"Where are you going today?" Clay asked.

"I'm not sure yet. I'll figure it out on the road."

"Jason, I don't think the answer you need is *where,* but *who* took JJ," Clay said and paused for several seconds before continuing. "I've been lying awake at night thinking about this, and for me, all roads lead to Senator Conrad. Our work for the senator may be related to your missing son."

"You sound like the FBI. How is it related?" Jason snapped.

"What if someone else from the Al Rashidi family is here trying to get revenge for taking out Amir and Jassim before they could assassinate Senator Conrad last summer?"

Jason took a deep breath and let it out. "I've thought about that, too, along with everybody else I've put behind bars or permanently neutralized as a PJ, DEA agent, PSD team member, even anyone I may have wronged in junior high. It's a longer list than expected, but nobody rises to the top as the most likely suspect to take my son. The Al Rashidi brothers are dead, and the State Department has flagged the rest of their family if they ever enter the United States. Donaldson from the DEA is still in prison, and all the cartel members are either dead or still in prison."

"What about the people that were negatively impacted? The Chinese drug cartel that lost their distribution network after you uncovered the corrupt DEA agents? Friends of the goons that tossed Molotov cocktails into your parents' house? A family member who thinks you railroaded Donaldson?"

Jason stood in stunned silence. During his frazzled mental state, he hadn't fully considered the tangled web of people with motives to kidnap his son. The mere thought of all the suspects was overwhelming.

"I don't know, Clay. The FBI is better suited to pull on all of those strings. I need to focus on one or two top suspects."

"What about the corrupt sheriff? He's as dirty as they get, and he may still have the means to get to you."

"Sheriff Kellerman?"

"Yeah, that guy."

Saying Kellerman's name aloud was akin to slicing off a scab with a dull blade. The former Navajo County sheriff was someone Jason had considered numerous times. His last stunt with the Chinese drug cartel had landed him in solitary confinement at the United States Penitentiary in Tucson, Arizona—a high-security federal prison. Kellerman had proven he'd let no law or person get in his way, and his additional twenty-five-year sentence gave him plenty of motivation to hurt Jason and his family—if he could.

"Yeah, I've considered Kellerman. If he weren't in solitary confinement in a federal pen, he'd be number one on my list."

"You should go down and pay him a visit," Clay suggested.

"He'll never admit to it even if he was involved."

"I know, but you can verify he's still in solitary confinement or isn't working with a guard or someone to do his bidding."

Clay brought one of Jason's concerns to the surface, and he could no longer ignore the fact that of all the people Jason has put behind bars, former sheriff Kellerman was the one man he knew would have no problem contracting someone to kidnap his son.

"You know, Clay, I'm going to do that. I need to see if I should either rule him out or make him my primary suspect in JJ's abduction."

Jason was already in his closet, changing from his cold-weather tactical gear to something he could wear to the federal prison in Tucson, Arizona.

"Keep me posted, Jason, and if there's anything else I can do, let me know."

Appreciation for his friend swelled in Jason like a rising tide. He knew this was also tough on Clay, and he had never asked how he was doing.

"Thanks, Clay. I appreciate it. How's everything going for you and the rest of the team in DC?"

"We're busier than a one-legged man in an ass-kicking contest, but we'll get through it like we always do."

"Thank you, brother. I'm going to find JJ and bring him home. After that, I'll return to DC to help the team."

Providing security for Senator Conrad was such a low priority right now that it almost seemed foreign to him. He was so laser-focused on finding JJ and his abductor that he couldn't imagine doing anything else, but he was loyal to his team, and once he found JJ, he intended to support the people who would cover for him as long as he needed.

"Sounds good. Go talk to the former sheriff and find your son."

Jason raised his arms for a physical pat-down to pass through the final checkpoint to the visitation room. He arrived at the sprawling 584-thousand-square-foot United States Penitentiary complex in Tucson three hours after he departed. It was across the freeway from his old Air Force Reserve unit at Davis-Monthan Air Force Base, sparking positive memories for a few miles before he took the exit for the penitentiary.

The visitation room was only a third of the size of the medium-security facility in Kingman, Arizona, because of the restrictions on the number of visitors an inmate could have at a high-security federal prison. Jason could only arrange the last-minute visit because he said it was part of his advanced security investigation for a future visit for Senator Conrad. He was pleasantly surprised that USP Tucson approved his request once they verified his credentials.

Nobody else was in the room, so Jason chose one of the eight open seats at the far right. He peered through the glass, waiting to see his old nemesis. The door opened, and a thin, gaunt man entered the room in shackles with a corrections officer on each side. At first, Jason thought someone else was coming to visit an inmate, but then Jason realized it was the former Navajo County sheriff. His puffy cheeks and barrel chest were gone, and Jason guessed that the former sheriff had lost about fifty pounds.

Kellerman's gaze floated around the room as if he were seeing it for the first time. He noticed Jason sitting on the other side of the glass, and his absent eyes immediately turned hard. The inmate said something to the guards that Jason couldn't hear but saw one of them shake his head and push Kellerman into his seat across the glass from Jason.

Jason picked up the phone, but Kellerman continued to stare him down. Jason motioned for him to pick up the phone, and several seconds later, he did.

"What the hell are you doing here?" Kellerman growled. His body had changed, but his gravelly, baritone voice still caused Jason's pulse to quicken.

"I'm here to ask you some questions."

"I'm not telling you shit. You put me here, and I still have six months of solitary confinement before I even get a cell."

"I didn't put you anywhere. You did this to yourself when you partnered with a Chinese drug cartel to traffic opioids across the country from your cushy cell in Kingman. You're lucky your attorney was able to negotiate a plea deal with the district attorney on the attempted-murder charge of a federal law enforcement agent, or you'd be sitting in Florence right now waiting for the needle."

Kellerman's face formed into a snarl but showed no other reaction to Jason's statement. The former lawman had lost some fight after so much solitary confinement.

"Who was your contact in the La Palma cartel?" Jason asked.

"He's dead."

"What about their Patrón? The man they call El Jaguar?"

"Why do you care? Everybody from that operation in the US is either in prison or dead."

"Because somebody abducted my son while he was sleeping in his bed earlier this week, and you and the cartel rise to the top of my list as the kind of people that would orchestrate something like that."

Jason thought he saw Kellerman wince and flash an expression of disgust.

"I know you're not very bright, son, but I'm in solitary confinement in a federal prison, so I didn't have anything to do with that."

"That's never stopped you in the past."

Kellerman leaned closer to the glass, allowing Jason to see the fiery red streaks in the whites of his eyes.

"I may be a lot of things, but child predator is not one of them."

"What about the cartel? Kidnapping is big business for many of them."

Kellerman's bushy gray eyebrows pinched toward the bridge of his nose as if seriously considering the question.

"I wouldn't put it past them, but they took me off their Christmas card list after I was arrested, so I wouldn't know."

"So you think they are capable?"

"Why don't you go down there and ask them yourself?" Keller-man said with a sinister chuckle.

"I'm here right now, so I'm asking you."

A ghastly grin flashed across Kellerman's face. "I did hear a rumor before I landed in solitary."

Jason waited to hear the rumor, but Kellerman's tired eyes stared back at him through the glass.

"What's the rumor?"

"I heard an old ghost may come back to haunt you."

"Who?"

"He wouldn't be a very good ghost if everyone knew about him."

"Tell me what you know!" Jason demanded.

Kellerman stood and shuffled back a step in his shackles.

"I'm done here." He slammed the phone down, and the two guards swooped in and escorted him from the visitation room.

Jason stared at the empty seat across the glass, replaying the conversation.

What did he mean by "an old ghost"? Did Kellerman know something, or was he taunting me the only way he could?

Despite Kellerman's history as a corrupt sheriff and hardened criminal, Jason believed he'd heard a rumor. It didn't help him pinpoint a suspect, but it narrowed the list of likely suspects to someone he'd put away in the past. Now Jason just had to find a ghost.

CHAPTER 11

Whispering Pines, Arizona

Jason pulled into his driveway in Whispering Pines in the early afternoon and turned off the ignition. He remained in his truck and stared out the windshield at the dry golden grass in his backyard surrounded by dull-green pine trees. His brain ached from spinning scenarios during his drive home from the Federal Penitentiary in Tucson. Although the sun was out, his truck cooled quickly, and Jason was chased inside once his breath was visible.

When he entered, he hung up his coat and noticed Shanna in the kitchen. Jason met his wife near the kitchen sink and kissed her forehead.

"I'm glad to see you up," Jason said.

"What's that supposed to mean?"

Jason was taken aback by the sharp edge in her voice. "You've been in bed a lot lately, and I am glad to see you up. That's all."

"I have things to do like laundry and picking up around here. Where were you?"

Jason recognized that Shanna was feeling the pain of JJ's absence, so he suppressed his instinct to become defensive despite feeling it well up inside him.

"I had to do something down in Tucson."

"Did you go down to your old Air Force Base?"

He couldn't lie to Shanna, but Jason also didn't want to reveal that he was talking to a man who tried to have him killed—twice. It would only make her more concerned about JJ, so he told her a partial truth.

"I was following up on a potential lead about JJ."

"Well, did you find anything?"

Jason shook his head and looked at the floor. "No, nothing concrete, but the drive back gave me time to think of new leads."

Shanna leaned against the counter and crossed her arms. "You know, Jason, not everyone handles trauma the same way. I know you've been out searching for JJ during every minute of daylight the last three days, and I appreciate it, but just because I wasn't out looking for him doesn't mean I'm not devastated that he's missing. I needed a few days to process that our JJ is out there waiting for us or the police to find him."

Jason's heart ached for his wife. She was in so much pain, and he'd do anything to make it go away.

"Did you think I was judging you for not putting on your boots and searching the forest high and low for JJ? Nothing could be further from the truth if that's what you thought. I know you're an amazing mom and would do anything, and I mean anything, to get your boy back. I understand everybody processes situations like this differently, and I have to keep charging ahead to solve the problem or complete the mission. I don't know what I would do if I—"

Jason trailed off as he choked back tears. Shanna crossed the kitchen, wrapped her arms around his torso, and leaned her wet cheeks against his chest. "I miss him so much."

"I do too," Jason said as he pulled Shanna closer.

After a long hug, Jason pulled away. "Have you heard anything from Reddy today?"

"I called her after I got up, and she said they're still working around the clock but have nothing new to report."

"Dammit. I hate feeling helpless!" Jason barked.

"Me too."

Jason wiped a tear from Shanna's chin and kissed her. "What can I do to help?"

"We're getting low on wood for the stove, and a cold snap is in the forecast for next week."

"I'll split enough wood to last us several weeks."

The pile of oak logs that Jason split grew near the back patio. The air was cool, but the mid-January sun was still warm on his head and neck. Jason took a break in the shade and thought more about what Kellerman said to him in Tucson. La Palma was still one of the top suspects in his mind. During the drive back to Whispering Pines, Jason committed to calling his old boss at the DEA to see if he knew anything about the La Palma cartel.

Jason left Special Agent Holland a voicemail and received a call back a half hour later.

"Thanks for calling me back so quickly," Jason said when he answered.

"How's the new gig going in DC? I meant to call you after you saved Senator Conrad from the terrorists in Las Vegas last summer."

Jason could hear the good-natured smile in Holland's voice but didn't have it in him to partake in small talk when his son was missing. He wanted to get right to the point.

"Everything's going fine with the senator, but I called you regarding something personal that happened to my family."

"What is it?" Holland asked tentatively.

Jason swallowed hard and sighed, knowing there was no easy way to share that your child was kidnapped.

"My son was abducted."

"What? You need to call the FBI right away because they have specialists for that kind of thing. The sooner they—"

Jason cut him off. "It happened three days ago, and the FBI is on it. They're doing the best they can, but all they can tell me is that they believe the kidnapper is no longer in the area and that they are doing everything they can to find my son."

"Understood," Holland quickly replied. "I'm so sorry to hear that terrible news. How can I help?"

"I think it may have something to do with former Sheriff Kellerman."

"No, not this time. He's in the hole in Tucson, and he could never coordinate something like that from there."

"I know. I went to visit him today to see if he knew anything about my son's abduction."

The call went silent for so long that Jason checked his phone to ensure he hadn't dropped the call. He was confident that Holland would help him as long as it fell within his role at the DEA. However, he also knew that Holland would be careful not to overstep his boundaries and risk a reprimand from his boss. It was another reason Jason was glad to be in the private sector.

"Did you learn anything when you spoke to him?"

"He didn't give anything up, and I don't think he was involved, but Kellerman confirmed my suspicion with another suspect."

"Who do you suspect?"

Jason knew it might sound crazy to Holland before he said it, but he thought about it a dozen times during his drive home and concluded they were prime suspects each time.

"The La Palma cartel."

"Why? How would they pull that off up here?" Holland asked in succession, sounding flustered.

"They have a motive because we dismantled their entire US operation, and I know they have no qualms abducting adults or children. Plus, Kellerman said he heard an old ghost was coming back to haunt me. I don't know what that means, but I figure it has something to do with the cartel."

"Okay," Holland replied slowly. "How could I help?"

"I'm sure you have access to some information or intelligence on the La Palma cartel in El Salvador," Jason started. "I was hoping you could get in touch with those assets and see if they've heard of any chatter about a kidnapping of an American boy."

Jason heard Holland's office chair creak as he rocked back and forth, considering the request.

"Yeah," Holland finally said. "Give me a couple of days. I'll make some calls."

"Thanks." Jason's voice was steady, but desperation lingered just beneath the surface. "I appreciate it and understand the sensitive nature of what you're doing—but please, hurry."

Holland's voice interrupted when he was on the verge of ending the call. "Jason, who do you think the ghost is?"

Jason hesitated, his mind reeling. He'd pondered that question countless times, but the answer always seemed elusive, like a mirage on a hot Arizona day.

"I don't know," Jason admitted. "I wish I did."

Holland cleared his throat. "What about Victor Romero?"

Jason blinked. "The guy who got swept over the waterfall unconscious? During a flash flood?"

"They never found his body," Holland said.

The words hit Jason like a gut punch, kicking open a door he thought had long since been closed. His memory of that day was vivid: Victor Romero's lifeless body suspended at the top of the waterfall, surrounded by brown mist from the massive amount of water plunging forty feet with a force that could crush steel.

"There's no way anyone could have survived that fall," Jason said, reliving that scene in his mind. "Or that amount of water."

"Maybe," Holland replied, though his tone suggested doubt. "I'll get back to you."

The line went dead, but Jason froze where he stood and stared at the tree line at the edge of his property. He raked a hand through his hair and exhaled.

"Could it be Victor Romero?"

Jason shook his head. "I saw him go over those falls. Don't waste time chasing that dead end," he muttered.

He turned his focus back to the list of suspects in his mind. One of them held the answers—and his son. Jason knew his instincts would have to lead him to the answer. And soon.

JJ was running out of time.

Chapter 12

Payson, Arizona

Jason poured himself and his mom a cup of coffee and carried them to the kitchen table. He placed one cup in front of his mom and sat in the same oak chair that supported him for thousands of meals in the home he grew up in until he left for the Air Force. Celeste had been calling several times a day to check on the status of her missing grandson, and Jason was concerned about his mom and the guilt she was unnecessarily putting on herself for JJ's abduction.

"How are you doing, Mom?"

Celeste stirred a single packet of sugar and two half-and-half creamers into her cup like she had since Jason could remember.

"I'm not worried about me. I'm worried about JJ and you and Shanna."

"We're concerned about you too. Are you okay?"

"I feel so horrible about what happened. Poor little JJ. I picture how scared he must be, alone and confused about what's happening."

"You can't put this on yourself. JJ was taken by scum of this earth, and there was nothing you could've done about it. We must be strong and persistent to find JJ and bring him home."

Celeste reached across the table and squeezed Jason's hand. A knock at the front door surprised everyone, and Jason leaped to his feet.

"Are you expecting anyone?"

Celeste shook her head.

"Stay here. I'm going to see who it is."

Jason still had Shanna's Glock tucked in his waist, so he removed it and crept to the family room. He took a quick peek through the front window and saw a black ponytail waving back and forth across an FBI logo on someone's jacket. Jason hid the gun under his shirt and opened the front door.

"Special Agent Reddy, what are you doing here?"

"May I come in?"

Jason opened the door and moved to the side to allow Reddy to enter. After she was inside, he closed the door and faced the FBI agent as he slid his hands into his front pockets. "What brings you up here today?"

Celeste entered the family room and noticed Special Agent Reddy. "Is everything okay?"

Reddy nodded. "Yes, I was back at the park this morning and noticed Jason's truck when I drove by, so I thought I would take advantage of a face-to-face conversation versus a phone call."

Celeste smiled. "Do you want anything, coffee, tea, water?"

"I'm fine, thank you."

Celeste returned to the kitchen, and Jason motioned toward the couch in the family room. They sat on opposite ends and turned toward each other.

"We positively identified the tire tracks at the park to a crossover SUV that is also one of the most rented vehicles," Reddy began. "Tecate police in Mexico found a burned-out SUV that matched the VIN number of a black SUV rented at Phoenix Sky Harbor Airport six days ago."

"Nobody was inside," Reddy was quick to add. "We think that vehicle belonged to our kidnapper."

Jason scooted closer, keenly interested in the new information. "Were they able to find any clues to verify JJ was with them or where they were headed?"

Reddy shook her head. "No evidence, but the Tecate police suspect they continued to Tijuana to link up with another mode of transportation like a flight or boat."

Jason rubbed the stubble on his cheek. "It seems all indications are the kidnapper fled south."

"That's not the only thing I stopped by to share. The lab came across something that piqued my interest, so I came up today to get a better look."

"What is it?"

"We matched a boot print in the bedroom here and at the park, so we know it belongs to the kidnapper, but the sole pattern doesn't match anything in our databases. They were both just partial prints, so I came up today to see if I could find another print that was larger and had more of the design, but I couldn't find anything."

Wrinkles formed on Jason's forehead as he processed the information.

"What do you make of a boot print not in the database?"

"It points to someone coming from another country to take your son."

Jason scooted closer. "More evidence the kidnapper is from Latin America?"

"It's hard to say until we identify the shoe manufacturer, and once we do, that will help narrow down where the abductor is from."

Jason's eyes drifted from Special Agent Reddy to the floor. "And where we may find JJ."

Reddy returned a subtle nod but did not speak. After a period of silence, the FBI agent stood and straightened her jacket. "That was all I wanted to share with you. We have a team working to identify the shoe print, and I'll let you know as soon as we do."

Jason remained seated, and his head bobbed up and down, confirming he understood. He saw Reddy moving to leave, so he jumped up and met her at the door. "Let me know as soon as you find out."

"We will."

Reddy's SUV disappeared around the corner, leaving Jason with his darkening thoughts. His mind circled back to La Palma. They'd already proven their willingness to destroy his family when their *sicarios* tried to burn them alive with Molotov cocktails. A local shoe manufacturer from Central or South America might slip through the FBI's database, but La Palma's fingerprints were all over this. They had the manpower, the motive, and most importantly, the capacity for unconscionable violence. With each passing minute, his certainty grew that La Palma either had JJ or knew who did.

The pump clicked rhythmically as Jason filled his gas tank, the sound matching his pulse. A black Toyota Rav 4 pulled up to the opposite pump, its tinted windows obscuring a clear interior view. Jason barely registered the vehicle until movement caught his eye—a small head visible through the back window, a child in a car seat.

His heart stopped.

Jason had just learned that authorities found the kidnapper's empty SUV burned to a crisp in Mexico, but he was still drawn to the back seat.

What if they were wrong?

Before Jason realized what he was doing, he stepped over the fuel hose and strode toward the SUV, his hands trembling. The world narrowed to that back window as he pressed closer, trying to see through the glare.

"Can I help you?"

The sharp female voice cut through his tunnel vision. Jason turned to find a woman watching him with a mixture of fear and protective anger. The look of a mother sensing a threat to her child. The reality of what he was doing hit him like a slap across his cheek.

"No, I—" Jason forced an embarrassed laugh. "I thought you were someone I knew."

The woman's eyes never left him as he backed away, her hand hovering near her purse. She didn't relax until he was well clear of her vehicle.

Jason returned to his truck, and once inside, he gripped the steering wheel until his knuckles went white. Every child he saw became JJ. Every black SUV could be holding his son. The rational part of his brain, the part trained for tactical thinking and cool decision-making, was being hijacked by a desperate father's grief.

I'm going to lose it if I don't find JJ soon.

He jammed the truck into gear and peeled out of the gas station, leaving strips of rubber on the asphalt. In his rearview mirror, he saw the woman pulling her phone out, probably calling the police about the suspicious man who'd approached her car.

Let her call. None of it mattered. The only thing that mattered was finding his son, and if that meant embracing the darkness growing inside him, so be it.

CHAPTER 13

Whispering Pines, Arizona

The steady beat of his footsteps on the pavement sent Jason into a contemplative state. Over the past week, he had experienced an overwhelming number of new situations. Boot prints, cartels, charred vehicles, and vague remarks from a corrupt former sheriff clung to his mind like prickly thistles on a sock.

Jason turned the corner and checked his GPS-enabled watch. He'd completed four of the planned five miles of his run and was sweating despite the temps in the forties. He needed the run to clear his head.

He slowed and turned into his driveway. Jason stopped beside his back patio and started pacing while he caught his breath. The five-mile run before breakfast provided Jason with the clarity he sought. It was painful to admit, but they were no closer to finding JJ or capturing his abductor than they were a week ago. It was time for a change.

Jason entered the house and found Shanna sipping tea at the dining room table. He leaned against the counter, ran his fingers through his hair, and sighed.

"What's wrong?" Shanna asked.

"I think JJ may be in El Salvador."

"Have you told Special Agent Reddy?"

Jason shook his head.

"Why not?" Shanna asked. Her voice was accusatory. "She's looking for our son and needs all the help she can get."

Jason's shoulders tensed, and he crossed his arms over his chest as he grew defensive. It was one part frustration, one part exhaustion, and one part fear.

"That's the problem. Don't you think they should have made more progress by now?"

"Then help them."

Jason opened his mouth to respond but stopped. He was trying to be strong for Shanna and his family while concentrating all his efforts on finding JJ. The agony of knowing his son was somewhere out there alone, afraid, and potentially injured was unbearable. Even with all of his training to remain calm and focused during times of chaos, Jason felt his self-control slipping. Each tick of the clock was like another razor-thin paper cut to his heart. The minutes of waiting for the next update from the FBI when he should be busting down doors in La Palma were the most excruciating of all. Jason felt the pilot light of adrenaline ignite in his gut, and once it reached a boil, he'd no longer be in control of his emotions.

"Shanna, our son has been missing for six days," Jason said through gritted teeth. "I know the FBI is doing all they can to find him, but that's not good enough. JJ needs to be home with us; I'm the best person to make that happen. I should go to El Salvador to find JJ."

Jason spoke calmly during his response, but he couldn't mask the rage dripping from each word.

Shanna stepped toward Jason as her hand moved to his face. She gently caressed his cheek while they locked eyes.

"We want the same thing, Jason. Nobody has the skills and desire to bring JJ home more than you do. I miss JJ so much, but I don't want to risk losing both of you. There has to be a better way to end this nightmare."

Jason pulled Shanna into his chest and held her tight. She didn't shed a single tear, and he assumed she'd also moved from the shock and denial stages to anger and action. "You're not going to lose JJ or me."

Shanna's phone rang, and she checked her caller ID. "If you want to share something with Special Agent Reddy, you can now. It's her."

Shanna put Reddy on speaker.

"Hi, I'm here with Jason."

"Hi, Shanna. Hi, Jason. I'm glad you can hear this too," Reddy said.

Shanna secured Jason's hand in hers, and they sat next to each other on the couch.

"Good news. We got a match on the partial boot print that came up empty when we put it through our CJIS database. The Scientific Working Group on Shoeprint and Tire Tread Evidence has tens of thousands of footwear designs but nothing similar to our print. We contacted our international partners. We just got a call back from DNI in Colombia, and they identified the manufacturer. It's from Guatemala."

"Guatemala?" Shanna asked. Her eyes were wide in surprise, but this revelation confirmed Jason's suspicions.

"Yeah," Reddy replied. "It's a custom shoe handcrafted by Adelante Shoe Company in Guatemala. Based on their website, whoever purchased the boot had to shell out over seven hundred dollars, so it was not a poor farmer. It was likely a—"

"Cartel member," Jason interrupted.

"Yes, a cartel member," Reddy echoed.

"That's good news though, right? Can't you get the shoe company to tell you who they made that shoe for and identify the kidnapper?" Shanna asked.

Reddy sighed into the phone. "That's where our luck ended. The shoe manufacturer has a strict confidentiality policy for all their wealthy clients. We must go through the Justice Department to get cooperation through the Guatemalan courts, which will take some time. I just wanted you to know this latest information as soon as I received it."

"What happens next?" Shanna asked.

"We have several people working on this new evidence, so something is bound to break soon. I'll contact you when we have something new to share."

The call ended, and Shanna rushed into the bedroom and shut the door. Jason leaned back on the couch and stared at the wood beams on the ceiling until his phone buzzed. It was Clay, so Jason stepped into the crisp air on his back patio. Jason assumed he was calling to check in on JJ like he had every morning since he went missing.

"The FBI found a shoe print from a manufacturer in Guatemala," Jason shared. "It points to a kidnapper who is not from the United States, and you know who that leads to?"

"La Palma cartel," Clay whispered.

"It's not much, but it's a small step forward," Jason said, trying to sound positive for his boss.

"I'm excited to hear you're getting better leads, but that's not why I called."

Jason pulled out a chair, turned it toward the river behind his house, and sat down. "Okay, what's up?"

"I wouldn't even think to ask this of you right now if it weren't absolutely necessary, but the presidential inauguration is in two days, and Conrad was invited to be on the main stage behind the president."

"Conrad? Why?" Jason asked.

"The new president ran on promoting more bipartisanship, and his team believes the POLAR Act cosponsored by Senator Conrad and Congresswoman Duarte is a prime example of what can be accomplished if Congress works across the aisle. They want Conrad and Duarte visible on TV across the country during the inauguration, but his chief of staff is concerned that will reignite tensions with the people opposed to the POLAR Act. My threat assessment came to the same conclusion, and we can't provide adequate protection with a three-man team."

In any other circumstance, Jason would have been on the next flight to Washington, DC, but now he couldn't imagine protecting an important principal like Senator Conrad when his mind would be on JJ.

"Can you contract someone in the area?" Jason asked.

Clay chuckled. "Not for the inauguration with over a hundred thousand people expected to attend. Everybody with a badge within ninety miles is already booked, and I'm not willing to put a warm body in the diamond after what happened during the campaign. We both know how desperate some of Conrad's opponents can be on this issue."

"I get it, I do," Jason replied, "But I'm not sure my head will be fully in it to protect the senator at such an important event. I can't take my mind off finding JJ."

"I'd already thought of that, and if you can come, I'd rather have half a Jason Mulder watching our flank than anyone else. We need you, man."

Jason took a deep breath as he ran his fingers through his hair.

"I need to talk to Shanna." Jason intended to speak with his wife, but it was more to buy him time before he declined Clay's invitation.

"I appreciate it, Jason, but don't take too long to decide. I need you on the first flight out tomorrow so we have time to get everyone on the same page."

Jason returned and found Shanna making a new cup of tea in the kitchen.

"Who were you talking to?" Shanna asked.

"That was Clay. He said he needs me back in Washington for the presidential inauguration."

"What did you say?"

Jason searched Shanna's face to determine if she was upset at the prospect of him leaving, but he couldn't read her emotions.

"I said I had to talk to you. I know they need me back there, but I can't fathom working while I could be searching for JJ."

Shanna met Jason near the door. "Have we found anything new today that will lead us to our son?"

"Just the information on the boot that you heard from Reddy. That's it."

Shanna put her hand on Jason's chest. "Help your team with an important event for this country, and then come back home and continue your search for JJ. We still have bills to pay, so you need to keep your job."

"I can't focus on work when all I can think about is finding JJ."

"Where would you search tomorrow if you told Clay no? Is there somewhere you haven't checked two or three times yet?"

Jason stared back at his wife. Shanna was right, but he couldn't fathom flying across the country to work while his son was still missing. She must have read his thoughts.

"Turn the trip into part of your search for JJ."

"What do you mean?"

"Check with your connections in DC to see if they can help. You work for a US Senator, and he must know some people who can help. You can meet up with Archie and see if he knows of any new angles to consider."

Jason had already considered reaching out to Special Agent Archie Woods. Even though Archie worked in a different division than Reddy at the FBI, he had a lot of connections in all the Washington agencies. Plus, he was a friend.

"Maybe that will help."

Shanna moved closer to Jason and slid one hand behind his neck.

"If I thought for a moment that you staying home and searching for JJ around here would bring him home faster, I'd tell you to stay, but that's not the case. The FBI and police have searched everywhere. He's no longer in this area."

Jason looked at the ceiling as tears welled up. "I know."

"Go to Washington, and I'll keep the pressure on the FBI while you're away."

Jason's hands rose to Shanna's face, and he kissed her. "I'm going for a walk."

"Is everything okay?"

"Yeah, I just need a few minutes to think."

"I'll make us an early lunch."

Gusty winds ruffled Jason's hair and tussled his flannel jacket as he walked to the East Verde River in his backyard. When he arrived at the bank, the leafless branches rattled above him like wooden swords. He slid his hands into his coat pockets as he watched the shallow, narrow river glide over the smooth boulders.

Everything points to La Palma. How can I find where they're holding JJ?

A crow landed on a branch twenty feet above Jason. It skirted back and forth, its eyes darting from Jason to the yellow grass around him as it searched for a meal. Jason moved from under the crow and ambled along the bank, thinking of how to locate JJ. Suddenly, he turned and jogged back to the house. He took the patio stairs two at a time and burst through the back door.

Shanna sat at the table with two plates covered with wheat bread sandwiches and potato chips.

Jason grabbed his wallet and the keys to his truck off the counter.

"Where are you going?"

"If I'm going to find our son, I need intelligence. I'm going to the DEA office in Camp Verde to see my old boss. After that, I'll call Archie to see if he knows anything new. And then I'm going to bring JJ home."

CHAPTER 14

Camp Verde, Arizona

Jason zipped past the mesquite and juniper trees lining the highway like sentries as he descended into Camp Verde, Arizona. Distant white-tipped mountains grew in his windshield before he turned into town. It was a familiar route after Jason worked out of the DEA duty office for over a year before he joined Senator Conrad's PSD team. He used the seventy-five-minute journey to think of how to approach his former boss with a delicate request.

The parking lot was full, so Jason parked in a visitor spot. He announced himself at the front door and entered once he was buzzed in. Steps inside, Jason was greeted by the smell of cleaning products, old carpet, and pungent coffee. The familiar scents boosted his confidence in his mission with Holland.

"Is Special Agent Holland available?" Jason asked the young lady at the desk nearest the door. He did not remember seeing the raven-haired woman while he worked there but knew she was likely assisting Holland.

"No, he's in a meeting right now. Is he expecting you?"

"Can I wait for him?"

"It could be an hour or two before he's available."

"Okay, I'll wait."

"Who should I say is here to meet with him?" the young lady asked.

"Tell him Mulder is here."

Jason scanned the area for a place to sit when he heard his name called from across a bank of desks. "Mulder, is that you?"

He turned to locate the voice and saw it was Special Agent Gary Carlson. They'd shared a workspace when Jason worked from the Camp Verde duty office.

Jason strode across the room and shook his hand. "Hey, Carlson, what's up?"

"Still chasing drug pushers across the state. Are you here to meet with Holland?"

"Yeah. It's a drop-in visit, so I have to wait for his meeting to end."

"In that case, sit down so we can catch up."

Jason sat in the same plastic chair Carlson had when he'd worked there, and it was still uncomfortable as hell.

"Are you still with the security team for the senator?"

"Yeah, it's a pretty good gig and a great team."

Carlson continued to pepper Jason with questions, but his focus was on Holland's door. He wanted to catch him as soon as he entered the hallway.

Thirty minutes after Jason sat down, he saw Holland exit his office.

"Take care, Carlson, and stay safe. I have to catch Holland."

Jason hustled toward his former boss before someone else could grab him with another question or problem. He tapped him on the arm and noted Holland's wide eyes when he turned around.

"Mulder, what are you doing here?"

"I have a quick question. Do you have a minute?"

Holland looked at his watch. "Actually, I don't. I have to take another call with Special Agent Hendrix. I wish you had called first. I could have saved you a trip."

"Can I wait in your office until you're done?" Jason asked.

Holland sighed. "I have to get to my son's basketball game in Prescott Valley, so I won't have much time after this meeting."

"That's okay," Jason replied. "It will be quick."

Jason sat in his office and scrolled through his phone. He was surprised when Holland returned after only twenty minutes.

"Okay, Mulder. I have a few minutes, and that's it, so what's up?" Holland said as he sat down behind his desk.

Jason charged ahead with the reason he showed up unannounced. "The FBI confirmed the kidnapper is from Central America."

Holland nodded. "You've suspected that from the beginning, didn't you?"

"I suspected it was the La Palma cartel, and now this essentially confirms it. I'm going down there and have one last favor to ask," Jason said.

Holland crossed his arms and leaned back in his chair. "What's the favor?"

"I need an address for Orlando Vasquez with La Palma. He'll know where they are keeping JJ."

"El Jaguar? The capo? Do you have a death wish?" Holland asked in rapid succession.

"No, I want to find my son."

"We don't have that type of information at the DEA."

A wry smile streaked across Jason's face. "Yes, you do. He's the leader of a cartel trafficking narcotics into the United States. You probably know what he had for dinner last night."

"Not for all the cartels."

"I need a place to start my search for JJ in El Salvador."

Holland stood and moved to the window, facing the silhouette of the jagged mountains outside. The sky was a faint blue after the sunset, but the streets were already dark. He spun around to face Jason.

"I don't want to provide you with information that will encourage you to go into enemy territory and get yourself killed."

"I'm going anyway. This information can help ensure I'm successful in finding my son."

Holland shook his head and resumed peering out his window, so Jason went all in with his next question.

He lifted his palm toward the family picture on Holland's desk. "What would you do if one of your four kids were kidnapped?"

Holland marched back to his desk and glared at Jason. "Don't go there, Mulder. That's a low blow."

"You're probably right, but if you think about it for two seconds, you'll know exactly why I'm asking you for this information."

Holland picked up the frame and stared at the picture of his wife and kids.

"Hang tight. I'll be back in a few minutes."

Jason's knee bounced wildly in anticipation of the information Holland could provide. He was closer to locating JJ now than at any other time since he was abducted.

Minutes later, Holland burst into his office and handed Jason a note scribbled on a slip of paper.

"This is the address for Orlando Vasquez's girlfriend's house. He goes there every other night. If you want information on the La Palma compound or anything else, you will have to get that from another three-letter agency. This is all we have."

Jason stared at the address.

"Memorize it quickly because I'm taking it with me. I'm going to be late for my son's game."

Jason memorized the address and handed the note back to Holland.

"This conversation never happened, and you never got this address from me," Holland said. "I hope you find your son, Mulder, but try not to get yourself killed."

Sitting in his truck in the parking lot, Jason repeated the address several times to ensure it was firmly engrained in his memory. He felt like he was finally progressing and thought more about what Holland said about getting additional intel from another three-letter agency. Going to the home of the La Palma cartel alone was borderline insane, but detailed schematics of the compound and surrounding property may make the mission slightly more favorable for his survival.

Could Archie get that kind of information from his contacts?

Archie was two hours ahead of Jason and probably home for the night, so he texted him.

`Call me whenever you have a minute.`

Less than a minute later, Archie called him.

"Hey, Mulder, I got your text. What's up?"

"A few minutes ago, I got some good information on where to find my son."

"That's great news, Mulder. Is Special Agent Reddy sending in the HRT?"

"No, but she confirmed JJ is in Central America, so I plan to fly down to find him."

The line was quiet for several seconds. "Is that a good idea?"

"Probably not, but letting JJ spend a minute more than he has to with his abductors seems like a much worse idea to me."

Archie sighed. "I can tell you're already committed to going, so how can I help?"

"Have you talked to any of your contacts in the other agencies?"

"I've put out some feelers. What are you looking for?"

"I need detailed maps of the La Palma compound. Is that something one of your contacts may be able to provide?"

The line fell silent again. Jason could hear Archie shuffling papers.

"Give me a couple of days to see what I can dig up."

"Thanks, Archie."

Jason remained in the parking lot for another minute. His conversations with Holland and Archie had solidified his plans.

The kitchen light was on when Jason parked in the driveway. He quietly entered through the back door and met Shanna's gaze. She was chopping vegetables on the counter, and a silent exchange passed between them.

"What's up?" Shanna asked.

"I'm going to El Salvador after Washington, DC. JJ needs me."

Shanna stared intently at Jason and met him on the other side of the counter. She moved close and rested her hands on his hips.

"I know. Please be safe."

"I'll try." Jason kissed her forehead and took a step back. "I'm taking my satellite phone and will check in with you every day."

Shanna moved to her tiptoes and kissed Jason on the lips. "Don't forget that we're in this together."

Jason nodded. "I'll let you know when I have our son."

CHAPTER 15

Washington, DC

Jason slid on his sunglasses and donned his tactical gloves as the midday sun reflected off the white marble of the Capitol Building in Washington, DC. He took his place at his post adjacent to the stands on the western side of the US Capitol, surveying the vast expanse of people gathered along the National Mall. The sunny but chilly day in late January made every exhale from the crowd visible, creating a collective breath that filled the area.

Ruben Zambrano, from Conrad's private security detail, appeared beside Jason before the event started. Zee chest-bumped Jason and pulled him in for a quick hug. "I'm glad you could be here. Clay told us that you had a family emergency but didn't give us any more details. Everything cool with your family?"

"We still have some things to work through, but my focus is on the inauguration today."

Zee studied Jason's face with a questioning gaze for a moment. "Okay, I get that you don't want to tell me. If anyone ever messes with you or your family and you need some muscle, you know how to reach me."

"I will."

Their earpieces crackled to life.

"Check-in," Clay's voice boomed, and Zee scampered to his assigned position.

"Central, in position."

"Zee, all clear."

"Mulder, in position."

Senator Conrad stood nearby, engaged in conversation with fellow lawmakers. Jason's gaze never stopped moving, constantly assessing potential threats in the crowd of politicians, dignitaries, and civilians. The challenge of protecting a high-profile individual in such a crowded, open space was immense. Every handshake and pat on the back presented a potential risk.

"Central, how's our exit route?" Clay asked over the comms.

"A few VIPs are loitering between the barricades, but we can still get through," Central replied from behind the risers and seats.

The inauguration ceremony was about to begin, and they'd need to move the Senator to his designated seating area three rows behind the main podium.

"Duke on the move," Clay reported. "Zee, take your position on the east, Central, maintain the rear, and Mulder, you've got the west. I'm on point."

A chorus of affirmatives sounded across the team's earpieces. As the senator reached the elevated and exposed platform, Jason felt the familiar surge of adrenaline. His senses were hyperaware of every face and threatening movement in the crowd.

Soft applause rang out for Senator Conrad as he waved and smiled at colleagues and constituents. Clay guided their principal to his designated seat next to Congresswoman Duarte. At the same time, Jason, Zee, and Central maintained their positions, creating a three-hundred-and-sixty-degree protective perimeter around the senator.

The ceremony began, and the new president stood ramrod straight across from the chief justice of the Supreme Court and placed his hand on the Bible to deliver his oath. He solemnly swore to preserve, protect, and defend the Constitution of the United States as Jason's eyes continuously swept the crowd. The new president also vowed to support and defend the Constitution of the United States against all enemies, foreign and domestic.

The mention of foreign enemies took Jason's mind from Washington, DC, to the jungles of El Salvador, where JJ could be held by his captors. He tried to blink away the image of JJ alone and scared in a rotting wood shanty.

Not now, Mulder, he scolded himself.

A sudden movement in the crowd drew Jason's attention back to the inauguration. He moved two steps to his right to get a clearer view of the disturbance.

"Mulder, sitrep?" Clay asked.

"Two photographers are jockeying with each other for a better position. All clear."

The ceremony ended, and the crowds began to disperse.

"Good work. Let's get the Senator to his vehicle," Clay announced to the team.

Conrad turned to Jason on his right as Clay, Zee, Central, and Jason converged in their diamond formation around the senator. "Smooth as always. I hardly noticed you guys were there."

Jason allowed himself a quick nod of acknowledgment. "That's the idea, sir."

The team exchanged glances of satisfaction, and Jason continued to scan the crowd as Clay and Zee stood outside the armored limousine while the senator climbed inside. He couldn't simply turn off his heightened awareness of the situation while adrenaline continued to pulse through his veins. Jason's ears heard the senator's vehicle depart the loading area while his eyes alerted him to a person of interest. The man strode with purpose toward the Capital Reflecting Pool behind the Ulysses S. Grant Memorial, so Jason left without a word to his team.

Navigating the crowd was like swimming upstream, and Jason didn't want to let the man slip away, so he pushed through. Once Jason had made it across the street, he noticed the man standing in the shadow of the towering statue of a former Union Army general and eighteenth president of the United States mounted on a bronze horse. The stoic-faced Ulysses S. Grant's gaze was fixed west towards the Lincoln Memorial at the other end of the National Mall, paying tribute to another former president, Abraham Lincoln. Jason charged across the marble platform and secured the man's arm.

"Hey, Archie, thanks for meeting me here," Jason told his FBI friend.

Archie spun around with a shocked expression but quickly opened his arms and pulled Mulder in for a hug.

"I'd never miss an opportunity to meet with my favorite former PJ."

The comment elicited Jason's first semblance of a grin since JJ was abducted. Archie waved toward the stairs. "Let's grab a seat by the reflecting pool."

A moment later, the two men looked across the silver water at the Washington Memorial soaring into the sky. Archie spoke first.

"I'm so sorry about what you and your wife are going through. I can't imagine the pain and anger I'd feel if someone took my child. Gloria and I are praying for his safe return every day."

"Thank you," Jason replied with an appreciative nod. "It's hard to describe how I feel, because I know JJ is gone but I still expect to hear him talk to himself in the morning and see him in his crib when I go into his room. I'm not sure the anger has hit me yet. I think I'm still in shock that he's gone, but I can feel the anger building."

Archie patted Jason's knee. "Harness that anger for good. Don't let it consume you or your wife. A traumatic event like this can put a serious strain on a marriage, so be sure you two tackle this as a team."

Jason felt the tension between Shanna and himself over the past few days and was glad Archie had brought it up. He had to do a better job of including Shanna in his efforts to bring JJ home.

"What are the chances we ever find JJ?" Jason asked.

Archie inhaled deeply and emptied his lungs. "Mind you, I don't work on kidnapping cases unless explosives are involved, which is rare, but I know that every case is unique. I spoke with Special Agent Reddy this morning, and I can confidently say that her team is doing all they can to find your boy and bring him home."

"I know they are, but I feel like everything is moving so slowly while my boy is out there alone with a psychopath that would take a kid. Is there anything I can do to speed things up?"

"I'm afraid not, my friend," Archie replied. "Things usually move faster once the investigative teams get the break they need, but until then, they methodically turn over every stone until they find that critical piece of evidence."

"I'm not sure how much longer I can sit around and wait for that break."

Archie turned toward Jason with a raised eyebrow. "What are you planning to do?"

"I don't know, but waiting for others to find JJ is eating me up inside."

"I understand, but I strongly suggest you let the FBI handle this. You don't want to get in the way of our progress or mess up the case against the person who abducted your son. Make sense?"

Jason forced himself to nod. "Yeah," Jason lied.

He felt Archie's investigative eyes on him, reading his body language.

"I don't believe you, but I still hope you'll heed my advice."

Jason stood while Archie pushed himself to his feet and stretched.

"Could you check—" Jason stopped before he could finish asking the question and awkwardly slid his hands into his coat pocket.

"What?" Archie asked.

"Nothing."

"You hate asking for help, don't you?"

"I do," Jason said. He shifted his weight and asked his question. "Could you ask around to see if any of your friends in agencies that might know things have any information on my son or the cartel that may have him?"

Archie rocked on his heels. "I will."

Jason extended his hand. "Thanks for meeting with me, Archie. Let me know if you hear anything about my son."

The two friends departed the Grant Memorial, and Jason caught a cab to his hotel. The trip to Washington, DC, for the inauguration was a welcome distraction for Jason, but he wanted to get home as soon as possible to continue his search for JJ. He placed his backpack on the bed and stuffed his dirty shirt and pants inside. Jason packed light for a brief trip, which also helped him avoid the baggage claim at both airports. His phone buzzed, and he saw it was Special Agent Holland from the DEA.

"I know you're at the inauguration, so do you have a minute to talk?" Holland asked after Jason answered.

"Yeah, I'm in my hotel now. What's up?"

"I just heard from my asset, and before I share anything, I need you to understand that this information is for your ears only. You can't share it with anyone, not even the FBI, because, officially, we don't have anyone in Central America," Holland said.

"Your secrets are safe with me. My only concern is my son," Jason quickly replied.

"Okay, I learned that abductions have skyrocketed in El Salvador recently, and my asset believes the La Palma cartel is a player in those abductions. Kidnappings shot up in the last year, and the authorities are unable to do much about it with all the corruption inside the local police departments."

"What about my son? JJ?" Jason asked.

"He doesn't have any specifics on any American adults or children being held in El Salvador or Central America."

Jason ran his fingers through his hair and began pacing around his couch. "Holland, what do you make of this information?"

"It doesn't prove anything, but I wouldn't take La Palma off your suspect list either."

Jason stared at the wall but said nothing. His mind was racing with countless scenarios.

"Mulder?" Holland said when he didn't answer.

"I'm here."

"That's all I have," Holland said. "What are you going to do now?"

"I'm going to El Salvador," Jason growled.

Chapter 16

El Salvador

A slit of sunlight stretched across the hastily made table as Paulina Almarez Garcia slid a plate of food to the other side. Jubilant calls of birds in the El Salvadoran jungle penetrated the thin wood walls and single-pane glass and filled the tiny room. Paulina watched the little boy examine the refried beans wrapped in a fresh flour tortilla, but he did not touch it.

"Eat it. It's a good breakfast," she said in heavily accented English.

The boy looked up at her, his brown eyes a mixture of fear and anger. She pushed the plate another inch closer to him and smiled. "It's good."

He curled his tiny hands around the tightly rolled tortilla and took a bite. It was a minor victory for Paulina because her boss made her responsible for the toddler, and she was concerned that he ate very little.

Paulina was fully aware of her boss's line of work and had come to terms with it, but this was the youngest person he'd abducted since she'd known him. The twenty-two-year-old had no children and wasn't sure how to care for such a young child. Her only experience with toddlers before this boy was her younger brothers and sisters raised by her aunts when her mother disappeared a decade ago.

She was first introduced to her boss fifteen months ago while Paulina lived in Santa Ana, the second-largest city in El Salvador. Her roommate was his original mistress, and he took an immediate interest in Paulina the first time he came over. The mutual flirting occurred every time he visited for over a month until one night, Paulina returned battered and bruised. When she entered the room, her boss sprang to his feet and held Paulina by her chin.

"Who did this to you?"

Paulina was a decade younger than him, and despite her physical attraction, she was also intimidated by the man. She didn't know his reputation then, but Paulina was sure he was someone not to cross.

"It's nothing," Paulina whimpered.

"Who did this to you?" he repeated slowly.

"My ex-boyfriend."

"Where is he?"

"You can't go after him. He's with all his friends, and they're bad people. They'll kill you."

Her boss stepped back, and his face stretched into a satisfied grin. "I'm not worried about them. Just tell me where he's at."

Paulina told him, and he left the apartment.

Two days later, the streets were buzzing with rumors of a man who butchered three young men to death with a knife, and one of them was Paulina's ex-boyfriend. They were all found gutted in the alley where she last saw them. Each corpse had both hands cut off at the wrist, an old cartel warning not to put their hands on certain people.

Her boss did not come around for several weeks, but when Paulina's roommate was at work one night, he let himself into their tiny house. Paulina feared for her life yet was drawn to his strength and charisma.

"What are you doing here?" Paulina asked. Her voice trembled as she searched for a place to run.

"I'm here to offer you a better life."

"What do you mean?"

"Come with me, and you'll never have to be afraid again."

He couldn't have offered a more appealing proposal to someone who had lived in fear for most of her two decades. Paulina understood she was trading her familiar fear for an unknown one and was satisfied with that exchange.

"I'll go with you."

Her boss took Paulina to a small house he owned in the jungle and then to his bed. Since that day, Paulina had been by his side, supporting her boss in any way he wished.

The little boy finished his bean burrito and drank all of his juice box. Paulina took the empty plate and placed it in the sink. The boy sat in a diaper and nothing else in the warm, humid house.

"I have to get you dressed."

His lips quivered, and he began sobbing. Paulina noticed her boss talking to another man outside her window. His shrieks were loud, so she quickly scooped up the boy and rocked him. Paulina whispered in his ear to calm him down.

"Shhh. Don't cry. It's okay," she repeated over and over.

She scurried to the other side of the room and sat on the bed with the boy cradled in her arms.

"I don't want him to hear you crying. I've seen what he's done to others he's held here. I don't want anything bad to happen to you."

CHAPTER 17

Washington, DC

Jason entered the sixteen-story Hyatt Hotel in Arlington, Virginia, and marched through the lobby as if he belonged there. He found Randy at the concierge desk, per Archie's instructions.

"I'm Stuart Kemper. I believe you have something for me," Jason said, hoping he remembered the alias correctly.

Randy opened a drawer and handed Jason an envelope with his alias scribbled on it.

"Will that be all, Mr. Kemper?" Randy asked. Jason felt he emphasized his last name too much and suspected this was a routine activity for the concierge attendant.

Jason stepped away from the busy lobby and searched the ceiling for cameras that could pick up the letter's contents. Seeing none, he opened the envelope and found a Metro card with a single sheet of paper that said: `Blue Line to Pentagon City then find a seat at the food court. Be there by 10:15.`

At ten o'clock sharp, Jason arrived at Pentagon City station. He found an open table and ordered a coffee to blend in with other patrons. At precisely 10:15 a.m., a janitor emptied the trash near him and dropped a newspaper on his table as he left. Jason waited thirty seconds and scanned the area to see if anyone else noticed before picking it up. It contained another note: *Walk to the Air Force Memorial, and you'll find us. Be sure you are not followed.*

Jason plugged in the address on his phone and shook his head in frustration. It was a twenty-minute walk to the Air Force Memorial, and he was wasting valuable time. He had to get to El Salvador as soon as possible and didn't need the cloak-and-dagger routine. However, Archie's message seemed urgent, so Jason decided to meet him and the contact he'd mentioned.

"This intel better be good," Jason muttered.

The crisp January air chased Jason along the sidewalk faster than expected, and he reached the Air Force Memorial five minutes early. He'd never been to the memorial before and was happy that he had a minute to enjoy it before meeting Archie.

The memorial's focal point was a trio of stainless-steel spires stretching over two hundred feet into the bright sky. They were named "Soaring to Glory," and they resembled the contrails of a bomb-burst formation, paying tribute to those who served in the military. Granite walls complemented the spires with inscriptions about the values and valor of aviation pioneers who supported the Air Force.

After circling the memorial twice to ensure he wasn't followed, Jason recognized Archie and another man standing before the memorial wall. Jason approached Archie, and his friend's typical easy smile was replaced with a look of concentration.

"You weren't followed?" Archie inquired.

"No. I did everything by the book. This seems like a lot of OPSEC for a quick meeting."

"I understand, but it's necessary in this town," Archie said. "Let's walk."

The trio rounded the corner and strolled behind the memorial, where they were free from prying eyes and ears.

"Mike, this is Jason Mulder," Archie said. "Jason, this is Mike. What he's about to tell you about La Palma cartel never leaves this spot."

Mike removed his hand from his coat pocket to shake Jason's hand and returned it to his gray wool trench coat. "Mr. Mulder, what do you know about Operation Green Serpent?"

"I've never heard of it."

"We call Central America from Guatemala to Panama the green serpent. The operation is a joint venture among the CIA, DEA, and Homeland Security to stifle the flow of contraband from South America to the United States through the Green Serpent. Ultimately, we want to cut the head off the snake, but we're still trying to identify all the players."

"Makes sense," Jason replied. "How does this involve La Palma?"

"As you know, La Palma is a small player in the massive drug trade flowing through that region, but recently, they've popped up on our radar for human trafficking."

Jason's eyebrows arched, and he stopped walking. Archie and Mike stopped beside him.

"We've attributed some of the uptick in abductions in the region to the La Palma cartel," Mike continued. "From what we can tell, they seem to stick to the Abduction 101 playbook by abducting company executives or high net-worth citizens and holding them for ransom."

"Neither my wife nor I have received a call for ransom."

Mike shot a glance at Archie and turned back to Jason. "I know, and that's why I agreed to meet with you today."

The response turned Jason's stomach into a boiling kettle of concern. He had an idea of where the conversation was going and hoped he was wrong.

"We don't have any confirmed evidence of La Palma taking children or babies, but that doesn't mean it hasn't happened before," Mike stated. "If this is a first for them, it likely means one of two things. One option is that this kidnapping is personal, and based on what Archie has told me, that's probably what it is."

"What's the other possibility?" Jason asked, dreading the answer.

Mike sighed and looked at the concrete pavement for a beat before he answered. "The other is that La Palma is getting into human trafficking."

The answer wasn't unexpected, but it still landed with the weight of a sledgehammer. Jason had considered the possibility but refused to let his mind go there.

That can't happen to JJ. It just can't.

"I have the address of a place I can find the La Palma leader, Orlando Vasquez, so I'm going down there tonight," Jason said with heat pulsing throughout his body.

"I have something else for you." Archie bumped into Mulder and handed him an envelope of photos. Jason peeked inside and looked at Archie. "Is this Orlando Vasquez on his compound?"

Archie's long index finger appeared and wagged before Jason's face. "You cannot take these, so hurry up and take a look. The US officially does not have any CIA or FBI assets in El Salvador, so if someone finds these photos missing, my source and I will be in a lot of deep shit. I wanted to give you a quick look at the man you're looking for and his compound. I hope this helps."

Jason flipped through several photos and stopped on one with a man standing confidently overlooking the compound. It was El

Jaguar, the leader of La Palma. "This is a lifesaver, Archie. Thank you."

Knowing his son could be sold into a human trafficking ring, Jason was ready to fly down to El Salvador and start his new search. "What suggestions do you have for me to get my son back?"

"Everything is interconnected down there," Mike said. "If you don't find your son at the compound, I'd recommend focusing on major transportation hubs like ports and bus stations in major cities. Many of the finest resorts are also transfer stations for human traffickers."

"Anything else?"

"Go now. If your son is sold to human traffickers, he may be gone forever."

"Not my son," Jason hissed. "I'll never let that happen."

CHAPTER 18

Washington, DC

The elevator doors opened on the fourth floor of Senator Conrad's Washington, DC, office, and Jason stepped out. He held on to hope that he would locate his son quickly during his upcoming trip to Central America and return to his job with the senator's PSD team. Jason knew his upcoming mission could be the most dangerous he had ever faced. It was realistic to assume that he could be in Central America for an extended period of time—or never return at all.

Clay's door was shut when Jason arrived. He considered knocking, but it was unusual for the head of Senator Conrad's PSD to work behind a closed door, so Jason decided to return later. He ambled past cubicles and offices filled with other senators' staff members. Jason received several nods, grins, and a couple of waves as he passed, but no sad eyes of dread he experienced whenever he entered a room of people who knew about his son.

Did Chief of Staff Crenshaw and Clay not tell anyone about JJ?

Jason was grateful for the reprieve. It was growing more challenging to retell the story and maintain his composure with the hurricane of despair swirling inside. He continued through the corridor until he reached one of four conference rooms. Jason searched each room until he reached one with Central and Zee sitting adjacent to one another, their attention focused on the laptop screen in front of them.

Central pointed to a spot on the monitor. "That's the choke point, right there. We need an alternative exfil route."

Zee leaned closer to the screen. "Yeah. How about the alley to the north?"

"Perfect. I'll put it into the plan," Central replied.

"Hey, guys," Jason interrupted.

Central and Zee looked over the laptop screen at their coworker. Central smiled, while Zee jumped to his feet. He strode around the table and pulled Jason in for a bear hug.

"Mulder, you're back!" Zee boomed. "I'm glad the team is at one hundred percent again to fend off all these wackos."

"Glad to be here, but I'm not staying long. I came in to tell Clay that I'm leaving again."

Neither Central nor Zee could hide their disappointment.

"Will you be back soon?" Central asked.

"I don't know."

The disappointment was replaced by confusion on Zee's face. Jason hated to let down his team and suspected they'd be supportive if they knew why he couldn't be with them.

"I'm going down to Central America."

"I get the weather sucks here right now, but is now the best time to take a vacation?" Zee questioned.

"It's not a vacation. My son was abducted, and the kidnappers are holding him in El Salvador."

Jason watched as both mouths opened simultaneously, and the room went utterly quiet.

Zee shook his head and stepped toward Jason. "I'm sorry, man. I didn't know."

"I know you didn't, and you deserve to know why I can't be here."

Central joined Jason and Zee near the conference room door.

"When did this happen?" Central asked.

Jason was about to provide a brief explanation when Clay entered the room.

"Hey, Jason, I didn't know you'd be here."

"I'm heading to El Salvador and wanted to tell you in person."

Clay's eyes swung from Jason to Central and Zee.

"They know," Jason said. "I just told them."

Clay shut the door and motioned for them to sit around the cherrywood conference room table. Once everyone was seated, Clay continued. "Jason, can't the FBI do this instead of you?"

"The FBI is doing their best, but now that they suspect JJ has been transported from the United States, things are complicated. Every country has its red tape that US law enforcement agencies have to work around, and I don't have time for it. I have an idea of where I can find JJ, so I'm going down there before—"

Jason trailed off and stopped talking. He didn't want to speak into existence the one thing that could make his living nightmare a living hell. He didn't have to say the words for Central, Zee, and Clay to understand his urgency.

"I hope they can break through all the bullshit to get your son back as soon as possible," Central said.

"Me too."

The room had a brief, uncomfortable pause, so Jason rose from his chair. "I'll touch base with you when I return."

"Are you going down there alone?" Zee inquired.

Jason shook hands with Clay and Central without responding to the former Ranger.

"That's messed up, Mulder. You can't go down there alone."

"Zee, I'm walking into the lion's den when I go to El Salvador. It's dumb enough that I'm going, and there's no way I would ask someone else to go with me. It's way too dangerous."

Zee's face turned hard. "I don't run from danger, Mulder. I destroy danger before it kills me. If you want my help, say the word."

Jason was touched and tempted by Zee's offer. It would have been great to have someone with his background and skills with him when he entered El Jaguar's compound, but he was serious about not wanting to put someone else in such a risky situation. Plus, he couldn't do that to Clay.

"I appreciate the offer, Zee, but you have your hands full with Clay and Central here. The hornets are buzzing about his CFO Act."

"How long do you think you'll be down there?" Clay asked.

"I'm not sure. It could be a few days. It could be a month."

Clay removed the trademark plastic straw that was a fixture between his lips. "Central and I could probably manage for a few days."

"Hell no!" Jason barked. "That would put you at fifty percent force capacity, and you can't risk that with the current threat assessment."

"Just because I'm from Louisiana doesn't mean I don't know how to divide," Clay retorted with a sly grin. "I also know that a team member is missing a family member, which takes precedence over everything else. Go do what you have to do, and we'll get by."

"But, that will—"

Clay's huge paw raised to stop Jason's rebuttal. "Remember what you told me in Phoenix when I found out my mom was sick?"

Jason stared blankly at Clay.

"You told me to take care of my family and you guys would figure it out. Now it's your turn to take your own advice."

The offer was almost too attractive to resist, but Jason's mind was made up. He wouldn't let Clay weaken the PSD team further and risk something devastating happening to Senator Conrad. Going to El Salvador to retrieve JJ was his mission, and he had to do it alone.

"I don't know what I'm up against and may not even need help. Let me get down there and assess the situation. If I can't save JJ alone, I'll call and ask for help," Jason lied.

"I'll go if you need help," Zee immediately responded.

"Then it's settled. You guys keep Conrad safe while I get my son."

After exiting the conference room, Jason stood and waited for the elevator. The doors opened with a familiar ding, but instead of stepping inside, he turned to look at the bustling activity of Senator Conrad's staff on the fourth floor. He couldn't shake the feeling that this could be his final time seeing the office and his colleagues.

Chapter 19

El Salvador

Jason watched the azure waters of the Pacific Ocean transition to hilly, green countryside through his portal as the plane descended to land at El Salvador International Airport. El Salvador was bordered by 190 miles of pristine Pacific Ocean coastline to the west, Guatemala to the north, and Honduras to the east. The Central American country known for its pupusas, volcanoes, and coffee was about the size of Vermont.

He drove his rental car into San Salvador, the largest city in the Central American country. He checked into his hotel east of the historic city center and connected to the local Wi-Fi network. He didn't have any messages, so he browsed the digital maps on his phone to identify the best place to get some local intel on the La Palma cartel. He noticed the Ilopango International Airport several miles to his south. While in the Air Force, Jason had spent three hours during a layover at the military and charter airport that once served the city as its international airport. He recalled the warning by his Combat Rescue Officer not to venture too far outside the airport grounds and, specifically, not go north and west because of rampant gang activity.

"Perfect," Jason said.

He slid his phone back into his pocket and splashed water on his face. Jason was about to embark on an extremely dangerous mission. Go into the heart of cartel territory and ask strangers for information about a ruthless cartel. Jason knew it was reckless and probably foolish to attempt such a feat but had convinced himself it was necessary to find his son.

After a quick change of clothes, Jason departed the hotel as the last rays of sunlight briefly transformed the clouds into bright swatches of gold and purple. Minutes later, the buildings appeared to age a decade with each mile until modern structures built within the last fifty years were no longer in sight. The local residences by his hotel with colorful stucco and glass transitioned exclusively to rusty tin roofs covering cinder block homes. Faded graffiti told years of stories on the crumbling walls, partially hidden by shadows cast by the rare streetlight. Stray dogs and cats replaced pedestrians on the sidewalks and in alleys.

Jason kept his speed slow until he noticed a flickering neon sign for the equivalent of a local bar and grill. After several passes, he parked a block away and sauntered to the bar. Upon stepping inside, Jason was greeted by half a dozen mismatched tables filling the dimly lit interior, with more scattered across an outdoor patio under vines of tangled string lights. A tiny stage for live music sat empty, and most of the patrons, a collection of lean, hard-faced men in their twenties and thirties, huddled in subdued clusters over drinks. The low murmur of conversation briefly paused as Jason entered, but the patrons quickly cast their gazes elsewhere.

He slid onto a stool at the bar and ordered a Centenario Pilsener and cheese-filled pupusas with chicharrón and refried beans. He hadn't realized how hungry he was until the food arrived, and the sight of it reminded him he hadn't eaten since morning. A few bites steadied the gnawing unease in his stomach, but it did nothing to quiet the tension thrumming in his mind.

As he polished off the last of his meal, he scanned the room subtly through the mirror behind the bar, watching the faces that filled the smoky haze. Hard stares. Mismatched clothes. Cheap tattoos marking arms and necks. He doubted any of these men would openly admit ties to La Palma, but he wanted local intelligence. As his Combat Rescue Officer used to say in Afghanistan, "Local knowledge always beats satellite images."

When an older man, likely in his fifties, rose from his table and walked toward the bathroom, Jason made his move. His graying temples gave him the look of someone who might know something but was past risking his neck for trouble. Jason cleared his throat and stepped into the narrow hallway, intercepting him just outside the door.

"Hola," Jason said, his voice low.

The man stopped as his gaze settled on an unfamiliar face.

"Do you live around here?"

The man hesitated. "Sí."

"I'm heading to La Palma tomorrow. Do you know anything about the town? Or its people?"

The question changed the man's face instantly. His brow furrowed, and his lips thinned. "Why would you go to La Palma?" Suspicion crept into his tone.

"I'm looking for someone. The leader of an organization."

"Don't be a fool!" The man turned and scurried back to his table.

When Jason finished his business in the bathroom and returned to his stool at the bar, the atmosphere felt different. The conversations were quieter and the eyes of several men never left him.

Jason noticed his half-full beer was missing, and a bill for the meal was in its place.

"One more beer," Jason said to the bartender in Spanish.

He drifted toward Jason, placed both palms on the counter, and leaned over the bar. "Pay up. You're done here."

He didn't want to take on the entire bar, who were now clearly unhappy with his presence, so Jason paid and left. He ambled back to his rental car and climbed inside.

"That went well."

He'd struck out gathering local intel, so he'd study more of the maps and satellite images back at the hotel. As he prepared to start the engine, a flicker of movement in his rearview mirror caught Jason's attention. Five silhouettes materialized from the shadows, approaching his car with purpose. Jason's gut told him they weren't coming to give him directions, and before he could react, his driver's side door flew open. Several hands grabbed his shirt and yanked him out of the vehicle. Jason's back slammed against the pavement, knocking the wind out of him. He blinked away the stars dancing in his vision and saw five figures looming over him.

"*¿Qué quieres con La Palma?*" one of the men growled. *What do you want with La Palma?*

Jason's mind raced to evaluate his options. He was sure the young men were *falcones* or scouts for La Palma, and he needed to neutralize them—at least some of them.

One of the men stepped toward Jason and extended his arm to pick him up. Jason turned to his side, raised onto an elbow, and kicked the attacker in the knee. A satisfying crunch was followed by a howl of pain that caused the others to stop and evaluate the situation. Jason rolled to his feet, assuming the fighting stance ingrained by years of Krav Maga training.

The dim light revealed eight eyes had turned their attention back to Jason like predators locking onto their prey. A second man moved toward him, slowly at first, but then he lowered his head and lunged forward. Jason sidestepped, grabbed the attacker's outstretched arm, and used the man's momentum to slam him face-first into the side of the rental car. The thug crumpled to the ground, unconscious.

Jason turned to the three remaining scouts, but an incoming fist had already been launched. The man's knuckles connected with Jason's jaw, snapping his head back. His legs immediately turned to rubber, and he fell back into the rental car, grateful that it prevented a backward fall to the ground. Jason returned to his fighting position with blood filling his mouth. He blocked a flurry of punches, but a boot to his midsection doubled him over, and a blow to the back of his head sent him sprawling. One man against five was too great to overcome, even with Jason's expertise in Krav Maga.

The men converged like wolves on wounded prey, boots and fists finding every exposed target. Jason curled tighter, using his forearms to shield his head while his ribs took the brunt of the assault. Blood from a split eyebrow burned his vision. Through the red haze of pain and growing unconsciousness, he heard words that chilled him more than the beating: "Finish him."

Time slowed. All he could think about was JJ and how he'd failed to find him.

Twenty seconds into the beating that felt like an eternity, a new sound penetrated the calamity of Jason's beating. A shriek pierced the night, causing his attackers to freeze. Through swollen eyes, Jason saw a man with long white hair and a beard brandishing a machete, the blade catching the dim streetlight.

The old man swung the machete in wide arcs, screaming incoherently until he charged the men. The young *falcones* scattered like roaches, disappearing into the shadows as quickly as they had appeared.

As they fled, one of them shouted back, "*¡No te metas con La Palma!" Don't mess with La Palma!*

Jason unfurled himself and stared at the machete-wielding man, unsure if he was there to help him or finish the job. The man stood still as a statue, so Jason stumbled to his feet. He limped toward his rental car when Machete Man moved to his side to help him lean against the vehicle.

"You ask too many questions, my friend," the man said in Spanish. His voice was deep and raspy. "La Palma has eyes and ears everywhere. Next time, there may be no one to save you."

Jason started to speak but winced and grabbed his left side. A beat later, he swallowed hard and tried again. "I'm just trying to find my son."

"If La Palma has your son, he will not be here. He will be in their compound in the mountains."

"I know. I'm going there tomorrow," Jason wheezed.

"You will be killed if you try to go there like this." The man motioned up and down toward Jason, whose bruised and bloodied body clung to his vehicle to prevent him from falling.

He'd tried to find actionable information from locals about the cartel. Instead, Jason almost took himself out of the search for JJ by getting attacked and nearly beaten to death if not for the timely arrival of Machete Man.

Jason limped to the driver's side door and pulled it open. "*Gracias,*" he choked out to the man.

Machete Man vanished as fast as he appeared, so Jason turned and fell back into his car, wincing at every movement. With his hands on the steering wheel, he stared ahead at the empty street.

"This is going to be much harder than I thought," Jason muttered, tasting blood. But as he started the engine, his resolve hardened. They'd meant to discourage him, but all they'd done was confirm he was on the right track. La Palma had his son, and no amount of beatings would stop him from bringing JJ home.

Chapter 20

Washington, DC

Clay Landry pushed the rock-hard crust of his half-eaten lunch sandwich to the edge of his desk and scanned the Washington, DC, landscape from his fourth-story office in the Dirksen Senate Office Building. The partly sunny morning had turned into a gray afternoon with skies threatening to snow. He leaned back in his chair and imagined the countless security tasks he'd yet to complete as he stared at the ceiling.

Senator Conrad's PSD team was stretched thin with the rash of new threats after the senator proposed the CFO Act, and manpower was already depleted with Jason's absence. The long hours were adding up with no end in sight. Exhaustion and frustration were growing within the team.

Clay returned his attention to his computer screen when he received a text. He leaned forward with alert eyes after the first sentence and reread it to ensure he correctly interpreted it. Clay typed two words in his return message: *Where? When?*

He read the response and left his chair. Clay blew out a breath and moved to the window in his office. The bad news in the text was shocking, but not a surprise, after Conrad's recent proposal of cutting off campaign funds to Congress from powerful lobbyists.

Clay knocked on the door of the small office down the hall shared by Central, Zee, and Jason. Central and Zee were debating the possibility of snow that evening when Clay arrived.

"We have a serious situation with the senator and don't have much time to prepare. Meet me in my office in two minutes."

Clay stood before the whiteboard on the wall, his arms crossed as he studied the scene mapped out in black dry-erase marker. Rough rectangles, squares, and circles were scribbled across the board with arrows and lines slashed all over the diagram. His brow remained furrowed, and his focus fixed on the board even after Zee and Central entered the room. They stood in silence for a half minute until Clay faced them.

"Guys, I just received word from the investigations division of the Capitol Police about an attack planned on Senator Conrad. They're certain the tip is credible, and it's going down before the dinner at the Family Business Caucus event tonight. According to the Capitol Police informant, a team of three or four hit men will ambush the senator in the parking garage when we drop him off at the restaurant entrance."

"Holy shit!" Zee chirped.

"We need to talk to Crenshaw and get Conrad to cancel," Central said.

Clay shook his head. "He'll never do it."

"Then we need to change the drop-off location and time," Zee suggested.

"I have a better idea."

Central and Zee moved beside the head of Conrad's PSD as he laid out the plan to ensure the senator's safety.

A black Chevy Suburban rolled into the dimly lit parking garage three blocks from the Capitol Building. Central drove, while Clay sat in the back. They passed SUVs and cars parked between support columns, most bearing a *G* on their license plates, indicating that they were government-issued vehicles. Clay studied the garage blueprints before they departed and knew they were two turns away from the attached Italian fine-dining restaurant with a direct entrance inside the parking structure. On any other night, this entrance was the most secure location to drop off a principal, but tonight, it was a death trap.

Clay's eyes swept the shadows between parked vehicles. His Heckler & Koch 416 rifle rested on the seat beside him that Senator Conrad would typically occupy. Before the final turn to the restaurant entrance, a white Chevy Tahoe SUV suddenly reversed out of a parking spot, blocking their way.

"This is it," Clay said calmly. "You know what to do."

Central stomped the accelerator and T-boned the SUV, collapsing the front and back driver's-side doors while shattering all the windows. Clay observed four silhouettes slide to the passenger side and exit the vehicle. Bursts of gunfire peppered the Suburban's armored panels as Clay and Central kicked open their doors, using them as cover. Clay identified muzzle flashes behind the Tahoe and concrete pillars to the right and left as the hit men fanned out. Clay aimed and returned fire. They were outnumbered, which Clay had expected and accounted for in his plan.

The sound of six semiautomatic rifles firing in rapid succession and spent shells hitting the concrete pavement was deafening. Sixty seconds into the firefight, neither side had hit an opposing target, and it was looking more and more like a stalemate could force them to retreat. He had also anticipated this, and that's when a seventh person arrived.

Zee exited the restaurant behind the four hit men, with all their attention focused on gunning down Central and Clay. He placed a violin case on the trunk of a Toyota Camry sedan and removed an M4 rifle with a folded butt stock. Zee leaned against the vehicle, acquired his first target, and dropped one of the hit men shooting from behind a pillar with a single pull of the trigger. He swung his rifle toward another hit man firing at Central from the cover of the damaged Chevy Tahoe. The former ranger exhaled and put the red dot from the reflex optics on the back of the hit man's head where it met the neck. Zee squeezed the trigger, and the shooter's medulla blew up like an exploding watermelon. The hit man died instantly and fell like a puppet with its strings cut.

The other two hit men noticed two of their comrades were out of the fight and stopped firing. Clay heard shouting, but his ringing ears wouldn't allow him to hear what they said. Suddenly, the hit man hiding behind a concrete pillar between two parked vehicles broke for the damaged Tahoe. Clay was ready and sent a three-round burst toward the bounding man. All three slugs connected center mass, and the hit man tumbled and fell, his MP5 clattering across the concrete.

The last hit man dropped his rifle and raised his hands. He stepped out from behind the white Tahoe and locked eyes with Clay.

"Don't shoot. Don't shoot."

Clay considered his next move. He heard the police sirens in the distance and knew he had little time to decide.

"Central, Zee, make sure he's clean and secure him."

Zee frisked the man and removed a pistol while Central kept his rifle aimed at his chest.

"I've got him," Clay said.

The hit man opened his mouth, but before he could talk, Clay grabbed him by the back of the neck and slammed his head into the Tahoe's side panel.

The sirens grew louder. Capitol Police would arrive soon, and Clay knew they needed answers from the hitman before this became an official crime scene.

"Who sent you?" Clay demanded.

A trickle of blood ran down the hit man's crooked nose as a confident smirk spread across his face. "I'm not telling you shit."

Clay replied with a lightning-quick right hook to the man's jaw, knocking him to the ground. He pulled the hit man off the pavement by his coat collar until he was kneeling.

"This is the last time I'm asking. Who sent you?"

The man stared back with contempt until Clay wrapped his gloved hand around his throat and squeezed. The man's eyes fluttered and looked like they might roll back into his head, so Clay let go of the man's throat and stepped back. The hit man rolled his neck and rubbed the skin on his throat that was still red from Clay's talon-like grip.

"You're messing with the wrong people," the hit man snarled. "You're going to—

Boom!

The report from Clay's SIG Sauer P226 echoed off the walls as the police sirens entered the parking garage. The hit man stiffened for a beat before he fell face-first onto the concrete floor. Blood spilled from the gaping hole in his head to quickly form a crimson lake.

"What the hell?" Central yelped. "Now we won't ever know who sent him."

"He was going for my gun," Clay replied coolly.

Central opened his mouth as if he might contest Clay's claim but closed it without saying anything.

Zee stood expressionless beside Central. "He was never going to talk."

The PSD team lowered their weapons and placed them on the ground as the Capital Police vehicles arrived.

Amid the shouts from the officers to put their hands up, Zee turned to Clay. "He never should have gone for your weapon."

Chapter 21

El Salvador

The streetlights of San Salvador shone brightly outside the window as Jason departed the El Salvadoran capital city on the last bus of the day. He'd nursed his injuries and returned the rental car earlier that day, believing he'd be better prepared for La Palma if somebody else drove the three hours to his destination.

He leaned back to rest, but too many scenarios of the obstacles he might encounter once he arrived in La Palma flashed through his mind. The persistent thought that he was being watched also lingered. Jason opened his eyes and scanned the other passengers in the dim light cast from under the overhead cargo bins. Everyone was looking at their phone, listening to headphones, or sleeping. However, one military-age male sitting in an aisle seat two rows ahead of Jason turned around multiple times to sneak looks at the lone American on the bus. Jason thought little of it the first time, but the second time the young man looked back in under five minutes, his heart raced. He reached for his backpack in the window seat beside him and pulled it closer. Jason didn't have time to file for the necessary permits to bring his gun to El Salvador, so he purchased a high-quality Condor Bushlore hunting knife at a San Salvador shop. The four-inch carbon-steel blade secured inside a sheath at the top of his bag was Jason's primary weapon against the La Palma cartel and its allies.

After the man turned around a third time, Jason unzipped his backpack to make his knife easily accessible. He scooted several inches forward in his seat to stand faster if the passenger came at him with a weapon of his own. Jason assumed the man was with the La Palma cartel and was ready to eliminate him on a public bus if necessary.

The man turned around a fourth time and pointed to his upper arm. Jason's forehead creased above his furrowed brows as the man continually pointed to his short shirt sleeve. Jason looked down at his shirt and saw the white Adidas Combat Sports logo on the black compression shirt he wore to Krav Maga training in Washington, DC. It was the closest thing he had to a clean tactical shirt in his apartment.

Jason turned back to the man, who stood in the aisle with a wide smile. He pulled down on his white shirt to better expose the large Adidas logo and gave Jason a thumbs up. Jason forced a smile and waved to the Adidas fan.

Focus and relax, Mulder. The guy was just admiring your shirt.

The rest of the ride was uneventful. Jason studied the maps he was provided by Archie's contact, Mike. The bus arrived at La Palma Station shortly before midnight, and the humid air smacked Jason like a wet towel when he stepped onto the pavement. The cartel compound was not his first target, so he hailed a cab and took it east to a late-night restaurant on the outskirts of the town of ten thousand residents. He was in enemy territory, likely with citizens either sympathetic to or fearful of the La Palma cartel. Jason had little doubt that the locals would report him to the cartel if he did anything to stand out.

Jason lingered in the parking lot until the taxi driver left and disappeared into the night. He began walking east, keeping to the shadows until the girlfriend's house on the outskirts of town came into view.

The house owned by El Jaguar's girlfriend was surrounded by trees and dense shrubs that provided complete privacy from the neighbors, only fifty feet away on each side. Among the other houses on the street, her one-story stucco home stood out as the most well maintained. A new metal roof protected the smooth walls painted in colorful swatches that resembled the stunning scarlet macaw bird commonly spotted in the surrounding jungle. Jason noted light beaming through the windows on the side of the house, which he assumed was a bedroom.

The former pararescueman dropped to a knee and switched to tactical-approach mode. He remained silent and still to observe the property for any signs of a security detail. None were spotted after fifteen minutes, which surprised Jason, so he cautiously approached the bedroom window.

Once Jason reached the house, he pressed his back against the cool stucco wall and removed his phone. He checked his tracking app to see if the *out-of-range* message displayed on the screen since the day JJ went missing was replaced by a blinking dot on a map. Shanna had placed a Bluetooth tracker inside JJ's favorite teddy bear to help her find the stuffed animal if it was left at daycare, a restaurant, or one of the grandparents' homes. Jason was using it to see if he could pinpoint JJ's exact location. Similar to the Bluetooth trackers for car keys, he had to be within two hundred feet of the teddy bear for it to work.

"Dammit. Still no signal," Jason whispered.

Jason didn't know if JJ and his teddy bear were still together but suspected they would be. The teddy bear was often the only thing to calm JJ down when upset.

JJ may not be here, but if La Palma has him, El Jaguar will know where they are holding him.

It was time for Jason to execute his plan. He'd wait for El Jaguar and his girlfriend to fall asleep, and then he'd sneak in and press his knife to the capo's throat to get answers on JJ's location. The plan was far more complex and riskier by a factor of one hundred without a gun, but it was Jason's only option. He couldn't wait any longer to find JJ.

Jason slunk below the bedroom window, slowly raising his head to look inside. He saw the naked ass of a muscular man cross the room and crawl into bed. Jason recognized his profile from the pictures Archie shared with him.

El Jaguar.

He continued to monitor the room when a younger woman, who was also naked, appeared from the bathroom and joined the man in bed.

"Please don't have sex," Jason whispered into the darkness.

He remained by the window for a half hour, waiting for the sicarios to reveal themselves and for El Jaguar to fall asleep. Jason saw multiple vehicles out front and was sure El Jaguar would have security, but he also knew that sicarios could be undisciplined and fall asleep on the job. Seeing no movement, Jason made his move once he heard snoring through the single-pane glass window.

Jason crept to the back door and slowly turned the knob. To his surprise, it opened into a dark kitchen. He entered and let his eyes adjust to the dark room illuminated only by a digital clock on the stove. Once Jason could see the outline of the room, he moved silently past a small table and removed the hunting knife from its sheath attached to his belt. The bedroom was steps away, and Jason was prepared to pounce on the cartel leader.

Steps before Jason entered the hallway, he bumped into a wooden chair, and it squealed as it lurched several inches across the tile floor. He froze and moved his knife into the ready position in case it woke El Jaguar. Jason didn't move a muscle as he listened for movement. A minute later, two people's snoring wafted from the bedroom, so Jason resumed his journey toward his target.

A rustling noise behind Jason caught his attention, but it was too late. He felt a sharp blow to the back of his head before everything plunged into darkness, and he lost consciousness.

Chapter 22

La Palma, El Salvador

Jason's eyes fluttered open, but he was met with total darkness. For a moment, he panicked that the blow to his skull may have rendered him blind until he felt the rough fabric covering his head. He sat in a hard chair with his hands secured behind his back with plastic zip ties. Every move made his head throb in excruciating pain. Jason felt dried, crusty blood crackling on his shirt whenever he moved his neck.

How long have I been out?

The last thing Jason remembered was moving through the kitchen and then feeling a sharp pain on the back of his head.

Has it been five minutes or five hours?

Jason wasn't sure but surmised by the hood, zip ties, and dried blood that it had been several hours. He heard muffled voices of people talking in Spanish from a nearby room. Jason tried to position his head to listen to the conversation better but gave up after the electric shock of pain shot down his spine.

Footsteps entered the room. "Is he awake yet?" a voice asked in Spanish.

"He's been out long enough. Wake him!" another voice commanded.

Jason tensed for a blow to his hooded head, but instead, cold water jolted him upright in his chair. He heard three voices laughing at his reaction.

"He's awake now."

"Get him out of here. Take him to the compound."

Jason felt weightless as a person on each side lifted him. His legs were still too wobbly to bear his weight, so they dragged him out of the building and shoved him inside a vehicle. Jason lay on his side with the hood still over his head as the vehicle bounced for what felt like an hour to its destination. When the vehicle door opened, Jason suspected he was at the La Palma compound.

The chorus of buzzing insects, croaking frogs, and calling birds was the first indication that he was in the jungle. A pungent, woody smell that reminded Jason of a greenhouse confirmed that a rainforest surrounded him. Jason felt a hand on his ankle, and then he was pulled from the vehicle and allowed to slam onto the moist jungle floor. Someone else grabbed his other ankle, and both individuals dragged Jason across wet grass until he heard the squeak of a door open. One of the people helped him to his feet and pushed Jason up two stairs and into a room. He could tell by the echo that it was a small room with a wooden floor. They sat Jason's muddy body onto another hard chair, then he heard footsteps and a door closed. Five minutes after Jason arrived at the compound, he was alone in a quiet room.

Jason had been in many dangerous situations, but this one felt the most ominous. He was battered, blindfolded, and disoriented, not to mention unarmed, inside a cartel compound.

This isn't going to end well.

His thoughts drifted from his meager chances of survival to Shanna. Visions of his wife pacing in their Whispering Pines home, wondering if her husband and son were still alive, made his heart sink. Jason vowed that if he ever got out alive and brought JJ home to her, he'd never put Shanna through anything like this again. Feelings of dread consumed Jason until he had a new thought.

JJ may be in this compound!

A jolt of adrenaline surged throughout his body, and Jason yanked on his restraints to break them. His captors used multiple zip ties around his wrists, and they didn't budge. Jason wiggled in his chair to find a better position to free himself when the door slammed open. Multiple people entered the room, but he couldn't tell how many. They gathered around Jason without saying a word.

"What do you want with me?" Jason asked shakily.

The room remained silent.

"I want to speak with Orlando Vasquez."

More silence.

"El Jaguar. Your capo."

Jason was struck with an initial blow above his left ear, and then a relentless assault of fists, elbows, knees, and feet followed. He could not lift his arms to protect himself and could only attempt to deflect the blows by bringing up his legs and tucking his head down. A push from the side knocked him off the chair, and Jason slammed onto the dusty wood floor.

The beating stopped as suddenly as it started. The only sound in the room was Jason writhing in pain on the floor and the panting of his attackers. Rolling onto his side, the coppery taste of blood filled his mouth from his upper lip that was sliced open. Every breath sent jolts of pain through his bruised ribs, and his left eye could barely open.

He heard footsteps approach him, and Jason tensed up, prepared to absorb another kick, but instead, his hood slid off and his wrists were freed. Jason squinted with the early-morning sun beaming into the room until his eyes adjusted to the light. Once

Jason opened his good eye, he counted five sicarios standing over him.

The man who removed his hood spoke first in broken English.

"You still want to see El Jaguar?"

Jason nodded.

The man squatted beside Jason. "Okay, it's your life."

Four men with Kalashnikov rifles remained in the room after their leader departed. Jason assumed he had left to inform El Jaguar that the intruder had requested to meet with him. The sicarios in the room did not know Jason spoke Spanish, and he heard them talking with each other.

"This fool asked to see the man who's killed more people than all of us combined," one of the sicarios said with a chuckle.

"How do you think he'll kill him?"

The sicario rubbed his chin as if deeply contemplating Jason's demise. "He usually guts them with his knife, but he'll probably shoot this one. It's quicker and easier to clean up."

The men laughed in unison as Jason questioned his decision to see the head of the La Palma cartel. He knew that anyone who rose to the position of capo in a cartel had to be a ruthless killer, but Jason also hoped that Orlando Vasquez, the father, would understand another father's need to bring his son home. Jason had received intelligence from Mike that El Jaguar had two sons and a daughter. The plan to appeal to a cartel leader's empathy for a father desperate to be reunited with his son sounded reasonable in his apartment in Washington, DC. Now under the watchful eye of four sicarios in the cartel's main compound in the El Salvadoran jungle, Jason realized the plan may have been overly ambitious.

The leader of the group pushed into the room and barked orders to the four sicarios in Spanish.

"El Jaguar will see him now. Get him up and follow me."

They put the blood-stained hood over Jason's head and pushed him out the door. Minutes later, he climbed a half dozen stone stairs and entered an area that echoed with each footfall. He sensed it was a larger room, and it was air-conditioned, a luxury Jason figured was reserved only for El Jaguar's quarters.

The hood was removed, and Jason instinctively scanned his surroundings. As expected, he was in a room that looked like the lobby of a five-star beach resort in Mexico. Jason faced a single man with six armed sicarios behind him. The man drank a caramel-colored liquid from a crystal glass while seated in a black leather chair. His crisp white dress shirt, unbuttoned to his midchest, remained perfectly pressed despite the oppressive humidity. A platinum Rolex gleamed on his wrist while a gold cross swung on a chain around his neck with every sip of his beverage. Jason was twenty feet from the man and felt he was in the presence of the cartel boss.

"I was told you want to see me."

Jason nodded. He was shocked at El Jaguar's near-perfect English.

"Why?"

It wasn't easy to speak to the man who could give him the location of his son or take his life. Plus, his left eye was still swollen shut, and his head throbbing with constant, dull pain. Jason swallowed hard.

"I am looking for my son."

El Jaguar's black eyebrows furrowed, and he leaned forward. "Why would I have your son?"

Jason sensed a hint of irritation in his voice. He had to tread lightly to push for answers while not angering the head of the La Palma cartel.

"I don't think you have him, but you may know where he's being held."

The capo leaned back into the plush chair and took another drink from his cocktail.

"So he was kidnapped, and you think I did it?"

Jason didn't respond.

"La Palma doesn't have kidnapping of children in our portfolio, but perhaps I should start. I heard it can be quite lucrative."

A couple of the sicarios behind Jason chuckled at the comment, which made the capo smile.

El Jaguar's thumb moved to his chin and index finger to his lips as he swung his gaze from Jason to the high corner of the room. His finger tapped his lips like a metronome while considering his next command. He stood and slid his hands into the pockets of his fine Italian dress pants.

"I don't have your son, but I have a good idea who has him."

An overwhelming sense of hope filled Jason, pulsing through every fiber of his being. His instinct was to charge forward and eliminate the space between himself and El Jaguar, but he knew that would be a deadly mistake.

"Who has my son?"

Chapter 23

Sunlight pierced through a high window, creating a pool of buttery light across the spacious room. From the next chamber, Jason heard the sounds of breakfast preparation in contrast to the thick tension in his room.

A new man entered the room and whispered in El Jaguar's ear. He handed the cartel leader a folded piece of paper that he scanned and put into his pocket.

El Jaguar stalked toward Jason. His demeanor quickly changed from amused to stern as his sicarios fell in behind him like shadows. The cartel leader unsheathed a knife, letting sunlight dance along its blade. Jason's throat went dry as he realized he might have pushed too far.

The capo reviewed the paper in his pocket again for several long seconds.

"I understand you are Jason Mulder. Did I pronounce that correctly?"

Jason nodded.

"You know a lot about our family here in La Palma. How did you find out about me?" El Jaguar asked.

Jason immediately knew he was in grave danger. El Jaguar's men had found his ID in his backpack and might already know more about him, but he could never tell them that he got his information from Special Agent Holland at the DEA.

"Someone told me in San Salvador."

"Liar!" El Jaguar thundered.

Jason doubled down. "It's the truth."

"Nobody in El Salvador would ever speak my name to an American stranger. They all know they'd have their tongues cut out and their family butchered. Get him out of here!"

Before Jason could protest, the hood returned over his head, and he was dragged out of the room. They pushed him into the corner of an adjacent bedroom.

No sicarios spoke, but Jason could hear at least two people shuffling around the room. Jason's thoughts turned to his fate. El Jaguar must want something from him, or he'd already be dead. He'd have to play ball with the cartel boss if he wanted to survive long enough to find JJ.

Minutes after Jason arrived in the bedroom, he was rushed back to the room with the echoes. The hood was removed, and Jason faced El Jaguar beside a sicario, an AK-47 pointed at his chest.

"Your answer to my next question will determine if you live or die. Do you understand?"

Jason nodded.

"You're Special Agent Mulder with the DEA, correct?"

"No."

"You disappoint me," El Jaguar hissed. He raised his finger to signal the sicario to shoot when Jason interrupted.

"I used to be in the DEA!" Jason shouted. "But now I provide security for a politician."

"So you were in the DEA?"

"Yes."

"What does the DEA know about La Palma?"

Jason inhaled deeply and let it out. "They know all about your former operation in Arizona and that you have a few routes through Mexico to the United States."

"That's it? They are not concerned about La Palma flooding the United States with narcotics?"

"Concerned, yes, but interested, no," Jason replied. He braced for an outburst or worse. When it didn't come, he continued. "La Palma is much smaller than the Mexican and new Chinese cartels. The DEA is so focused on them that La Palma rarely appears on their radar. If you don't grow too big and don't pull any more stunts in the United States like you did in Arizona, the DEA will probably pay little attention to La Palma."

"If you are lying, I will also have my men hunt down your family in the United States and kill them too," El Jaguar threatened.

"You know that is the truth. You're a smart man, and I simply confirmed what you already know."

A genuine smile stretched across the cartel leader's face. "That is true. So you really came here to find your son?"

"Yes. As I told you, my son was abducted and moved to Central America. I thought La Palma may know where I could find him."

El Jaguar strutted beside Jason, put his arm around him, and turned him to face the armed sicarios in the room.

"Can you believe the *cajónes* on this guy? He wants answers about where to find his son, so he comes here to find them," El Jaguar jeered in Spanish.

The room erupted in laughter.

El Jaguar's lips curved into a predatory smile. "I can only think of one man who would abduct a child from Arizona. Find Victor Romero, and you'll find your boy."

"Víctor Romero is dead!"

"No, amigo. He's alive—and he has your son."

Fury surged through Jason as he lunged forward. "If he touches my boy, I'll—"

A rifle stock slammed into his back, driving him to his knees. Pain exploded through his spine as Jason wobbled back to his feet, but the physical agony was nothing compared to the knowledge that Victor lived—and had JJ.

"Save your strength," El Jaguar said. "Víctor is no longer part of the La Palma family. After he failed in Arizona, I ordered his death. But like a cockroach, he scurried away before we could finish him."

"Where is he now?"

"If I knew, he'd already be dead. Rumors say he's hiding in the mountains near the border with Honduras. He knows returning here means death."

"When I get my son to safety, I promise Victor will receive a painful death," Jason stated. It was a brazen attempt to show El Jaguar he was an ally.

"So you know of Victor Romero?"

"Yes, I was the one that sent him over the waterfall in Arizona."

"He has your son. I am sure of it," El Jaguar reminded Jason. "If you find him, what will you do?"

Jason sensed his time with El Jaguar was coming to an end. He didn't yet know if it would lead to his release or death. He looked up at the stone arches supporting the ceiling as he carefully considered his response. "After I find Victor Romero, I guarantee he'll never take another breath in this life."

The cartel boss drew a knife from the leather sheath at his waist. The sharp steel glinted as he lifted it before Jason's face.

"Should I use my knife?"

Jason swallowed hard as El Jaguar moved behind him. He felt a firm grip around his wrist and tensed up, preparing to get stabbed in the back, but the tip of the blade never entered his flesh. Instead,

Jason felt freedom after El Jaguar cut his zip ties. Now Jason was more suspicious of his intentions.

El Jaguar put the knife back in the sheath and stepped away from Jason. His right hand remained behind his back. He strode toward Jason, and when his hand became visible again, it held a Glock 17 pistol.

"Or my pistol?"

"Shit!" Jason muttered.

He raised the weapon and aimed it between Jason's eyes. Every muscle in Jason's body tensed, but he continued to stare defiantly at the cartel leader. Seconds felt like minutes as Jason gazed at the ruthless expression of a man who had surely pulled the trigger before in this situation.

Instead of firing, El Jaguar flipped the gun in his hand and offered the grip to Jason. "You'll need this. Promise you'll put an extra bullet in Victor's head for me," El Jaguar said coolly.

Jason stared at the Glock in his hand for a beat. He ejected the magazine, confirmed it was full, and secured the pistol in his front waistband.

"Count on it."

Chapter 24

La Palma Cartel Compound, El Salvador

Jason stood alone in the same spot where he'd received a weapon minutes earlier. The determined father was relieved to be alive but also surprised by the fact that he now held the cartel leader's pistol. Unsure about what to do next, Jason remained still as a statue as he pondered whether he was allowed to go or if he should stay until they returned.

El Jaguar had moved to an adjacent dining room where he sat at the head of a long, handcrafted wooden table set with fine China plates, silver cutlery, and crystal glasses. A sicario flanked each side of the capo. The compound food staff placed silver platters of pastries, bowls of colorful fresh fruit, and steaming carafes among the trio. The scent of freshly brewed coffee and sizzling meats wafted toward Jason, reminding him that he hadn't eaten in a day and was famished.

"Are you going just to stand there, or are you going to kill Victor Romero?" El Jaguar shouted from across the room.

Jason spun to address the familiar voice and took several steps toward the table.

"I don't know where I am or how to get out of here."

The cartel boss stabbed some fluffy scrambled eggs and fried plantain with a fork and pointed the utensil full of food at Jason.

"Go out front and tell the driver to take you back into town."

Jason nodded and shuffled toward the door.

"Never come back here again. Don't even think about me," El Jaguar warned. "You won't be as lucky in the future as you were this time."

Jason didn't stop to acknowledge the threat. He knew he was fortunate to be walking out of El Jaguar's compound instead of leaving feet-first in a body bag. He had no intention of visiting La Palma in the future.

Once he passed through the ornate metal door, Jason ambled to the circular driveway in front of the beautiful building. He looked in both directions and noticed a Black Yukon Denali XL at the end of the driveway. One of the sicarios from inside, a man with salt-and-pepper hair pulled back into a ponytail, was smoking a few feet from the SUV, which was glistening in the sun.

That must be the vehicle that will take me back to town.

Jason couldn't see through the dark tinted windows and strode to the front of the vehicle. He kept an eye on the sicario, who leaned against a wrought-iron fence with an air of disinterest. Jason found the front seat empty and scanned the area for the driver.

"I know the man you seek," the sicario called out in Spanish.

Jason turned and replied in Spanish. "Are you the driver?"

"I will get him for you. I know Victor Romero."

Intrigued, Jason trained his intense gaze on the man. "Do you know where I can find him?"

"*Sí,*" the sicario responded. He looked around to see if anyone else was watching and stepped off the sidewalk to the driveway beside Jason.

"My cousin is Victor's ex-wife. She stays with us now after their divorce, and last month, she got an envelope in the mail with some money but no letter or note. It was from Victor for their sons. The letter was sent from Corinto."

"I'm not familiar with Corinto. Is it in El Salvador?"

"Yes, it's a medium-sized village in the southern jungle near the Honduran border. It's very remote and a good place to hide out."

Jason nodded. "Yes, but if El Jaguar wants him dead, he may constantly be on the move."

"She received at least two other letters from Corinto in the last six months. Victor is definitely there."

Jason was grateful for the news and planned to check out Corinto as soon as possible. However, he didn't want to cross El Jaguar again while in El Salvador.

"I appreciate the information, but you must know that if I find your cousin's ex-husband, I will kill him."

The sicario smiled, exposing a missing incisor in his top row of teeth.

"I know. That is why I am telling you this."

"Can you find my driver now?" Jason asked.

Additional missing teeth were exposed when the sicario's smile widened. "I'm your driver. We can go now."

Jason returned through the jungle that he missed with the hood over his head earlier that morning. No words were spoken during the seventy-minute commute until the cartel driver announced that he'd arrived at the bus station in La Palma. Jason purchased a ticket and boarded a bus to San Salvador less than an hour later.

During the return trip to the nation's capital city, Jason leaned his head against the glass as he considered his next mission. He understood he was lucky to be alive after his encounter with the head of the La Palma cartel and that luck would be in short supply going forward. It would take all of Jason's knowledge and experience as an Air Force pararescueman, DEA Special Agent, and PSD member to find JJ's captor and bring home his son.

Small towns and patches of forest passed outside his window as Jason mentally ran through a half dozen scenarios. They were all unique, but he always arrived at the same conclusion.

I can't do this alone.

Jason didn't want this to be true. He prided himself on being self-sufficient and not relying on others to do the job. However, this mission wasn't about Jason; it was about JJ. His probability of success would improve greatly if someone else were there to help him, and that was all the convincing he needed to conclude that he would ask for help. But who?

After a short stop to drop off and pick up more passengers in a far-flung suburb of San Salvador, Jason turned his thoughts back to who could help him navigate what he expected to be a heavily guarded compound to reach his son.

Should I ask Clay, Zee, or Central to fly down to help? Could Noah be an option?

He immediately ruled out his brother. Although Noah would eagerly hop on the next flight to Central America, he didn't have the skills to help Jason breach a fortified compound. Plus, he didn't want to risk losing another brother. His teammates on Senator Conrad's security team certainly had the skills, but Jason knew they couldn't afford to leave their principal at such a chaotic time.

The bus arrived at its final destination in San Salvador, and Jason waited until everyone exited. He slung the backpack that a sicario returned to him over his shoulder and strolled down the bustling street. Jason always found it easier to think while running or walking. He needed to figure out who would be best suited for his upcoming mission and who could come before he hailed a taxi to take him to the airport car-rental lot.

Jason stopped at a street vendor and bought five cheese-and-bean pupusas and some coconut-based candy. He continued to walk and eat until he inhaled every crumb in the bag two blocks later. The surge of energy was instant, and Jason felt his strength return after a draining night. It could be zapped quickly by the humid heat, so he stayed in the cooler shade of high-rise apartments and leafy trees as the late morning temps soared into the high eighties. A list of names flickered through his thoughts like a news ticker at the bottom of a TV screen. He bounded past a shady enclave, stopped, and checked his phone for a signal. It had four of five possible bars, so Jason stepped beside an empty bench and dialed a number. He'd identified the best person to help him bring JJ home.

"Where are you?" A voice answered after two rings.

"I'm in the capital city of El Salvador."

"Have you found JJ yet?"

"Shanna," Jason started. "I'm on my way to investigate a promising lead now. I don't have much time to talk, but I need you to do something for me."

"Okay, what is it?"

"Pack a travel bag and ask my dad to drive you to the Phoenix airport."

"Why?"

"I need your help in Central America."

CHAPTER 25

San Salvador, El Salvador

Jason stepped out of the taxi and onto the blistering asphalt of the airport parking lot. He strode past rows of parked cars as commercial airliners thundered overhead as they ascended through the fluffy clouds into the blue sky.

He reviewed his decision to ask Shanna to come to El Salvador every mile of his journey from central San Salvador to the airport, twenty-five miles south of town. Jason understood his request for Shanna's help put the mother of his child and wife at risk, but he couldn't think of anyone better suited for the mission he had in mind. She wouldn't arrive in the country for another thirty-six hours, and Jason intended to scout Victor's compound in Corinto while he waited.

Jason arrived at a single-lane road connecting two airport parking lots. Other travelers going to the rental car lot were coming from the terminal shuttle buses, not trekking across a massive concrete slab covered in parked vehicles.

The refreshing blast of cold air cooled his warm skin as he stepped into the rental car center at El Salvador International Airport. The air-conditioned modern building provided a welcome reprieve from the hot and humid weather outside. He paused for a moment to let his body adjust to the temperature before joining the line for his rental car in the terminal. Ten minutes later, Jason snagged the keys the rental car agent pushed toward him on the counter. He deposited them in his pocket as the young lady tapped the computer monitor with her long nails.

"We recommend adding the additional insurance even if you have a policy in the United States while you're here in El Salvador," the agent said in perfect English. "Would you like both the supplemental liability protection and loss-damage waiver insurance?"

Jason nearly declined the insurance, like he always did in the US, but thought better of it.

I'm driving to the compound of a former cartel member in the middle of the jungle in Central America. The probability of my vehicle getting damaged has to be close to one hundred percent.

"Yes. I'll take both."

"Do you know how much coverage you'd like?" the agent inquired with an enthusiastic smile.

"I'll take the maximum amount you can provide on the vehicle."

The response caused a double-take from the clerk before she completed the transaction.

Jason secured his rental agreement and marched into the lot to locate the Jeep Grand Cherokee he'd rented. He spotted the hunter-green four-by-four vehicle, and just as he opened the driver's door, a firm hand grabbed his arm. Jason jerked away and spun around, primed to defend himself. He was prepared to encounter a sicario or gang member seeking to harm him. But that's not who he saw. It took Jason a few moments to process the confusing signals his eyes relayed to his brain.

"Zee? What are you doing here?"

"It's great to see you too, Mulder."

Jason stood with his mouth agape, shocked to see his PSD team-mate from Senator Conrad's security team. He pulled Zee in for a quick hug.

"I'm thrilled to see you, but why are you in El Salvador?"

"I knew you were lying about calling us for help when it was clear you needed it, so I came down to lend a hand. I figured you could use the help."

Help is an understatement, Jason thought. *I could use a small army.*

Zee pointed to the bruises on Jason's face and arms. "It looks like I should have come a little sooner."

Jason touched the gash on his forehead that was still tender. "What about protecting Senator Conrad? Does Clay know you're here?"

"Yeah, Clay knows. It puts them in a bind, but he understands."

"If it puts them in a bind, why'd you come?"

Zee looked to the ground and sighed. "Mulder, you know that a US Senator has the money and resources to have plenty of people to protect him. Clay can find some local help if he needs additional bodies. After you told me you were coming down here alone to find your son, I knew I had to help you find him."

As the shock wore off that a former Army Ranger was standing beside him and willing to help find JJ, Jason switched to the other question on his mind.

"I appreciate you coming down here, but how'd you find me?"

A sinister grin formed below Zee's dark mustache. "You're not the only investigator on the team. I called your wife, who told me she was coming down here to meet you. Shanna shared that her flight would have to connect through Dallas, so I knew I could beat her on the direct flight. She said that you planned to pick her up at the terminal, and I knew you'd have to rent a car, so I've been waiting out here since I arrived last night."

"I'm glad you're here," Jason said sincerely. He meant it, but the gratitude was tinged with guilt. It was one of the reasons Jason hated to ask for help.

"Zee, my next mission is very dangerous. I'm willing to risk anything because it's my son, but I would never ask you to do the same. I'd understand if you wanted to sit this next mission out."

A fist flew through the air and connected with Jason's arm.

"Are you out of your mind, Mulder? I live for this shit," Zee asserted. "If I hear another butthurt member of Congress whine about how they can't serve their constituents without the lobbyist or PAC money going into their campaign because of Conrad's CFO bill, I'm going to lose it. Down here, I can help you do some real good, so I'm in no matter how much danger is involved."

Jason didn't expect any other response from Zee, but it helped alleviate the guilt. He rubbed his aching bicep from Zee's punch and opened the rear hatch of the Jeep. Zee tossed his travel bag into the back. It was bursting at the seams.

"Plan on staying a few months?" Jason joked.

"Half that is your shit."

"My shit?"

"Yeah. When I was in the locker room packing, I saw you still had your good tactical gear in your locker, so I grabbed your stuff too."

Jason extended his hand for an arm-wrestle handshake with Zee. "Thanks, man. I was in such a big hurry to get down here I forgot some pretty important stuff. We can change on the way.

He shut the hatch and checked his watch.

"We have to get going. I'll explain the mission during our drive to Corinto."

CHAPTER 26

Jason and Zee passed the time driving to Corinto with stories of past adventures. At the halfway point to their destination, Zee leaned his seat back.

"I'm a little tired from the flight," Zee stated. "I'm going to rest my eyes for a few minutes."

"Good night," Jason chided his teammate and friend.

"I'm not going to sleep, just rest a little bit."

Moments later, Jason heard soft snoring coming from the passenger seat. Jason welcomed the temporary quiet, constant conversation replaced by the soothing hum from the Jeep's air conditioner working hard to keep the cabin cool as he put more miles of concrete behind them.

An armadillo appeared and scuttled across the highway, its suit of armor gleaming in the afternoon sun. The dinosaur-like mammal spurred a memory of JJ from a happier time in his life.

It was a fall morning at the Phoenix Zoo, days before Jason moved into his new apartment in Washington, DC. JJ rode high on his father's shoulders, his tiny hands drumming excitedly on his father's head as they approached the Desert Lives exhibit. They secured a seat in the front row for the live animal encounter, where JJ bounced on Jason's lap in anticipation. JJ was entranced when the zookeeper arrived with her first animal, a white-nosed coatimundi with a long snout, ringed tail, and brown fur. As more desert-dwelling critters arrived, Jason leaned back to watch his son's eyes widen and lips curl skyward at the sight of each creature. JJ loved all animals but had a clear favorite, and the zookeeper arrived with the baseball-sized creature.

"This is Dilly, our three-banded armadillo."

JJ's eyes grew wide as saucers. "Ball!" he said excitedly, pointing at the armadillo curled into a perfect sphere.

"He does look like a ball, doesn't he?" Shanna laughed as Jason held him to get a closer look.

The zookeeper knelt before JJ. "Would you like to touch him? He's very gentle."

Jason guided JJ's tiny hand toward Dilly as he uncurled, his pointed nose twitching curiously. JJ gasped in delight as his fingers brushed against his smooth armor.

He turned to his parents, beaming with pride, and then returned his focus to Dilly's nose investigating his palm. It was the highlight of all JJ's animal encounters that day.

Later, in the gift shop, JJ reached from his stroller and clutched a stuffed armadillo nearly as big as himself. Shanna bought it for JJ, and they named it Dilly Junior, or DJ for short. He refused to let it go during the two-hour ride home. DJ occupied the place of honor on JJ's bed until his father brought home a teddy bear from Washington, DC.

"Remember, buddy?" Shanna had said one night while tucking him in with Jason. "The real Dilly curled up into a ball just like this." She demonstrated with the stuffed armadillo, making JJ laugh over and over.

Jason blinked away the moisture in his eyes as he had to brake for a passing vehicle swerving into his lane. He could still hear

JJ's musical laugh, and the sting of his absence that Jason had temporarily suppressed bubbled to the surface.

The armadillo memory worked into his mind like a barbed splinter. The small moments with the most important people in his life reminded Jason precisely what he was fighting for.

"Mulder, is everything okay?" Zee asked.

Jason turned to see Zee staring at him.

"Yeah, why?"

"I've been asking you a question, and you seem out of it."

"I'm good." Jason offered his reassurance with a fake smile. "Just thinking about our mission. What's up?"

"Why, exactly, are we going to Corinto?" Zee asked.

"I know who took my son," Jason replied. He kept his gaze on the faded asphalt road with no lane lines and heavy traffic. "It's the same man I thought was dead, but somehow, he rose from the ashes and took JJ. His name is Victor Romero."

"You thought he was dead?"

"Remember the story Clay and I told you about the cartel we hunted down in Arizona after they murdered my brother?"

"Yeah, how could I forget?"

"I watched Victor's body cascade over a raging waterfall forty feet high during a flash flood. I have no idea how he survived."

"So he came back for revenge?"

Zee's question was more of a statement that Jason had finally accepted. He blamed himself for not finishing the job once JJ went missing, but he stopped beating himself up after his last trip to El Salvador. He'd face off with Victor Romero again; this time, it would truly be a final showdown. Only one of them would leave Central America alive.

"I used Google Maps to view the satellite imagery outside of Corinto, and I found an area that looks like it could be the compound," Jason said, changing the subject. "I want to conduct recon of the site and then develop a plan to extract my son."

"Let's do it."

The coastal plains turned into hills, and eventually, mountains carpeted with trees as they neared Corinto. Traffic thinned, and the road narrowed as they approached the community of ten thousand residents tucked in the country's northeast corner. Lush trees formed a continuous canopy over the road, stealing most of the sunlight hours before dark. The eerie atmosphere only heightened the tension of their high-stakes mission.

Once past Corinto, Jason turned off the paved road onto a path with grass growing between two thin slits of dirt. It was not a well-traveled route, and he was glad he had chosen to upgrade to a four-wheel-drive Jeep. Even with all four wheels engaged, the SUV slid right and left in the soft mud, narrowly missing the trees surrounding the path.

"Are you sure this is the right way?" Zee questioned.

"Yeah, it's either this or hump the last five clicks in this heat to the compound."

Zee held tightly to the handle above his head. "I'm beginning to think five clicks don't sound so bad right now."

Jason chuckled at the thought that Zee had no problem confronting a cartel in a remote jungle but was afraid of a vehicle slamming into a tree. "I'm trying to get us as close as possible so it's not such a long trek."

They reached a muddy hill three clicks later that even a four-by-four vehicle couldn't climb. Jason parked the Jeep and turned off the ignition.

"Now we get to hump through the jungle."

Zee and Jason secured their gear and met behind the locked vehicle.

"Anything dangerous out there?" Zee inquired.

"You mean other than an armed cartel?"

"Yeah. I mean, like, snakes and shit."

Jason raised his hand to the jungle to the right. "There are all kinds of venomous spiders and snakes in there. The pit vipers are the worst of the bunch."

Zee's face blanched as his eyes widened. "What do they look like?"

"They're all different shapes, sizes, and colors, so try to avoid anything that slithers."

"Roger that. You don't have to tell me twice," Zee chirped.

Jason took a reading with his compass, and his demeanor immediately turned serious. He was close to finding JJ, and every fiber of his being was focused on the safe retrieval of his son.

"The Jeep is our FRV, and we'll establish the RV when we get closer to the compound," Jason said of the rendezvous and final rendezvous points.

"Got it," Zee replied. "After we finish the recon mission, I want to go into town and try some famous pupusas I've read about."

"I had some earlier today, and they were excellent."

"Okay, now I really want some. We're going to the first street vendor we find in Corinto."

"Let's do it," Jason said, leaving the clearing. Every step into the darkening jungle brought Jason closer to JJ, but it also sparked a growing doubt that he'd ever share pupusas with Zee.

Chapter 27

Corinto, El Salvador

Sweat trickled down Jason's neck as he followed ten paces behind Zee through the dense jungle flora. The humid air clung to them like a second skin, darkening their tactical clothing with moisture. Zee took the point while Jason continually verified their location with his compass.

Jason stepped carefully on the undulating forest floor, testing each step before committing his weight to the muddy surface. Zee chose to advance through the jungle at a deliberate pace to avoid detection while still arriving with enough daylight to observe the compound.

They stealthily covered two of the three kilometers when Zee suddenly raised his fist—the signal to freeze. Jason immediately dropped to one knee, eyes scanning their sector while Zee maintained his gaze on the forest before him. After thirty seconds, Jason moved beside Zee.

"Got anything?" he whispered.

"I counted two clicks, so we need to switch to hand signals the rest of the way."

"Roger," Jason replied. He noted they were on a flat area near the bend of a small stream. "This will be our rendezvous location if we need to abort."

Zee nodded. "Got it. You ready to go?"

Jason was ready, but he had to voice a concern eating at him like the tropical biting insects attacking him throughout their trek through the jungle.

"I don't like that you only have a knife. Take my pistol," Jason said while presenting the Glock to Zee.

His teammate refused to take it. "It sucks that we couldn't bring our weapons here, but I'm good with my knife. It's quiet but deadly."

"We're likely going to run into sicarios with rifles," Jason reminded him.

"I hope so. I'll take one of them by surprise, and then I'll have a rifle."

Jason knew Zee couldn't be swayed once he'd made up his mind, but he tried one final time.

"You're on point. Are you sure you don't want the Glock?"

"The only thing I'm sure of is that we're wasting time. I'll be fine, so let's go find these bastards."

Jason nodded, and Zee bounded ahead.

The duo pressed through the dense foliage until Zee halted again, dropping into the prone position behind a fallen tree. Jason followed suit, crawling forward until he was parallel with his teammate. Zee tapped his chest twice and pointed forward with two fingers spread, indicating it was time to move up for visual confirmation. They belly-crawled through the undergrowth until they reached a clearing.

Jason peered through gaps in the foliage and noted a main structure with three outbuildings. The weather-beaten wooden structures surrounded an animal pen enclosed by a hasty barbed-wire fence.

That's where they must be holding JJ.

The compound appeared deserted initially, but then two armed sentries walked from behind the main building. Jason pulled binoculars from his pack and scanned the compound property. It was a little larger than a football field, and he spotted two additional guards walking the perimeter at the opposite end of the clearing.

They'll eventually investigate this end.

Jason removed his phone and opened the app to check for the tracker in JJ's teddy bear. The application opened but a spinning wheel appeared in the middle of the phone screen where he should have seen a blinking blue dot for the tracker.

"Dammit. I only have one bar," Jason whispered to himself.

Despite the weak signal, Jason kept his eyes glued to the screen. The wheel disappeared, and a blue dot appeared for the first time since JJ went missing. Jason's breath caught, and he blinked to be sure his mind wasn't showing him what he wanted to see. A second later, the spinning wheel returned for good.

His first reaction was to smash the useless phone into a billion pieces, but then hope slammed into his chest like a giant fist.

"JJ's in there."

Technology may have confirmed his son was nearby, but Jason didn't need it—he felt JJ. He was sure his son was just over fifty yards away in one of the buildings, and determination-fueled adrenaline flooded his body. Jason pictured JJ's tear-filled hazel eyes peeking through his light brown locks, willing his mother and father to burst through the door and save him. He was so close to the moment he'd dreamt about since JJ went missing, but he still couldn't swoop his son into his arms. It took all the self-control Jason could muster to prevent himself from charging ahead to retrieve his son.

Focus. JJ needs you, so don't rush this.

Zee tapped Jason and pointed with two fingers toward more armed men milling around the outbuildings. That was six sicarios carrying AK-47 rifles they would have to overcome with knives and a pistol. The numerical superiority of the sicarios did not provide encouraging odds for Jason and Zee, but it was possible to eliminate all of them with the right people and plan. Jason was confident he had both.

A goat in the pen between the buildings bleated, and a pig squealed. Seconds later, the animals in the pen erupted into chaos.

"Shit! The animals caught our scent," Jason whispered.

Six more men poured out of the buildings with their Kalashnikov rifles at the ready. They fanned out in all directions of the compound, looking for the source of the animal's concern. One sicario headed straight toward Jason and Zee.

"Back to the RV!" Jason said.

He pushed back on his belly until the clearing was out of view. Jason stood and took several steps through the underbrush when he noticed Zee wasn't behind him.

"Come on, Zee. We need to move."

"Your son is in there. We can get him," Zee whispered back.

Jason desperately wanted to side with Zee. He desired nothing more than to have JJ in his arms that moment, but he knew that if something were to happen to him, his son would have no chance of surviving. Jason locked his gaze on the tree line where he last saw the sicario. He hoped their whispers didn't give away their location.

"We need to split up. I'll take another look and meet you back at the RV," Zee said and darted into the forest in a different direction.

"Zee! Zee!"

He tried to stop his PSD teammate, but it was too late. Zee was on the move while a dozen guards combed the property, searching for intruders. He waited as long as possible for Zee to return. Jason fell deeper into the jungle when Zee didn't appear as a sicario pushed through the brush where he'd been lying prone seconds earlier.

Jason arrived at the rendezvous point after ensuring no guards followed him and found cover while he waited for Zee. After fifteen minutes had passed, he began to worry that his teammate might be in trouble.

"Zee's a former ranger, so I know he wouldn't get lost," Jason tried to assure himself.

A half hour after Jason had returned, he knew something was wrong. He cautiously returned to the compound but veered to the left of the previous spot to get a better view of the main building. Shouts in Spanish wafted through the trees before Jason reached the clearing. He couldn't make out what they were saying, but their hoots and joyous tones of victory were concerning.

Jason returned to his stomach as he approached the clearing. He pushed forward to the previously sunny open area engulfed in shade as the sun descended below the jungle canopy.

A figure appeared from the main building, but unlike the sicarios, he was not armed with a rifle. He walked with a sense of authority toward a cluster of guards gathered in a circle.

A twinge of familiarity fluttered inside Jason as the man drew closer.

The voices of the sicarios hushed as the man scanned the surrounding jungle as if looking for someone. Jason's chest constricted, and his stomach churned as the man's piercing gaze landed in his direction.

"Victor Romero!"

CHAPTER 28

The jungle appeared to hold its breath as Jason watched his nemesis strut around the compound. He was relieved to have chosen a spot downwind, preventing the farm animals from sounding an early warning. This strategic position enabled him to overhear conversations from forty yards away.

The former La Palma cartel lieutenant returned his attention to the sicarios huddled nearby. He reached into his waistline and withdrew a matte black pistol. At the tip of his chin, a half dozen sicarios stepped back to present their catch on a wooden chair—Ruben "Zee" Zambrano.

Jason's breath caught in his throat at the sight of Zee's bloodied face through an opening among the guards.

"Shit! They have Zee!" Jason muttered to himself.

The former ranger's head dangled to the left while the rest of his body slumped in the same direction. A sicario's hand pressed against Zee's shirtless body was the only thing preventing him from collapsing to the muddy earth.

Jason watched Zee's ribs expand and contract as his lungs yearned for oxygen in the oppressive heat. Blood streamed from his head like tributaries until they joined on his left cheek and ran like a mighty river down his neck. Jason guessed the sicarios pistol-whipped his PSD teammate multiple times to generate that much blood.

"Who are you with?" a voice asked in Spanish.

Jason watched Zee straighten, but he did not respond.

"If you want to live, you better start talking. Who sent you?"

Zee blinked at the question but remained silent.

Victor rushed past the sicarios and slammed the barrel of his gun into Zee's temple. "We're not going to keep asking you. Who sent you?"

The former cartel lieutenant suddenly spun around and scanned the tree line. "Who else is with you?"

Jason got a good look at the man responsible for his missing son. Overall, he looked like Jason remembered from their last encounter, except for an area on his head above his right eyebrow and ear. It looked sunken in, like a baseball bat had smashed into his skull.

How did he survive going over those falls?

The sight of Victor Romero standing next to his teammate and friend filled him with anger, but the knowledge that he had taken his sleeping son from his bedroom in his parents' house generated a wave of rage that Jason struggled to control. He brought the Glock gifted to him from El Jaguar up from his waist and aimed it at the head of JJ's abductor. His finger hovered near the trigger as Jason weighed the consequences of giving away his position and jeopardizing JJ's safety if he were in the compound, for the sweet satisfaction of putting a full magazine of rounds between Victor's eyes. Jason could picture Victor's head snapping back and exploding into a red mist if he fired. It should have been an easy decision, knowing that killing Victor would immediately place JJ in grave danger, but Jason eased his finger closer to the trigger until he felt cold steel on his skin. Jason breathed in the moist air and exhaled slowly as he settled the stubby front sight on his target.

Victor waved to the tree line surrounding the compound. "He didn't come here alone. Search the area."

Four sicarios went in different directions, while three stayed with Victor and Zee. Jason watched one of the men step into the trees thirty yards away from him and move in his direction. He stuck his head into the jungle to look and listen every five or six paces. Jason slid back several feet from the clearing and wiggled himself under the broad leaves of the jungle undergrowth. The former PJ held his breath and pressed his cheek against the mud to become as flat as possible.

The sicario stopped steps from where Jason had been and leaned into the jungle. He seemed to linger in the area longer than his previous stops, causing Jason to lower his hand to his pants pocket. The guard took another step into the jungle and looked in all directions. Three more steps, and the sicario would step on him. Jason worried that his heart pounding in his chest would give away his position.

The sentry took a single step back as Jason wrapped his fingers around the handle of his knife and prepared to thrust the blade into the sicario's neck. The sentry backed completely out and moved further down the tree line. Jason remained frozen until his heart rate and breathing returned to normal.

Victor kicked Zee, knocking him off the chair with his hands tied behind his back.

"On your knees!" Victor yelled in Spanish.

Victor swung around to the other side of Zee and pressed the barrel of his pistol against his jaw, pushing Zee's head upright.

"I will give you one final chance to talk or die. Who sent you, and where are the people who came with you?"

Jason sensed, from Victor's tone, that he was serious about pulling the trigger and that Zee was in mortal danger.

Dammit. I never should have let Zee come with me on this mission.

Zee's eyes glanced toward the tree line near where Jason had recently watched from a prone position and then settled on the area where they had originally scanned the compound earlier to the south.

Did Zee see me?

Victor noticed the shift in his gaze and turned to face the same direction.

"Are they waiting for you over there?" Victor asked.

Zee remained silent.

Victor stepped back and aimed at Zee's forehead.

He's going to shoot. I have to do something.

The sicario checking the perimeter near Jason a minute earlier had returned, inspiring a bold plan.

If I can secure his AK-47, I can take out Victor and the sicarios before they get to JJ.

The desperate situation led Jason to believe this plan was possible against over twelve armed cartel hit men. He pulled his knees under him so he could quickly reach the throat of the sicario with his knife. The guard stepped into the brush near Jason again.

Come on. Come in a little deeper.

The sicario's instincts were on high alert. He sensed the hidden danger, but the fading sunlight prevented him from seeing the predator lurking in the shadows, waiting patiently to take his life.

Two more steps, and you're mine.

The guard stopped, focused on the ground, and aimed his rifle at Jason.

Boom!

A thunderous blast rocked the jungle.

Chapter 29

The world around Jason went dark for a beat as the pistol report reverberated in his unprotected ears. He lifted his head from the jungle floor to see the stunned gunman gazing back at the source of the blast. At that moment, Jason knew he had a brief window of opportunity before the guard turned his rifle back on him, so he sprang up with his knife, aiming for the guard's throat. The sicario's eyes widened in surprise as he saw the razor-sharp blade closing in on him like a guided missile. Jason used his free hand to push the barrel of the AK-47 away from his chest and drive the combat knife through the sicario's Adam's apple until only the hilt was visible. The former PJ twisted it to ensure the man couldn't yell for help and yanked the knife out. The guard's death was quick and silent.

Jason secured the AK-47 from the dead man's cooling hands and swung the sights toward Victor. That's when he saw Zee wobble and fall forward. The left side of his forehead was missing.

"No!" Jason yelled. It came out louder than he intended.

Victor spun in the direction of the voice. "The others are out there. Find them and bring them back to me."

Jason dropped to the ground and high-crawled for several yards until he was out of sight of the men approaching from the clearing.

Once he had ample cover from the jungle underbrush, he stood and bolted deep into the jungle.

The sicarios gave chase, but Jason was already eighty yards ahead of them. He moved through the jungle swiftly, barely registering the leaves, vines, and branches striking him as he passed. The image of Zee's lifeless body tumbling to the ground replayed in his mind over and over like a looped video.

Why did you have to go back?

Zee's classic smile replaced the gruesome scene of his teammate's death, and Jason continued to put more distance between himself and the pursuing sicarios. A thought popped into Jason's head so profound he stopped running.

Zee saved me.

Jason turned back to where he'd last seen his PSD teammate.

He knew I was in the tree line and deliberately looked at the other end of the clearing to throw Victor off of me.

A wave of nausea overcame Jason at the realization that Zee had sacrificed himself to protect Jason and JJ from Victor and the sicarios. It was a sacrifice Jason never wanted from his former Army Ranger friend, and he struggled to reconcile conflicting emotions of anger and gratitude toward Zee for his ultimate sacrifice.

The sounds of snapping branches and ruffling leaves grew louder, so Jason resumed his retreat from the sicarios. He didn't notice the steep, slippery slope during his sudden start and tumbled down the muddy embankment. Jason used the AK-47 to slow and eventually stop his slide, but that filled the barrel with mud and rendered the rifle useless until it was cleaned.

"Shit, now I just have my knife and pistol against a squad of sicarios," Jason muttered.

He'd landed at the bottom of a narrow wash filled with mud an inch thick. The fall into the wash allowed Victor's goons to catch up with Jason, so he had no choice but to hide and hope they passed him by.

His mud-caked tactical pants and shirt provided the perfect camouflage when the sicarios arrived. Jason estimated that six or seven men were pursuing him, but they did not have the discipline of trained soldiers searching for a target. They moved in a straight-line formation ten yards apart and moved around obstacles, like the wash, instead of moving through them to ensure every inch of ground was clear of the enemy.

Jason kept his head down and slowed his breathing until the sounds of men moving through the jungle like predators were gone. As he slowly raised his head to scan the area, he heard faint ruffling nearby.

Are they circling back?

Surprised they'd return so quickly, Jason pushed himself up to crawl out of the wash when he saw the source of the sound. A rainforest hog-nosed viper slithered straight toward him. Jason pushed away and landed on his haunches without taking his eyes off the viper still barreling toward him. He removed his knife and rose to his feet. Jason planned to cut off the viper's head to eliminate the threat but was inspired by another idea.

Jason swung the AK-47 sling over his shoulder and aimed the rifle barrel at the snake. His goal wasn't to shoot it but to pin its head down and allow Jason to pick up the serpent. The snake slithered out from under the pressure of the barrel several times, and Jason wondered if the risk was worth it. He pressed the barrel harder into the snake's neck right behind its triangular-shaped head, and it worked. Jason maintained pressure on the barrel as he reached down and secured the viper behind the head.

An involuntary wave of adrenaline slammed into Jason's gut as he let go of the AK-47 and stood with the pissed-off pit viper between his thumb and index finger. Millennia of humans dying agonizing deaths from the venom of lethal snakes embedded instructions into our DNA not to do exactly what Jason had done.

The adult rainforest hog-nosed viper was only twenty inches long but was highly venomous. A single bite would cause intense pain, motor impairment, hemorrhage, and even death. It wrapped its body with a pattern of alternating cream and dark-brown rectangular marks around Jason's wrist. The viper opened and closed its mouth, hoping to find the flesh of its attacker to send a flood of toxic venom into his veins. The locals knew that the pattern and distinctive upturned snout of the rainforest hog-nosed viper meant grave danger and avoided encounters at all costs.

Jason's ears picked up a new sound in the jungle.

Someone is coming.

He reached into his pack with his free hand and slowly squatted to reach the bottom, careful to keep his body out of reach of the viper's fangs. His fingers found the item he wanted, and Jason stood and moved stealthily to the edge of the wash. The former PJ peered through the stand of trees and shrubs at the lone sicario stalking toward him. He pulled himself out of the wash with his free hand and hid behind the trunk of a ceiba tree soaring two hundred feet into the sky.

The sicarios must have split up and sent a lone sentry in each direction to find the missing intruder. He approached more cautiously this time, so Jason had to time his countering movements around the trunk with each step of the sicario. Once the gunman passed the ceiba tree, Jason ambushed him from behind. He covered his mouth with one hand and jammed the head of the viper into the sicario's bare forearm. The viper did its job and instinctively buried its fangs deep into the nearest flesh. Jason held the sicario's mouth tighter as his blood-curdling screams nearly escaped through his fingers. He tossed the viper a safe distance into the jungle before he secured the AK-47 and swung the shocked sicario around to face him. Jason kept his hand over his mouth as he pressed the rifle barrel under his chin.

"Make a sound, and I'll blow your head off," Jason growled in Spanish.

The sicario panted heavily, almost to the point of hyperventilating. Jason assumed he was most concerned about the deadly venom pumping throughout his body and moved to step two of his plan.

"I have antivenom, but you have to promise not to yell," Jason whispered in his ear. "Do you promise not to yell?"

The sicario's head wagged up and down.

Jason slowly removed his hand and backed away several steps with the AK-47 pointed at his chest. He removed a small, clear bottle of liquid from his pocket and held it to eye level for the sicario to see.

"This is the antivenom. If you answer all my questions, I'll give it to you and let you go free."

Hope replaced deep concern on the sicario's face.

"Are you willing to tell me what I need to know?"

"*Sí, sí,*" the sicario replied. "What do you want to know?"

"Does Victor Romero have a small boy he's holding up there that's a little over one year old?"

The sicario's gaze shifted from Jason to the ground below his feet then back to the man who held the life-saving antivenom in his hand.

"Yes. The little boy is with Victor's girlfriend in the small building west of the main building," the sicario replied shakily.

It was the answer Jason had hoped to hear, but the knowledge that he was fifty or sixty yards from JJ before his retreat stung like an angry wasp. The shock and sadness of Zee's death were replaced by a boiling fury at the people holding his son.

"How many people are guarding that building?"

The sicario shook his head. "It won't matter. They are already gone."

Jason lunged forward and returned the barrel of the rifle under his chin. He pressed so hard that the stubby, metal front sight post wasn't visible. "What do you mean they're gone?"

"Victor trained us to immediately move any hostages into the vehicles and leave as fast as possible if we were ever discovered. The other men not looking for you are doing that right now."

Jason leaned within a few inches of the sicario's face. "If anything happens to my son, you'll all pay the price."

"I-I've told you all I know. Can I have the antivenom now?" the sicario pleaded with Jason.

"You haven't told me everything yet. Where are they taking my son?"

The sicario winced in pain, and his expression changed. Jason wasn't sure if it was due to the viper toxin in his blood or if he was also considering the ramifications of ratting out Victor Romero. It didn't matter. Jason was committed to getting the answers he needed by any means necessary.

Jason raised the clear bottle to make it visible to the bitten man and placed it in his pocket.

"If you don't want to tell me, I'll take my antivenom and go look for them."

The sicario raised his hands in surrender. Jason saw that the bite mark was fire-engine red and swollen to the size of a golf ball. "Okay, I'll tell you. We were told to drive to Costa Rica, and Victor will contact us there."

Jason removed the bottle from his pocket and extended it toward the sicario to show he was close to receiving the antivenom.

"Where in Costa Rica?"

"I don't know."

Jason turned and began to walk away.

"I don't know. Victor said he'd contact us once he's in Costa Rica," the man shouted.

Jason looked around and listened to the jungle. He didn't hear anyone else approaching but knew he'd already spent too much time with this sicario. He strode back to the man leaning against the tree trunk as his organs began to shut down.

"Where are they taking my son?"

"I don't know. I'd tell you if I knew," the sicario mumbled. His speech was slow and slurred.

It wasn't as much information as Jason wanted, but he knew his next destination was Costa Rica. He tossed the clear bottle to the sicario. It bounced off his chest and fell to the jungle floor. The sicario picked it up and looked at the plastic bottle.

"How do I take the antivenom?"

A sinister smile swept across Jason's face. "That will help if one of your symptoms is dry eye."

The sicario gazed at the useless bottle of eye-wetting drops, and his lips trembled. Jason took another step closer to the dying man.

"The nearest hospital is about two hundred kilometers from here, so hopefully, they'll have antivenom. If you make it there and survive, which I doubt, tell your friends not to mess with Jason Mulder's family—or friends."

Jason turned and vanished through the trees. He heard the sicario yelp in pain and cry for help for over a minute until the screams stopped, and the sounds of the jungle took over again.

Chapter 30

Corinto, El Salvador

Victor Romero watched his band of sicarios disappear into the jungle to capture the other intruders. The singed-metal-and-gunpowder aroma hung in the air as Victor considered who was behind the unexpected intrusion. He'd chosen the location to avoid an unwanted encounter with El Jaguar and his men, but every operation in the area involving human trafficking or narcotics was at risk. Victor was responsible for both, so the list of potential enemies was long.

He exhaled and returned his pistol to the small of his back. Men and women had exited the compound buildings to investigate the gunshot that rocked the compound.

"Go back inside. There is nothing for you to see out here," Victor barked.

A few lingered longer than Victor liked, but they quickly relented under the weight of his stare and returned to the structures.

The compound boss turned to the Hispanic male he'd shot lying awkwardly near his boots.

"Which cartel are you from?" Victor asked the limp body.

He could be from the rival gang of narcotics traffickers who operated just across the border in Honduras, or it could be some of the new arrivals from South America attracted to his human contraband. Either way, Victor would make them pay for their foolish attempt to ambush his operation.

He straddled the man and rifled through his pockets. There was no wallet or identification, but Victor found something more problematic.

"He's American."

The clothing on the deceased man displayed the logos of American brands that were not commonly found in Central America. This surprising discovery caused a surge of concern to shoot throughout Victor's body.

"Is it the DEA or CIA?"

He faced the jungle, awash in twilight, where the sicarios had entered minutes earlier. After a quick glance, he pivoted and hurried toward the main house. Victor burst through the front door, startling two sicarios playing cards. "Pack everything up! The DEA is onto us!"

The men sprang to their feet as Victor snagged his go-bag from the nearby table, barking orders as he strode through the house. He stopped outside the storage room protected by a metal door with multiple deadbolt locks.

"Juan Pablo, get these packages into the trucks! Everything goes to Bravo Site across the border like we discussed."

Victor had had his men prebuild hidden compartments in two produce trucks. Moments after his order, workers transported fentanyl pills hidden inside two-kilogram bags of coffee beans to the vehicles.

"Leave nothing for them to find."

Satisfied the narcotics were moving as planned, Victor turned his focus to the most profitable product line on the compound—human cargo. He marched to the second building, where sicarios were already herding a half dozen hooded men, mostly business owners and CEOs waiting for ransom payments, toward a convoy of black SUVs.

"Faster!" Victor commanded.

The third building housed more VIPs that could fetch enormous sums of money for their safe release, and Victor's lieutenant, Carlos Saldiva.

"Jefe, has the strike team found the other intruders?" Carlos asked his boss.

"Not yet, but I'm confident they will," Victor replied.

"Should we wait to see if they catch all of them before we abandon this operation? We will have to start over from scratch."

Victor stomped across the tiny room until his chest bumped Carlos. Despite his three-inch and twenty-pound advantage over his boss, Carlos took several steps back.

"If it's the DEA, they've already called us in. I'm not taking chances. Move everything south, and do it now! Do you understand?"

Carlos raised his hands in surrender. "Yes, yes, I understand."

"I want them in the Nicaragua safe house before dawn."

"Not Costa Rica, like we planned?" Carlos asked tentatively.

"If the DEA found us here, they may also know about our contingency in Costa Rica. Tell everyone else we are moving to the Nicaragua location."

"Got it. The evacuation will be complete in thirty minutes."

Victor checked his watch. Now that everything Victor needed to get his operation reestablished in a new location was moving to their designated vehicles, he could focus on the last building. Having Mulder's son complicated the evacuation, but he wasn't about to lose his trump card.

Victor's hand instinctively went to the scarred depression on his head whenever he thought of the man responsible for his disfiguration. He gently traced his fingertips over the wound, relishing the thought of revenge. The thought of the agonizing pain Mulder must be feeling prompted a quick smirk from JJ's abductor. He'd planned his vengeance on the American since he washed up on the shore two hundred yards downstream from the waterfall that nearly killed him. Victor wanted Jason Mulder's pain to be deep and everlasting.

He arrived at the last building and entered. Unlike the other structures, it was quiet, with only two occupants. Paulina Almarez Garcia rose from one of the two beds in the room and kissed Victor.

"*Mi amor*, what is happening?"

"We are leaving. The Americans are coming to raid this compound."

"Where are we going?"

"Get the boy ready and meet me at my vehicle in ten minutes. We are leaving El Salvador."

Paulina turned to the little boy lying on his bed, cradling his teddy bear. She crossed her arms and paced inside the small room. Victor noticed her apprehension and gently took her by her shoulders. He met her brown eyes and spoke calmly. "I know this is sudden, but we will all be in a US prison soon if we don't go now."

Paulina nodded, rushed to the bag at the foot of her bed, and began packing.

"Ten minutes," Victor reminded her. "Don't be late."

The boss of the remote compound stepped out and watched the frantic activity through narrowed eyes. He hadn't survived this long by ignoring his instincts. In less than half an hour, he'd have his entire operation vacated, leaving nothing but empty buildings for the DEA to find. He'd regroup in their new location south of the border, and then Victor would deal with the Mulder kid. He had no intention of seeking a ransom for the boy. Victor plotted to cause Jason Mulder maximum suffering and pierce his heart like a sharp spear.

CHAPTER 31

One Hour South of Corinto, El Salvador

Jason parked his Jeep along a residential street in Santa Rosa de Lima, El Salvador, one hour south of Corinto. He watched the locals form a line under a streetlight to order pupusas from a street vendor. Judging by the consistent crowd, Jason assumed the food was excellent. The joyous laughter of young families and couples reminded Jason of the future Zee would never experience.

We'd be in line together now if Zee hadn't sacrificed himself to help me.

He shook off the somber thoughts and refocused on the present situation. Jason chose Santa Rosa de Lima because he knew the sicarios he managed to lose in the jungle would have allies and connections in Corinto. He needed a safer place to stop and make several calls. The locals passing by on the sidewalk didn't pay any attention to Jason or his vehicle, so he took his phone out of his backpack. He found a medium-strength signal, which beat the intermittent single bar he had in the Corinto area.

Jason opened the map app on his phone and plugged in the distance from Santa Rosa de Lima, El Salvador, to San José, Costa Rica.

"Twelve hours."

He pinched the screen to zoom in and out to confirm he'd selected the fastest route. It would have been much quicker to fly, but Jason wanted to keep both guns that he'd picked up in El Salvador, especially with how difficult they were to acquire. Jason knew what Victor was capable of and didn't want to pursue him unarmed.

Once Jason saved the directions to San José, he scrolled through his contacts to make a call. He found the contact he wanted and dialed.

"Hey, Mulder, tell me you have some good news," Archie said when he answered.

Jason shook his head and sighed. "Only bad news."

"What happened?"

"I found the compound where they are holding my son, but I couldn't get to him."

"Is it the cartel you thought it was?" the FBI special agent asked.

"Not exactly. Victor Romero has him. He's a former member of the La Palma cartel and someone I thought was dead. He's the one I told you about that floated over a waterfall in Arizona a couple of years ago after a fight in the middle of a flash flood."

"Oh yeah," Archie replied. "I remember that story."

"His body was never found, and the police assumed he was dead, and so did I. Apparently, he lived and left La Palma to start his own offshoot organization with a remote compound in southern El Salvador. Now he has JJ."

"So that's why he took your son. He wanted revenge."

Jason closed his eyes tightly and then slowly opened them.

"That's not all the bad news. Do you remember Zee, Ruben Zambrano from Conrad's PSD team?"

"Yeah. Why?" Archie asked with genuine concern in his voice.

Jason struggled to get the words out. The finality of Zee's death stuck in his throat. "Zee is dead. The sicarios caught him conducting recon around their compound, and Victor shot Zee."

The line fell silent for several seconds.

"That son of a bitch is going to pay for what he's done to JJ and Zee!" Jason shouted, his voice cracking with emotion.

"I'm sorry, Mulder. Is there anything I can do to help?"

Jason straightened and cleared his throat. "Yes, that's why I called. I'm texting you the coordinates of the compound. I'm sure Victor is long gone, but I want someone to retrieve Zee's body and bring it back to the US so his family and friends can have some closure."

"I know someone who can help. I'll take care of it."

"Thanks."

"Where are you going from here?" Archie asked.

"I got a lead that Victor's contingency location is in or around Costa Rica. It's my best lead, so I'm driving there tonight."

"I'll make some calls and get someone to that compound. Be safe, Mulder."

Archie hung up, but Jason continued to stare at his phone. He checked Shanna's flight, and she'd landed at the Dallas-Fort Worth Airport forty minutes earlier. Her connecting flight to San Salvador wasn't scheduled to depart for another two hours, so he checked on flights from DFW to San José, Costa Rica. One departed early the following day.

Jason texted Shanna: *Change of plans. Cancel your flight to El Salvador and book the flight to San José, Costa Rica, that leaves at 7:05 tomorrow morning.*

The response came seconds later. *Why?*

I'm leaving El Salvador, and I'll be in San José by the time you land so I can pick you up.

Why are you leaving El Salvador? Did you find JJ?

Jason didn't want to have this conversation by text or phone call. It was a discussion best handled in person, but he had to give her something.

I know where JJ is, but I don't have him. It's a long story. I'll explain when I pick you up.

His text did not elicit a response for several minutes. He wasn't sure if Shanna was angry, upset, or a spicy cocktail of many emotions. Jason's phone buzzed five minutes after his text, and he quickly read the message.

I changed flights. I'm heading out now to find a hotel near the airport. I want to know everything when I arrive in Costa Rica tomorrow.

Jason quickly responded. *I'll see you at the airport tomorrow morning.*

Once he confirmed that his text had been delivered, Jason placed his phone in the cupholder and slid the transmission into drive. Minutes later, he turned onto Highway 1 toward his destination in Costa Rica, but first, he had to slip through El Amatillo, one of the busiest border crossings between El Salvador and Honduras. Similar to the country Jason would be soon leaving, Honduras strictly enforced laws that prohibited the possession of a gun without a permit and all automatic weapons.

Bright-white lights interrupted miles of intense darkness as Jason inched toward the border crossing at El Amatillo. He hid the rifle and pistol in the third row of seats inside the Jeep Grand Cherokee and folded them down. It effectively kept the weapons out of view from watchful eyes as he passed through a security checkpoint, but it would merely be a speedbump if the border guards entered his vehicle for an enhanced inspection. Prison was a certainty if Jason was caught with weapons, but he couldn't risk being unarmed in Costa Rica.

A burly border guard manning a booth under a large "Bienvenidos a Honduras" sign motioned for Jason to drive forward. Jason felt he was sweating more than usual and turned up the air conditioner.

"Documentos, por favor."

Jason handed over his passport with a forced smile, fighting to keep his hands from shaking. The guard studied the passport longer than necessary, glancing between the photo and Jason's face.

"Americano? Holiday or business?" he asked in heavily accented English.

"Both," Jason replied casually. "I'm meeting my wife in Costa Rica after a business meeting, and then we'll spend a few days at the coast."

The guard's eyes narrowed. "Rental car?"

"Yes, from San Salvador airport."

The guard left his booth and made a slow, careful circle around the vehicle, shining his flashlight into the Jeep's interior. Jason's pulse raced as the beam of light stopped on his backpack sitting atop the third row of seats concealing the AK-47.

"Pull over," the guard pointed to a secondary inspection area. "With the dog."

Jason's stomach dropped as he parked beside two other vehicles. A different guard wearing a tactical vest with "FRONTERAS" emblazoned across the front approached with a Belgian Malinois straining at its leash.

"Step out of the vehicle," the guard ordered in Spanish.

A third guard arrived beside Jason, a young man who looked no more than twenty years old. He held a Beretta AR 70/90 assault rifle at the ready. Standing a dozen feet from the Jeep, Jason watched the drug-sniffing canine eagerly begin the inspection. The Malinois sniffed along the doors, under the chassis, around the wheel wells. Jason knew the service dog was trained to identify narcotics, but his breath caught as it approached the rear lift gate. Jason's checkered past with service dogs inspecting vehicles only heightened his concern.

The dog circled back, nose twitching until it sat quietly near the driver's side door. The handler moved one gloved hand around the door handle. Jason's eyes darted to the young guard beside him and across the street at the dark tree line just beyond the checkpoint lights. In seconds, the former PJ concluded he could overpower the young guard, take his rifle, and escape into the jungle.

Jason slid his hands into his pockets to appear casual, but his shirt was soaked with sweat that had nothing to do with the heat in Honduras. The driver's door to the Jeep opened, and the Malinois leaped inside. Jason's hands shot out of his pockets, and he turned toward the young guard. He was ready to pounce when the canine jumped out of the vehicle onto the pavement.

"Clean," the handler announced. He moved toward the next vehicle as the young guard returned Jason's passport.

Jason slid behind the wheel, his hands trembling slightly. He forced himself to drive unhurried through the checkpoint, fighting the urge to floor the accelerator. His pulse returned to normal only when the border crossing disappeared from his rearview mirror.

The weapons were secure, but his nerves were shot. He had two more border crossings before Jason would be in Costa Rica. The thought of crossing through more checkpoints was daunting.

"This is going to suck," Jason said to the empty SUV.

The blinking blue dot on his tracker app appeared in Jason's mind. He tightened his grip on the steering wheel and applied more pressure to the gas pedal. The blue dot that represented JJ was all Jason needed to fight through the living hell waiting for him in Costa Rica.

CHAPTER 32

Costa Rica Border

Jason glanced at the rearview mirror and watched the armed border guards who'd waved him through his final checkpoint disappear over the horizon. His heart rate slowed with each mile he drove further into Costa Rica. It returned to once the blue, white, and red of the Costa Rican flags waving above the border crossing were no longer in sight. Driving south from the border with Nicaragua, lush green lowlands dotted the landscape with farms and small villages beaming under the morning sun. Prominent volcano peaks were visible in every direction.

It was the least stressful crossing on his journey from El Salvador, and Jason was grateful to give his nerves a break with his wife. It had been five days since Jason last saw Shanna, but it felt like a month.

Jason navigated the airport traffic and drove cautiously through the arrival lanes. Shanna had landed thirty minutes before he arrived, and he didn't want her to wait alone too long. He leaned forward to reduce the glare of the sun off his windshield, and that's when he noticed a stunning woman with raven-black hair in a white top standing by the curb.

"Shanna!"

Jason pulled over so fast that he nearly clipped the quarter panel of another vehicle. He slammed the transmission into park and rushed to meet his wife without closing the door. Shanna saw Jason's abrupt approach and jumped into his open arms. Jason squeezed Shanna tight as she buried her face in his chest. Jason didn't just want to see his wife; he needed Shanna, but he didn't realize how much until he saw her.

Their embrace was interrupted by a uniformed police officer.

"You can't park there. Get moving!" he barked in Spanish.

Shanna left the embrace while Jason grabbed her suitcase and placed it in the back seat of the Jeep. She held Jason's hand as they drove out of the airport.

"How was your flight?"

"It was fine. What's going on with JJ? Why are we in Costa Rica?"

Shanna deserved to know everything he knew about their son, but Jason didn't want to tell her while he drove through a new city for the first time.

"I haven't slept or showered for days, and I'm starving. I booked a hotel downtown, so let's get settled, and I'll tell you everything I've learned since I arrived in Central America."

After lunch, Jason and Shanna moved to the balcony of their hotel room on the twenty-first floor, overlooking La Sabana Park in the heart of San José, the largest public space in the city. A glass of red wine sat on the end table beside Shanna, while Jason cradled a cold beer. He took a long draw and began his recap.

"A lot has happened since I arrived in El Salvador earlier this week. I was almost killed—more than once, but it was worth it. I was finally able to track down JJ."

Shanna leaned forward with wide eyes. "You did? Where is he?"

"I believe he's in Costa Rica."

"Can we go get him now?"

Jason pursed his lips. "I don't know exactly where he is."

"I don't understand. I thought you said you found him and that JJ is in Costa Rica."

"I did, but give me a few minutes to tell you the whole story, and everything will make more sense."

Shanna leaned back into the cushions of her chair. She sipped her wine and crossed her legs. "Okay, I'm ready."

"Do you remember the La Palma cartel that was behind Josh's death?"

Shanna nodded, and Jason told her about his turbulent encounter with El Jaguar, the shocking news that Victor Romero was still alive, and the intel that led him to Corinto.

"When I was outside the compound, I pulled out my app to see if JJ was nearby, and I saw the blinking blue light in one of the buildings. The cell signal sucked, so it only lasted a couple of seconds, but I knew he was there. JJ had to be less than two hundred feet away from me to get that blue dot on the tracker we installed."

Jason paused to provide Shanna with the opportunity to comment on the good news, but her face turned cold.

"You were that close to JJ?"

"Yeah, I got to the edge of the compound and saw Victor with his guards. I didn't see JJ, but I know he was there."

"Why didn't you get him while you had the chance?" Shanna asked. Her accusatory tone caught Jason off balance.

"Why didn't I get JJ?"

"Yeah. If you were that close, why don't we have JJ with us right now?"

Heat wrapped around Jason's neck, and he crossed his arms defensively in front of him.

"I didn't get JJ because the compound had a dozen armed guards with assault rifles. Even with Zee, there was no way we could get him."

Shanna looked hurt. "Zee was with you, too, and you still couldn't get him?"

"No, Shanna, I couldn't get him. The sicarios caught Zee, and there was nothing I could do against a freaking cartel," Jason replied. His voice rose with each word.

"Where is Zee now? Can he help us in Costa Rica?"

Jason's chin hit his chest. He inhaled deeply and locked eyes with Shanna. "No, Zee's dead," he said coolly. "Victor Romero killed him."

Shanna jumped up from her chair. "What? Oh my gosh. "Are you sure?"

Jason scooted to the edge of his seat and leaned toward Shanna. "I watched him get his head blown off, Shanna. That's the kind of people we're dealing with. They're drug smugglers and human traffickers, and they'll do anything to defend their shitty way of life. If they also killed me, who knows what would have happened—" His voice cracked until it trailed off. Jason leaned back in his chair and gazed over the peaceful park.

The balcony was silent for a full minute until Shanna stood and put her arms around Jason. "I'm so sorry you had to see that, honey. Everything about this sucks."

Shanna squeezed her husband tight. "I'm also sorry if it seemed like I was questioning you. I know you'd do anything to save JJ. What should we do now?"

Jason drained his beer and turned to Shanna. "I had twelve hours during my drive here to think about how we find JJ. I learned from one of his guards that the compound had a contingency plan in case the authorities discovered them. They were told to flee south with their hostages, and Victor would meet up with them in Costa Rica. That's all I got, but it's something, so we have to find a way to pick up their trail down here."

Shanna put her hands on her hips and bit her lip. "I have an idea."

She left the balcony and picked up her phone inside the hotel room. Jason followed her inside. "What are you doing?"

"We should search for any news about kidnappings or abductions. Stories about human trafficking arrests are ideal."

"How's that going to help us find JJ?" Jason asked.

"I had a case a couple of years ago where a young girl was abducted from a mall in Tucson by a human trafficking ring. I was there to help her with the trauma she suffered before the police recovered her, so I don't know all the details. However, I clearly remember in the police report that her abductors were involved in a human trafficking superhighway of sorts. The report said certain ports, resorts, bus stations, airports, and similar hubs were hotbeds of human trafficking. Do you know if JJ's abductor had other victims on the compound?"

Shanna asked in a calm tone, but the mere mention of JJ possibly being involved in human trafficking was unsettling for Jason to consider.

"I don't think so. Victor Romero was in a drug cartel, but I don't think he's involved in human trafficking. He took JJ to hurt me. It was personal."

"Well, any news of abductions in or near Costa Rica is probably still our best chance to find a lead on where Victor and JJ are right now."

Jason nodded and watched Shanna scroll through her phone. Past conversations with DEA Special Agent Holland and Archie's CIA friend Mike about abductions in Central America resurfaced.

"Wait, it's possible that Victor Romero has been involved with human trafficking. The DEA and CIA said abductions spiked in the last year, and that coincides with Victor's return to El Salvador and exile from La Palma. The feds think La Palma is behind the abductions, but they probably don't know that Victor is no longer part of the cartel. El Jaguar said kidnapping is not part of his portfolio, and I believe him. Victor Romero must be the culprit behind all the recent abductions. He had more buildings on his compound that could have held more people."

Shanna looked over her phone into Jason's eyes. "If we both start looking, we may find something. You can speak Spanish, so you take the local newspapers, and I'll search the national and international wires."

Jason sat in a chair and began searching through pages of articles involving reports of kidnappings or abductions. He wrote down every town or business where the kidnappings were reported.

The sun dropped below the mountains outside San José before Jason or Shanna spoke again. Jason reviewed his notes and didn't notice any patterns or common links, when his stomach growled.

"We should take a quick break and get some dinner," Jason suggested.

Shanna continued to shift her focus back and forth between her notes and her phone. "Order room service. I think I'm close and don't want to stop now."

Jason found a menu on the cabinet below the TV and opened it. "What do you want?"

"I think I found something!" Shanna cried out.

Jason dropped the menu and rushed to her side. "What?"

"I didn't find a pattern of human trafficking stories in Costa Rica, but I found three stories about stings that took down middlemen trying to connect buyers with sellers in the past decade.

One story was from eight years ago, the second one five years ago, and the last one happened two years ago. I think this is the superhighway my patient was talking about. In every instance, a seller approached an undercover agent of the Public Force of Costa Rica, their version of the FBI, about buying someone that was abducted," Shanna said.

"That sounds promising. How are they connected?" Jason asked.

"All three stings were at a luxury resort on the Pacific Coast. Of course, the government doesn't want to hurt tourism, so they didn't reveal the resort in the news story. However, I did some additional digging, and it seems one luxury resort has a reputation for facilitating transactions among human traffickers—Eternal Seas Resort in Guanacaste Province."

Jason stretched his neck and interlocked his fingers behind his head. He paced back and forth in the room until his arms dropped to his side.

"I have a plan."

Shanna stood and joined him. "What is it?"

"I think if we pose as an American couple who traveled to the Eternal Sea Resort to find a little boy to adopt because we can't have kids, we may get a lead that takes us to JJ. It will be very dangerous, but I think it's our best shot to find JJ if he's involved in a trafficking ring."

"How dangerous?" Shanna asked.

"I saw what these people did to Zee, so I don't think anything is off the table with them. I debated asking you to be part of this plan because I vowed never to put my family in harm's way, but you have something nobody else has other than me."

"What's that?"

"You love JJ so much that you'd do anything to bring him home."

Tears welled up and ran down Shanna's face. "That's true. I'd change places with him in a second right now if I could."

Jason pulled her close. "I know you would. That's why you and I are the best team for this plan. Is that something you're willing to do?"

Shanna stepped back from Jason, her tears replaced with determination.

"Let's do it."

Chapter 33

Pacific Coast, Costa Rica

Jason guided the Jeep down the rain-slicked road after an early-afternoon shower while Shanna read more news articles on her phone. The clearing skies allowed him to catch glimpses of the Pacific through gaps in the trees as he descended the mountains toward the coast. Despite the gravity of their mission, Jason couldn't help but marvel at the white-capped waves crashing against volcanic rock jetties carpeted with lush vegetation.

Shanna looked up from her phone. "Oh, Jason, this place would be paradise if circumstances were different."

Jason gave a brief nod but remained silent. His mind had moved to mentally conducting a risk assessment of the resort based on the images he found online. He'd considered potential chokepoints, sightlines for a shooter on a balcony, and all the entry and exit points. Jason had to be prepared for everything during this mission. This time, it wasn't just the principal, his team, or his own life that he had to consider. Shanna's life depended on it.

They pulled into the quaint Sol del Pacifico hotel, chosen specifically for its proximity to the Eternal Seas Resort without being on the target property. Their third-floor room offered a stunning view of the horseshoe-shaped bay, but neither had time to appreciate it.

Shanna unzipped the shopping bags draped over the queen-sized bed. Before departing for the coast, they'd visited a shopping mall on the outskirts of San José to purchase the necessary attire for their ruse at the resort. She handed Jason new shoes, tan dress pants, and an eggshell-white short-sleeved button-down shirt. He put them on while Shanna slipped on a floral sundress that made her look like every other American tourist soaking up the Costa Rican sun. She moved to the full-length mirror on the wall and turned side to side to check the fit. Shanna caught Jason adjusting his new shirt in the reflection.

"Ready to become Mr. and Mrs. Adam Delgado from Oceanside, California?"

Jason couldn't help but smile at the sight of his wife's beauty, but it quickly faded as the immense sense of emptiness darkened his mood like storm clouds blocking out the sun.

"You don't have to do this. We can find another way."

"I thought we had already agreed on a plan. Are you second-guessing it?" Shanna asked.

Jason ran his fingers through his short hair. "The plan is solid, but I am second-guessing asking you to help. I can't bear the thought of losing JJ—and you."

Shanna stopped applying her lipstick and put her arms around Jason's waist.

"We're doing this together for our son. It's what we have to do to get him back, and there is nobody else on this planet that I trust more than you to keep me safe. Let's finish getting ready, and together, we will find the scumbags who can lead us to JJ."

It was what Jason needed to hear. He swelled with confidence and kissed Shanna.

"That's why I love you so much. Let's find our son."

Armed with nothing but their cover story and their determination, they headed for the Eternal Seas Resort.

The marble floors of the Eternal Seas Resort echoed with Jason and Shanna's footsteps as they stepped into the lobby. She slid her arm through his as they strode confidently past the other guests and staff of the luxury seaside resort. Jason tasted the salt and felt the cool breeze on his face before he saw it. They turned a corner to see the endless horizon of the Pacific Ocean basking in the purple and orange light of the sunset.

Sounds of music and clinking glasses drew their attention to the resort's open-air bar and restaurant overlooking the gentle waves lapping on the beach. Patrons filled nearly every seat in the elaborate bar as the palm-thatched roof swayed in the ocean breeze. Servers whisked mouthwatering food to eager guests sitting at white-clothed tables in the restaurant.

"This is where the men in the articles were arrested," Shanna whispered to Jason.

"Let's sit in the bar," Jason replied.

Jason found the last open table and pulled out a chair for Shanna. He immediately scanned his surroundings to verify that his risk assessment based on the online images was still valid. Everything looked as he'd hoped, so Jason turned his attention to the crowded bar.

Which one of you is here to traffic innocent women and children?

Jason reached across the table and took Shanna's hand into his. He leaned forward and whispered. "Remember, no elaborate lies. They are too hard to remember if they try to trip us up. Tell the truth as much as possible, but change names and locations. We need these people to trust us."

"I remember."

Minutes later, the server delivered the drinks they ordered. After a toast, they turned their attention back to the guests, silently assessing each one on the likelihood they could be involved with JJ's abduction.

"Do you see anyone suspicious?" Shanna whispered.

"Not yet."

Over the next three hours, they ate dinner, drank cocktails, and talked while carefully scanning the restaurant and bar for anyone paying attention to them. They'd scare off anyone connected to JJ's abduction if they eagerly started asking around about adopting a child, so they had to draw the traffickers to them.

"Last call," the bartender yelled to the handful of patrons still in the bar.

"Let's go," Jason said as he stood up. He grabbed the table to steady himself after consuming five drinks. The former PJ felt the heat of a gaze on his skin, so he turned and saw a man sitting by himself at the bar, staring directly at him. The fit man in his upper thirties had an intensity in his eyes that was different than everyone else, but Jason couldn't tell if it was the alcohol or a potential trafficker. He was too buzzed to initiate a conversation without blowing his cover, so Jason grabbed Shanna's hand, and they left.

All their frustrations spilled out to each other once they arrived back in their room at the Sol del Pacifico hotel.

"Shit! I didn't see anyone suspicious the entire night," Shanna bellowed.

"If the traffickers are there, they must be watching us from a distance."

"What are we going to do, Jason? This was our best option."

He was also down on their failed attempt to find a link to JJ, but Jason maintained hope based on the solo man at the bar. "I saw one guy at the end that caught my eye."

"What did he look like?"

"It was a quick glance, but something about him caught my attention. I can't really put my finger on it. Let's go back tomorrow, sit at the bar, and talk about how we hope to find a little boy to adopt so the bartender can overhear us. He may be a spotter for the traffickers."

Mr. and Mrs. Delgado returned to Endless Seas Resort the next evening and sat at the bar. Once again, they ate, drank, and discussed their life loudly like couples who'd enjoyed too many cocktails. This time, Jason paced himself with his drinks and carefully poured some of them out when he went to the restroom.

"Last call," the bartender announced.

Jason couldn't believe they'd failed for a second night. Maybe the traffickers were too careful to approach a new couple, or the entire plan was a bad idea. He tossed a five-dollar bill onto the bar, but someone appeared on the empty barstool next to him before Jason stood.

"I'm sorry to intrude, but I couldn't help but overhear your conversation. Did you two lose a son in a tragic accident?" a male voice asked in English with a slight Spanish accent.

Jason swung his gaze in the direction of the voice and noticed it was the same man from last night. His intense eyes were replaced by a friendly face that looked incapable of causing harm to anyone.

Shanna lowered her eyes. "Yes. I'm sorry we were talking so loudly. It's still very raw."

"Losing a child is one of the most difficult things a parent can endure."

"It's the most difficult thing we've ever had to deal with," Jason added.

"I know how you feel. I've lost a child myself, but I had to be there physically and mentally for my other children, which helped me get through it," the man said thoughtfully. "Do you have any other kids?"

The man raised his hand to stop Jason and Shanna from answering. "Again, I must apologize for my directness. I'm just very passionate about children."

He extended his hand to Jason. "I'm Claudio Rodriguez. I've lived all over the United States and Latin America but made this seaside village my permanent home a few years ago."

Jason shook his hand. "I'm Adam Delgado, and this is my wife, Ana. We're both from the Southwest US but settled in Oceanside, California, after we got married."

"Nice to meet you, Adam and Ana."

Nobody spoke for a half minute until Shanna broke the silence.

"To answer your question, no, we don't have any other children. My pregnancy with Liam was complicated. Now I can't have any more kids of my own."

The man leaned on the bar and spoke directly to Shanna, who sat on the other side of Jason.

"I'm so sorry to hear that. Have you considered adoption? There are many children who want wonderful parents, such as yourselves, to take them into a loving home.

Shanna exchanged a glance with Jason and then turned back to the man.

"We've looked into it, but it's very expensive and takes a long time with no guarantee we'll ever get to adopt the little boy we want. We have a little money, but not enough to adopt in America. That's why we—"

Jason was sure this man was involved with human trafficking. He seemed so sympathetic to a vulnerable couple suffering unimaginable pain, but Jason knew a predator existed beneath the façade of a caring bystander. Now he had to reel him in without seeming too interested.

"Honey, we shouldn't burden this nice man with our problems. We should go."

Jason put his arm around Shanna and led her away.

The man stood as the couple passed. His tone shifted from soft and compassionate to one that sounded more businesslike.

"If you're serious about adoption, be here at ten tomorrow night."

CHAPTER 34

New Safehouse in Central America

Paulina made her bed and smoothed out a blanket in the crib for the little boy. The conditions of the new safe house were far superior to the weathered wood structures in the Corinto compound. The bedroom Victor assigned her was in a casita nestled among the palm trees behind the main structure. The gold walls and red-tiled roof of the hacienda stood prominently over a short dock extending into the steel-blue water. Views of mist-covered mountains were visible in all directions from the property.

The little boy played on the floor with his new toys while Paulina set up their new quarters. He seemed relaxed and happy for the first time since she met the little boy. It had only been three weeks, but she was growing attached to him.

A light knock on the door was followed by someone entering the bedroom. Victor arrived to check on his girlfriend and the boy.

"How do you like your new room?"

Paulina went to the window and turned to face Victor. "I love it. It's so much more peaceful in this location."

Victor nodded. "How is the boy doing?"

"He seems happier here. He loves playing with his new toys in the yard and watching the boats."

"Don't get too attached to him. He's not going to be here much longer."

The words had weight to them. They were like a cement block thrown at her from across the room, and they caught Paulina by surprise. "Are we moving again?"

"The Americans are on to us, and at some point, they'll track us down here too. Plus, keeping the boy is a liability we don't need now."

"I don't think they'll find us down here," Paulina said. Her statement was more optimistic than she believed, but she hoped to convince Victor it was true.

"They will surely track us down here at some point, and the local police may also grow suspicious if we are spotted with a fair-skinned boy with brown hair. In case you haven't noticed, we both have brown skin and black hair," Victor hissed.

Paulina's heart sank, and her legs felt weak. "I will keep him inside so nobody on the passing boats will see him."

The intensity of Victor's icy stare was like a physical blow, and Paulina knew it was time to stop arguing. She didn't want to subject herself to another one of his angry outbursts. "What do you plan to do with him?"

Victor crossed his arms and tilted his head. "You're already attached to him."

Paulina's eyes widened in shock. His accusation made her feel naked and exposed. He was right about her feelings for the boy, but Paulina thought she was doing a good job hiding them from Victor.

"You said to keep him safe and happy so he doesn't cry, and that's what I'm doing."

Victor stared at his girlfriend for a beat and nodded. "In any case, he'll be leaving us. I have a call later today with someone who can help me."

"A call? With whom?"

"A broker."

Paulina knew what type of broker it was, and she hated this about Victor.

"Get him cleaned up and dressed to travel. I'll be back later."

Paulina dropped to her haunches beside the boy after Victor left the room. His brown eyes looked from his toy truck, and he flashed a toothless smile. She had to choke back tears at the affectionate display from the boy.

"I won't let anything happen to you," she lied to the boy.

Paulina finished setting up their room and made the boy lunch in the modern kitchen in the main building. She was careful not to walk by any windows that would allow onlookers to see the boy. The new safe house felt like a real home, and Paulina allowed herself to dream that maybe Victor would give up the narcotics and human trafficking so they could start a family and live in the hacienda. It was a short-lived dream when common sense prevailed over her delusion that Victor could ever change. Paulina knew that any future with him meant a life of crime.

"Stop it!" Paulina scolded herself. Her sudden outburst caused the boy to stop playing with his toy and look up at his caretaker.

"It's okay," she reassured him. "I need to stop thinking about the future and focus on getting through today."

Paulina served the boy his food in the bedroom so she'd be prepared to eat dinner with Victor. Once the boy was fed and cleaned up, she heard a light tap on the door. Paulina opened the door to another woman from the compound. She was in her forties and worked in the kitchen. "Victor is ready for you. I'll watch the boy while you have dinner."

Victor's girlfriend arrived in the red dress he had his staff send to her room. She applied ruby-red lipstick and pulled her hair back to how he liked it. Paulina hoped to charm Victor and persuade him not to sell the boy.

"*Mi amor*, you look beautiful," Victor said when she entered the room.

Paulina returned a flirtatious smile and sat in the chair Victor had pulled out for her at the small dining room table.

After appetizers and drinks, she couldn't wait any longer. Paulina had to know what Victor had planned for the boy.

"Did your friend help you?" she asked.

"Who?"

"The broker."

Victor put his fork down and glared at Paulina. "Why are you so concerned?"

"I'm not. I just want to know what is going on."

He wiped his hands on the napkin on his lap and tossed it onto his plate.

"He found a buyer for the boy."

Paulina tried to hide her concern with every fiber in her body. "Where?"

"Venezuela. We're meeting him in Panama on Sunday."

"That's five days from today!" Paulina cried.

"And we'll leave in three to be sure we arrive on time."

"But—"

Paulina began to protest, but Victor raised his hand to stop her.

"It is already done and can't be stopped."

Victor stood and moved behind her. He leaned over until his lips were inches from her ear and whispered, "Don't think just because you're my girlfriend, you won't face the same fate as others who defy me."

Paulina swallowed hard, and her entire body tensed up. She wanted to reassure Victor that she'd comply with his wishes, but her voice was trapped in her throat.

"Be sure the boy is ready to go in three days, or I'll find someone who will."

CHAPTER 35

Pacific Coast, Costa Rica

Jason stepped onto the balcony to witness a clear sky exposing millions of stars shimmering over the bay. A full moon rose over the black waters of the Pacific Ocean, casting warm, silvery moonlight that projected his shadow onto the tile floor. The gentle breeze rustling the palm fronds and faint ocean waves created a tranquil atmosphere, in stark contrast to the storm of anxiety swirling inside him.

He'd spent the day reviewing the buildings, beaches, hills, and valleys surrounding the resort. The member of Senator Conrad's security team responsible for advanced scouting was well aware that a foolproof escape route when the shit hit the fan could be the difference between life and death.

Jason returned to the room and found Shanna fidgeting with the buttons on her shirt. He considered retrieving his Glock pistol from his vehicle in the hotel parking lot but concluded that if Claudio was the professional he suspected, he'd notice the firearm. Jason chose to attend the meeting armed only with his knife and ensure his wife was prepared for a speedy retreat if needed.

"Do you remember the plan if our cover is blown during our meeting with Claudio?" Jason asked.

Shanna looked to the ceiling as if trying to find the correct answer. "Yes, take the quickest exit that allows me to run north of the resort into the jungle. If we get split up, I'll do everything possible to avoid letting anyone follow me and meet you at the clearing about one hundred yards from the road. If you don't show up at the meeting, I'll make sure I'm clear and come back here."

"Perfect," Jason said, kissing her forehead. "I want to get there early in case Claudio tries to position some of his goons at the bar before we arrive."

Adam and Ana Delgado sat in the same seats they occupied the previous evening. They sipped their drinks and casually watched the bar entrances for a familiar face to arrive. Twenty minutes past ten, Jason grew concerned that Claudio wouldn't show up.

Did he research us and find out we were lying to him?

Jason chose the aliases of Adam and Ana Delgado because they were real people who lived in Oceanside, California. They had one joint social media profile that Jason found online, but fortunately, they posted no identifying pictures.

Am I just being paranoid?

He relaxed his shoulders when he saw Claudio step off the beach, brush the sand off his shoes, and strut toward Jason.

"Sorry I'm late," Claudio started. "It's too loud here to talk, so I took the liberty to reserve a table for us in the restaurant. Follow me."

He led them to an outdoor table in the far corner of the restaurant that was less than half-full. Claudio waved his hand toward two open chairs and motioned for Shanna and Jason to sit. A server arrived moments later.

"Sebastian, a bottle of champagne, please," Claudio said.

It was immediately apparent that Claudio was a regular feature in that corner of the restaurant, which meant they were on his home turf.

Claudio raised his glass to toast. "To new beginnings."

"What are we celebrating?" Shanna inquired.

"Because you are here, I assume you are open to an international adoption."

Shanna sipped her champagne. "Adam and I discussed it last night, and we'd like to know more about it."

Jason saw a flicker of irritation on Claudio's face before he caught himself and replied with the toothy smile of a car salesman. "Of course. What questions do you have for me?"

"If we proceed, how long does it take before we'd have a little boy to take home?"

"It doesn't take very long," Claudio stated. "Once all the paperwork is signed and the payment is made, you can have your new son in about one week."

"Wow, that's fast. Why does it take years in the United States?"

Claudio chuckled. "That's all the government red tape that only hurts the kids. Here, we have orphaned children that the government would rather have with new parents."

"Makes sense," Shanna said. "Adam, do you have any questions?"

"You mentioned a payment. How much is it?" Jason asked.

Claudio did not flinch at the direct question. He maintained his relaxed posture and calmly responded. "Like many adoption agencies in the United States, there is a fee for our services that we feel is commensurate with the speed, thoroughness, and ease of our adoptions. We require payment of twenty-eight thousand US dollars in advance before we start the paperwork to adopt your son."

Shanna placed her hand on Jason's forearm. "Honey, do we have that kind of money?"

Jason shook his head. "Not in the bank, but I can probably get it from my retirement account."

"We can help you with that," Claudio said. "Do you have any other questions, Adam?"

Jason understood how families desperate to adopt a child that had run into brick wall after brick wall could turn to a shady figure like Claudio for assistance. If Jason didn't know better, he might have fallen for the smooth-talking trafficker of innocent women and children as if it were a legitimate organization helping parents skirt the bureaucratic nightmare of adoption in the US. However, Jason wasn't there to adopt; he was meeting with a human trafficker in a Costa Rican restaurant to find information that could lead him to his son.

"Can we pick the boy we want?"

Claudio's brow furrowed. "I'm not sure what you mean."

"We'd like a little boy about the same age as Liam with light-brown eyes and brown hair," Jason stated.

A pained expression spread across Claudio's face. "Why so specific? Most adoptive parents are happy with any healthy boy or girl they can love and take home."

Shanna quickly responded. "I have a very conservative family, and if we go home with a baby with blue eyes and light hair, my family may not accept him," Shanna lied. "I'm sad that is the case, but it's true."

Claudio eyed Shanna for several seconds and nodded. "My parents are the same way."

He removed his phone and scrolled for a minute. "Yeah, we have several boys that fit that profile."

"Are those pictures of the boys available for adoption? Can we see them?"

Jason knew that was probably pushing Claudio too far, but the fact that JJ could be one of those pictures was too much to resist.

"No, not until we get payment," Claudio responded coolly.

A spark of desperation ignited and surged inside Jason.

This guy may know where JJ is right now.

"I won't pay in advance if we're not certain the boy we want is available. Can we go somewhere to see them?"

Jason saw Claudio stiffen, and his intense eyes returned.

"You want to see all the orphaned boys in Central America before you commit to an adoption? I thought you two were serious about finding a new child," Claudio growled.

Jason didn't respond. The request to see the children hit a nerve with Claudio, and Jason knew he was pulling the right strings. He decided to end the meeting as quickly as possible and follow Claudio home to see if that would lead him directly to JJ.

"We are serious, but I should verify I can get that kind of money."

Jason turned to Shanna to suggest they leave, but Claudio chimed in before he had a chance.

"First, I have some questions for you two."

"That's fair," Jason responded. "What do you want to know about us?"

"Where are you staying?"

"We're staying here," Jason responded with a chuckle to insinuate the answer was obvious.

"Then why doesn't the front desk have any record of an Adam or Ana Delgado staying here?"

Jason assumed this question might arise and followed his rule with a partial truth.

"We're staying down the street. This resort is too expensive for us."

"Then why do you keep coming to this bar every night?"

Jason suspected their cover was blown. He stood and feigned offense at the question.

"We didn't come here to be interrogated. We have to leave now. Shanna, let's go."

Shanna's eyes widened in surprise, and Jason instantly realized his mistake.

Shit! Shit! Shit!

"Who's Shanna?" Claudio snapped.

"I never said Shanna. I said Ana."

Claudio opened his sports coat and exposed a pistol in a shoulder holster. "Sit down. You two aren't going anywhere."

The silhouettes of four bulky men strutted along the sandy beach ten yards from the restaurant patio. Jason noticed them in his peripheral vision and was confident they were Claudio's security goons coming for Shanna and him. He had to act quickly before they were severely outnumbered and outgunned by Claudio's men. Faster than a rattlesnake strike, Jason lifted the table and shoved it on top of Claudio. Porcelain plates and champagne glasses crashed to the patio floor, breaking into hundreds of pieces.

"Run, Shanna. Run!"

Chapter 36

Jason put all his weight on the overturned table with Claudio pinned below to provide Shanna more time to escape. He watched her weave through the restaurant and into the lobby toward the north exit of the resort like they had discussed. The four security guys charged toward the commotion with their guns drawn. Jason desperately held Claudio in place, but he knew he had to retreat before he was caught—or shot.

"Get them!" Claudio yelled from the restaurant floor.

The former PJ bolted in the opposite direction of Shanna, hoping to attract the security detail to pursue him instead of his wife.

"Come on, Shanna. Get into the jungle."

Jason sprinted past rows of parked vehicles with loose asphalt crunching under his feet. He turned back at the edge of the parking lot and noted two shadowy figures passing the first row of cars.

"Shit, the other two guys must have gone after Shanna."

The men had closed the gap on Jason, so he vaulted over a low wall and dashed across the deserted street toward the shadowy Costa Rican jungle. The dense foliage blocked out much of the bright moonlight, making navigation through the rainforest treacherous, but he didn't slow down. He crashed through thorny vines and sharp branches that tore his skin.

Satisfied he'd put enough distance between himself and his pursuers, Jason stopped in the small clearing he and Shanna had previously agreed would be their rendezvous point if anything went wrong.

She had a head start, so why isn't she here?

Jason scanned the shadows, hoping to see Shanna emerge from the undergrowth at any second. He slowed his breathing to listen, but only the chirping of insects and distant howler monkeys interrupted the stillness.

She should be here by now.

Dread crept down Jason's spine as he was forced to accept the painful reality that Shanna must have been captured.

"Dammit! I never should have asked her to come down here!"

He didn't have time to question his earlier decision. Jason had to find and recover Shanna as quickly as possible or face having a second family member in the hands of Victor Romero.

Jason backtracked through the undergrowth, moving parallel to the resort's perimeter, looking for any sign of Shanna or the security team. Seeing neither, he continued until he reached the beach behind the resort and scanned the area. The northern part of the bay was pitch-black, where the jungle met the shore. On the southern end, scattered lights from buildings glimmered in the distance, so Jason started toward them. He passed the empty Eternal Seas Resort restaurant and continually looked over his shoulder to ensure Claudio's security detail hadn't snuck up behind him.

Floodlights from the resort reflected off an object in the sand. Jason picked it up and recognized it as the bracelet Shanna had worn that evening. The silver bracelet was broken, confirming his suspicion that Claudio's security team had caught her.

Hurry! She doesn't have much time.

Jason's brisk walk escalated into a full sprint on the sandy shoreline as he tried to catch up with Shanna's captors. He ran past numerous hotels and rental homes until he spotted movement ahead. As he drew nearer, the moonlight illuminated two stout figures dragging a smaller person between them. Even in the dim light, Jason immediately recognized his wife.

"Shanna."

The other two guards had joined them, and together, the four-person security team formed a diamond-shaped pattern used to transfer principals through hostile or high-risk environments.

These guys are professionals.

This new information about Shanna's captors forced Jason to slow down and assess the situation. He noted that he was close to the hotel where he was staying and, therefore, his weapons cache in the Jeep. Jason could retrieve the rifle and pistol and return in under ten minutes. The prospect of gaining his weapons while losing direct sight of Shanna was not worth the risk, especially while four armed professionals still outnumbered him.

As Jason considered his next move, he saw the group turn onto a dock. They passed under a dim light on the dock, and Jason saw them slide Shanna into a boat tied up forty yards from the shore. Jason assumed the modest vessel was for fishing in local waters or diving excursions. Either way, if they left with Shanna by boat, Jason might never see her again.

Two men climbed into the boat with Shanna, while the other two moved back to the beach and stood guard at the dock entrance. Jason moved inland to avoid being seen by the guards and hid behind a small shack on the edge of the beach.

"They're waiting for Claudio," Jason whispered to the wind.

Jason moved around the tiny thatch-roof structure to get a better vantage point of Shanna, and that's when he realized it was a shop that rented surfboards and snorkeling gear to tourists. He pushed lightly on the door and confirmed it was locked. Jason found traction for both feet and put his shoulder into it until he heard wood splintering. The door burst open, and Jason crawled inside. The walls were filled with flippers, goggles, and snorkels. He quickly removed his shirt and shoes but kept his pants on. The knife in his pocket was his only weapon and best tool to save Shanna.

Jason crept out of the hut and focused on the guards on the shore and the boat. Everyone was still where they were when he'd entered the shack. Jason waddled like a baby penguin into the ocean until it was chest-deep. The water felt cool on his skin, although the sun had warmed it to over eighty degrees earlier that day. He watched the light on the dock disappear with each passing wave and realized how easy it would be to miss his target.

He pulled his goggles over his eyes and took one last look at his destination. Jason panned over the bay teeming with blacktip, reef, and tiger sharks actively hunting for their next meal. He had a healthy respect for sharks and would typically never swim in those waters alone at night, but his biggest concerns were the sharks in the boat with Shanna.

Jason dove in and deployed the stealth swimming techniques he learned as a PJ. He'd perfected strokes designed to minimize splashing and disruption of the water's surface while swimming in hostile environments. If he could swim undetected through two hundred yards of inky-black water before the boat departed, he might be able to save Shanna.

CHAPTER 37

Jason held on to the dock with one hand and bobbed with the surf. He could see during the swells that the two guards at the dock entrance were still there. During one swell, he observed a car pulling into a nearby parking lot and figured it might be Claudio.

He inched closer and heard fragments of Spanish carried through the breeze. The person from the car and the guards began shouting back and forth. It was Claudio, and he was on his way to inspect the prisoner.

Jason dove under the dock and surfaced near the vessel that held Shanna and the two guards. The thirty-five-foot charter boat with twin outboard engines was more modern than he'd estimated from the shore. It could ferry Shanna anywhere up or down the Pacific Coast of Central America.

Light from the dock lamp revealed one guard smoking near the stern while the other kept Shanna seated on a cushioned bench as he held on to her wrist. Her expression was a mixture of fear and determination, and Jason was pleasantly surprised to see that her hands were not zip-tied.

Jason eased to the boat's stern, timing his movement with the gentle swells. The smoking guard sat on the aft gunwale and flicked his cigarette into the water. In one fluid motion, Jason's arm rocketed through the air, grabbed the man by the back of his collar, and yanked him backward into the Pacific.

Screams encapsulated in bubbles rose to the surface as the guard's arms flailed to slow his descent to the sandy bottom. Jason dragged him under like a killer whale drowning its prey until the man's survival instinct kicked in. He fought like an eel in a snare, writhing and breaking the grip of the other man pulling him under. The guard twisted enough to knee Jason in the ribs and push himself away from his attacker. They plunged deeper, trading positions in a violent underwater battle. The guard's elbow smashed into Jason's mask, stunning him just long enough to get his hands around Jason's throat.

In the PJ pipeline outside San Antonio, Texas, Jason had trained in the pool for situations like this many times—except for the over-sized goon trying to strangle him. Every instinct in his body wanted to fight back with all his might, but that would only expedite his demise. Jason relaxed and fell limp for several seconds, encouraging the guard to think he was losing consciousness. The guard went for the bait, let go, and kicked aggressively toward the surface to refill his lungs with oxygen. Before he could get to the prize, Jason caught his foot and yanked him back down.

Jason's lungs were burning, and he knew the guard had to be close to oxygen deprivation. Once they were at the same depth, Jason exploded into action and drove his knee into the man's solar plexus. Large bubbles ricocheted off Jason's face and neck as the last remnants of air were forced from the guard's lungs. As his consciousness faded, the guard clawed at Jason, scratching his arm with his nails like a cornered alley cat.

The roar of two outboard boat engines interrupted Jason's focus on the drowning guard. He'd opted to drown the first guard in the hope it would be quiet and quick, but it was neither. The two idling engines meant the other guard was aware of something awry taking place off the stern of their boat and was preparing to speed away. The element of surprise was Jason's primary advantage over the guards in the boat, and now it was gone.

The guard's strikes grew weaker until they slowed and stopped. Only when the body went completely limp did Jason release his grip, watching the dark shape drift into the depths under the moonlight.

Jason's lungs nearly burst as he struggled to orient himself and kicked for the surface. He was immediately aware of the consequences of his botched drowning. The second guard stood at the stern with his pistol aimed at the water and shouted an alarm to the others. Claudio and the remaining guards would be there in seconds. Jason had surfaced alongside the boat, feet from the stern, and didn't have the opportunity to board the vessel without getting shot. He searched for another option, and that's when his eyes met Shanna's.

She stood behind the armed guard in a wide stance like a football linebacker. In the dim light, Jason saw the resolution in her face before she started toward the guard. He wanted to yell and tell her not to do it, but it was too late.

Shanna drove her shoulder into his lower back, and the guard toppled overboard with a splash, his pistol clattering onto the deck. Jason was ready, meeting him in the water. This time, Jason couldn't afford to waste a single second and swiftly removed his knife from his pants pocket. The moment the guard's head emerged from the water to catch his breath, Jason drove the blade into his chest up to the hilt.

Death was nearly instant. The guard gasped, and his entire body spasmed until he disappeared below the ripples.

The shouts in Spanish grew closer, and Jason knew they had to flee or get shot when Claudio and the guards arrived. He swam to Shanna, who was treading water nearby, and sensed something was wrong.

"Are you okay?"

"I think so," Shanna said shakily.

"We need to dive before they get here, or they'll see us. Hang on to me and tap my arm three times when you need to come back up for air."

Shanna was still nodding when Jason took her arm and dove under the dock. He could hear shouting as he swam between the piling until the dock ended at the open sea. Shanna tapped his arm three times, and he surfaced slowly under the cover of the wood planks. Jason saw flashlight beams illuminating the inky black water near other boats tied to the dock as the men stomped in their direction.

"Can you hold your breath any longer?" Jason whispered over the lapping water.

"I don't know. That was pretty long for me."

"We have to go far enough out underwater so they can't see us with their flashlights. I will stay under a little longer this time, so tap on my arm when you have to come up."

Jason dove deep with Shanna. He pushed as much water with one arm as possible but knew they weren't getting far against the current. A new surge of adrenaline pumped through his veins, and Jason kicked harder with his flippers.

Shanna tapped his arm three times, but Jason didn't think he was far enough, so he kept swimming away from the dock. Seconds later, she tapped again more aggressively. Jason wanted to give her the oxygen she desperately needed but didn't want them to get shot in the process. Shanna's grip loosened ten seconds later, and Jason knew he had to surface immediately.

They popped to the surface twenty yards from the dock with a bigger splash than desired. As soon as Shanna's face was above water, she took in a massive gulp of Costa Rican air. The ruckus caught the attention of one of the guards, and he fired at them. After two shots missed them by inches, Jason had them underwater again, heading toward the south jetty.

Claudio and the guards raced back to the boat, and when Jason resurfaced, he heard it speeding toward their last location. Jason dove again and swam in a different direction, intending to confuse the guards—and it worked.

The boat sped over them and slowed near where the guard last saw them. Jason rose to the surface sooner than previous dives, giving Shanna a chance to get her breath. He heard shouts from Claudio and the guards as they bobbed silently in their wake.

"They dove again."

"Which way did they go?"

"I don't know, but they couldn't have gone too far."

Jason watched their flashlight beam dart left and right of the bow but never toward them near the stern. He rotated in the water and identified mangroves two hundred yards to the south. Jason tapped Shanna gently on her cheek and pointed toward the south shore. She nodded, and Jason turned to one side and paddled stealthily with Shanna in tow, leaving nothing but ripples behind.

Claudio and his men had drifted further to sea when Jason stopped swimming to gauge his distance from the shore. Shanna's grip felt weak, and he wanted to give her a minute to rest before the final push.

"Let's rest for a minute," Jason whispered. "You seem tired."

"I just need a couple of minutes."

Something seemed off with Shanna. "Are you hurt?"

She was breathing heavily, and Jason noticed her grimace. "I think I cut my leg pretty bad when I fell off the boat."

"Are you bleeding?"

"Maybe," Shanna replied. "I'm not sure."

Jason turned again to the destination. "One more minute, and we'll head to shore to check it out."

A powerful bump that felt like a punch from a gigantic fist connected with Jason's calf. A moment later, it happened again just above his knee.

"Why are you kicking me?" Jason whispered.

"I'm not," Shanna responded sharply.

Jason searched the waves in the moonlight for the source of his pain. He recalled his pararescue combat-dive training in Florida and pulled Shanna toward the shore.

"What's wrong?" Shanna asked.

"Shark!"

CHAPTER 38

Pacific Coast, Costa Rica

Jason pushed himself to swim faster than ever before, only stopping when his body collided with the thin tendrils of mangrove trees. He understood he couldn't outswim a shark, but Jason recalled that many species bump their prey to examine it before attacking. During combat-dive training, he was taught to remain calm, maintain eye contact, swim away slowly, and get out of the water after a bump. Jason couldn't perform any of those actions, so he committed to keep moving and make the shark work harder for its next meal. Fortunately, the shark, or whatever had bumped Jason, didn't attack, and they made it safely into the tangled roots of mangrove branches on the rocky shoreline.

The waves lapped at their feet as Jason helped Shanna onto the narrow peninsula. He noticed her limping while she hobbled to sit on a large, smooth boulder. She bit back a cry of pain, clutching her leg where the boat's cleat had torn through her dress and into her flesh.

Jason freed himself from the mangroves and hurried to Shanna's side. The wet dress clung to her thigh, and after she removed her hand, a shaft of moonlight revealed a concerning dark spot growing on her white dress.

"You have a nasty gash on your left thigh," Jason said calmly to reassure Shanna. "We need to get back to the hotel room so I can clean it up and take a better look at it."

Jason scanned the bay and saw Claudio and the guards in the boat still shining their flashlights several hundred yards from the dock. He turned back to Shanna and saw her rocking in pain. Jason's jaw tightened. The wound needed immediate attention, but they had to get off the rocky shoreline. They could sneak back to their hotel while their pursuers were still fixated on searching the bay if they were careful to be quiet.

"Can you walk?" Jason asked, already sliding his arm around her waist.

Shanna winced after taking a small step. "Just don't let go of me."

They moved through the jungle's edge, using the vegetation as cover. Every few steps, Jason paused to listen for their pursuers. Shanna's breathing grew more labored, but she didn't complain. After twenty grueling minutes, they reached the hotel's service entrance.

At that late hour, they reached their room without being noticed by the staff or guests. Once inside, Jason locked the door and drew the curtains. Shanna leaned against the wall to avoid collapsing onto the hotel floor.

"Let's get into the shower to clean you off."

Jason let the water warm for several seconds before helping Shanna into the walk-in shower. He laid her down on her good side and let the spray wash off the blood and dirt concealing her wound. Jason peeled back her dress and saw the four-inch gash split wide open.

"Shit!"

"What's wrong?" Shanna cried.

"Nothing, honey." The stress of the moment made him forget it was his job to keep wounded individuals calm.

"You're going to need a few stitches, and you'll be fine."

The sharp pain caused Shanna to squeeze her eyes shut and take deep breaths.

"How's the pain on the scale from one to ten?"

"Pretty bad. I'd give it a seven," Shanna croaked.

Jason knew his wife was tough, but this was another example of her tenacity. He figured he'd rate the pain a ten if he were in her position.

"Hang on a second. I'll be right back."

He bolted out of the shower soaking wet and returned with a hotel sewing kit, a clean white T-shirt, and four airplane-sized bottles of hard alcohol from the minifridge. Jason placed the bottles on the sink and folded the T-shirt into a tight rectangle. He applied it to Shanna's bloody thigh.

"Hold this to apply pressure to the wound while I get everything else ready."

Her hand replaced Jason's over the T-shirt. "What's with the bottles?"

"I'm going to use some of the vodka to disinfect the sewing needle, and the rest will be for you."

"For me? Why?"

"To help dull the pain. This is going to hurt like hell."

"What kind is it?"

Jason read each bottle. "We have bottles of vodka, bourbon, tequila, and whiskey."

"I don't like any of that stuff," Shanna said, her face pinched as if she'd eaten something very sour. "I've given birth, so I can handle pain. Let's just get started."

The former PJ turned off the water and dropped to his haunches beside Shanna. He handed her a damp washcloth. "Bite down on this."

Jason's hands moved with practiced precision, each stitch bringing the wound closer to closure. He'd performed this task countless times while serving in the Air Force but never before on someone he loved. He often stopped to check on Shanna and ensure she wasn't in too much pain.

"I'll live. Just hurry," Shanna groaned through the towel.

Nine stitches later, Jason tied the final knot. He covered the wound with strips from a clean hotel towel and secured them with the belt from the hotel robe.

"All done," Jason whispered, helping Shanna sit up. He handed her a glass of water and two ibuprofen pills. "Take these. They'll help a little."

Shanna tried to stand but yelped in pain and fell back to the wet shower floor with a thud. "Where are those bottles of hard alcohol?"

Jason pointed to the four bottles aligned on the bathroom sink like soldiers.

"I'll take them."

"Which one?"

"All of them."

Jason sat beside Shanna as she finished all four bottles. It took her less than ten minutes. They sat in silence for a moment, foreheads touching, allowing themselves this brief respite.

Shanna touched his face. "Thank you for fixing me up."

"Thanks for coming down to help," Jason said while returning the gesture. "I needed you here with me more than I realized."

Shanna responded with a groggy grin.

"You'll still have to see a real doctor when we get home."

She yawned. "Okay. I'm exhausted. Help me to the bed."

Once in bed, Jason held Shanna, and she immediately fell asleep. He drifted into and out of sleep over several hours because he couldn't stop thinking about the missed opportunity to follow Claudio home and potentially find JJ.

Is he still on the boat looking for us in the bay? Could I follow him to JJ's location?

Jason gently rolled Shanna to her good side and moved to the patio overlooking the bay. He located the dock and strained to see the lights from boats in the water.

"Dammit. They're gone."

He stared into the inky blackness until a shrill scream interrupted the stillness of the dawn. Jason rushed inside and found Shanna thrashing in bed.

"No!" She repeated over and over.

Jason hurried to her side and shook her awake. She attempted to sit up but cried out in pain and collapsed back onto the bed, gasping for breath.

"Honey, it's okay. You're here with me. It's okay," Jason reassured her.

Her eyes were wide as she scanned the room. "Where are we?"

"We're still in the hotel. You were injured, and I had to stitch you up."

Shanna's tense body relaxed, and her breathing slowed. Jason knew she was back in the present after a terrifying nightmare.

"Jason, I saw JJ. It was horrible. I was there but couldn't do anything. I—"

He took her hand and whispered. "I know. It was just a nightmare."

Jason recognized the signs of PTSD. He'd seen it countless times among fellow pararescuemen and DEA agents.

"Once we find JJ and get back home, you need to talk to someone about all this. It can leave a lasting mark on your mental health."

Shanna glared at her husband. "Me? What about JJ? I'm afraid he's going to be an emotional wreck the rest of his life because of this."

Jason hesitated to share that he believed JJ's young age might be a benefit in this life-changing ordeal for the Mulder family. "I'm worried about both of you."

His wife nodded and propped herself up on an elbow. "Were you out on the patio?"

"Yeah, I was scanning the bay for Claudio's boat. I'm still pissed that I blew the opportunity to follow him to JJ tonight."

Shanna patted the comforter. "I'm worried about you too. Come sit by me."

Jason sat next to Shanna and crossed his arms. "We were so close a few hours ago, and now I don't know where to go from here."

"I do," Shanna said softly.

Jason spun to explore Shanna's face. "What do you mean?"

"I don't understand Spanish very well, but I could make out bits and pieces of the conversations between the two guards with me on the boat. I think they were talking about JJ and where he is being held."

Jason raised an eyebrow in disbelief. "Honey, they could have been talking about anything. Are you sure they were talking about JJ?"

"They mentioned Victor."

His heart raced with anticipation as he sprang to his feet. "Victor Romero?"

Behind a confident grin, Shanna nodded. "Yes."

CHAPTER 39

Pacific Coast, Costa Rica

Jubilant calls from seagulls circling the bay announced the approaching sunrise as the first hints of daylight appeared in the sky. Hotel doors slammed, elevators dinged, and garbage trucks emptied dumpsters as the seaside town woke up. Jason pulled a chair next to Shanna's side of the bed.

"Tell me everything you heard."

Shanna pushed herself to a sitting position while Jason positioned pillows behind her. "Can I have more ibuprofen and a fresh glass of water?"

Before Jason could leave, Shanna's tender fingers touched his forearm. "Can you also make me some tea?"

Minutes later, Jason set Shanna's hot tea on the nightstand next to her ice water. He'd also brewed a cup of coffee in the hotel coffee maker. Despite his low expectations, the local Costa Rican harvested coffee provided a delicious jolt to start the day. Jason returned to his chair beside Shanna.

"Okay, tell me what they said."

Shanna blew into her mug and took a quick sip. "The guards didn't say much until we got to the dock. Once I was in the boat and the other two left, they started talking. I think they were discussing where they were taking me. I heard them say *'Isla de las*

Sombras' and 'Victor Romero' multiple times. I know '*isla*' is an island, but I wasn't sure about '*de las Sombras*.'"

"That's Shadow Island."

"Where's Shadow Island?"

"I don't know, but we'll find it. What else did they say?" Jason asked.

"I heard '*el niño pequeño*' several times, and I know '*niño*' is 'boy.' I'm pretty sure they were saying 'little boy.'"

Jason's pensive expression transformed into a genuine grin. "You know more Spanish than you thought." He leaned back in the hotel chair until the front legs lifted off the carpet.

"This gives us a new lead. Now we know Claudio works with Victor, and Shadow Island is involved."

"What should we do now?"

"We need to find Shadow Island."

Jason searched for places named Shadow Island in Costa Rica on his phone, but none popped up. "I'm not finding it. I wonder if Shadow Island is just a nickname and not the actual name of the place."

"Hand me my phone," Shanna said. "I'll help you look."

They searched until the sun moved overhead, and Jason's neck grew stiff from looking at his phone. He'd tried every online map search of Costa Rica, but nothing provided a target. His brows furrowed, and his jaw clenched in frustration. Jason shook his head in disbelief and began pacing in the hotel room.

Why can't I find my son when he needs me most? What am I doing wrong?

He searched again, hoping for a different outcome on the same query, but was met with the same websites he'd seen a half dozen times.

"I need a break," Jason said. "I'm going to grab some lunch. Do you want anything?"

Shanna remained silent, her gaze locked on her phone's screen.

"Shanna? Do you want anything to eat?"

When she didn't answer, Jason stomped to the door.

"Wait!" Shanna yelled out.

Jason removed his hand from the door handle and turned back to his wife.

"I think I found it."

A second later, Jason was in bed next to Shanna. "Where is it?"

"I found a place called Shadow Island in Nicaragua. However, it's not an island but a specific area in the southwest corner of Ometepe Island that's in the shadow of a nearby volcanic cone every morning. The main structure on Shadow Island is a former hacienda with multiple buildings that were converted into a vacation rental. Surprisingly, after years of regular guest reviews, they stopped for this rental nine months ago, and the calendar shows it booked for the next year. It's situated within Lake Nicaragua about twenty miles offshore from a town called San Jorge."

"I never thought to look outside Costa Rica," Jason chirped as he pinched his phone screen. "Wow, that's a massive lake."

"I read that it's the largest freshwater lake in Central America, so we'll need a boat."

For several minutes, Jason carefully analyzed the target property using the various online resources he could access with his phone. "It's the perfect place to hide JJ and other hostages. It's on the island's southeastern tip with a rocky cliff behind it. Nobody could sneak up on the property without being detected if they have an ounce of security."

The rhythmic sound of the surf filled their room as Jason and Shanna considered their next move.

"How does your leg feel?"

Shanna scooted to the side and swung her legs over the edge of the bed, placing her feet on the floor. She stood and balanced herself by holding her arms like she was walking on a narrow beam. As she took a step, Shanna winced in pain, causing Jason to rush toward her. But she gestured for him to stay away. "I've got it."

"Can you walk?"

"Y-yeah," she stammered. "I'll need more ibuprofen, but I can walk."

Jason moved to his travel bag. "It's a four-hour drive, so let's pack everything up."

"When do you want to leave?"

"As soon as possible."

"Right now?" Shanna questioned.

Jason's face hardened with determination. "I don't want JJ to spend another night with that monster."

Chapter 40

Safehouse in Central America

Paulina was startled awake by a scream. She sat up in bed and turned to the little boy in the crib. He was stirring on his mattress but still asleep with his favorite teddy bear. Victor's girlfriend rose and moved to a chair beside her bed. She crossed her legs and looked out the window at the palm fronds still wet after an afternoon shower. Paulina's dream came rushing back to her. A group of men had broken into the casita, beaten her, and snatched the little boy. She screamed for them to stop and for someone to help, but in her dream, nobody came to her aid.

She chuckled quietly. "I must have screamed during my sleep."

Victor was right. She was getting too attached to the little boy.

What would Victor do if he knew?

Paulina already knew the answer—he'd do nothing. Victor was already aware of her attachment to the little boy and still gave her the same amount of freedom and privacy as before. Paulina chuckled again at the thought of her privacy and freedom. She was not too different than the other men and women in the compound held for ransom, but instead of seeking money, Victor expected sex from Paulina. Her cheeks warmed and her chest tightened at the realization she was just as much a captive as the little boy.

Should I escape with the boy before Victor sells him?

Paulina admonished herself for even thinking of leaving Victor, especially with the little boy. He had saved her from an abusive boyfriend in San Salvador and provided her with a better life. She couldn't betray Victor—or he'd kill her.

She sat quietly in the chair until the little boy woke and made babbling sounds. Paulina scooped up the little boy, his arms wrapped tightly around his beloved teddy bear. She pried the toy from his grasp, causing him to let out a cry of frustration as he reached out to retrieve it.

"No! The bear is dirty. You can't sleep with it anymore until I wash it."

The little boy kept his eyes locked on the bear as Paulina set it next to the sink and turned on the hot water. Wisps of steam rose above the half-full basin when she added some soap.

"Mine!" the little boy shouted.

"I know. I'll wash it now so it's dry for your nap later."

"Mine!"

Paulina sighed and started to dip the bear into the sink when she heard a knock on the door. Victor was several steps into the casita before she had a chance to check on the visitor.

"*Buenos dias, mi amor*," Victor said as he kissed Paulina on both cheeks.

She returned a genuine smile and drifted back to the little boy standing inside the crib. Paulina always felt a need to put herself between Victor and the boy when he was around.

"Are you here to check on us?" Paulina asked with a playful smile.

"No, I'm here to let you know that today is our last day with the boy. My contact from Venezuela said he'd come here to pick up the boy, so we no longer have to travel to Panama."

"He's coming here?"

"Not on Shadow Island," Victor corrected himself. "We're making the exchange at the harbor in San Juan del Sur, so only a one-hour boat ride and a ninety-minute drive instead of days to Panama."

Paulina felt panic ignite and spread inside her stomach, but now was not the time to let Victor see it. "That is good news. Saves us from a long trip to Panama."

Victor stepped closer to Paulina but looked past her toward the boy.

"Mine!" the little boy howled.

"What's this?" Victor asked as he raised his hands in amusement. "The little boy thinks he's running the place now. I'm not surprised, though, because you've been very soft on him."

Paulina's face and neck turned red in embarrassment. She didn't have a good rebuttal to his claim, so she chose to stay silent.

"Mine!" the boy repeated.

A scowl stretched across Victor's face as he leaned over the crib until his nose was less than a foot away from the boy. Paulina wanted to pull him away but didn't dare interfere.

"No, little boy, you are mine, but soon you will belong to someone else."

Victor leaned so close his breath ruffled the little boy's hair when he spoke. "Losing you forever will only inflict a fraction of the pain your father deserves, but it's a start."

Seemingly proud of himself, Victor backed away from the crib and did a lap around the small room. He stared out the window at the mountain behind the casita until two guards entered.

"Señor, you asked to see us."

"Yes, the boy will be leaving tomorrow, so I don't want anything to interfere with his final day at the compound. I want you to put an extra guard on the hacienda tonight and tell the local police working with us to be extra vigilant for any unexpected visitors."

"Yes, sir!"

The guards left, and Victor turned to Paulina. "I know this is not what you want, but it must be done. The boy's father must be punished for what he did to me," Victor hissed. "He left me for dead and permanently disfigured. The pain Jason Mulder will experience from the loss of his son is just the beginning of what I have in store for him."

"I-I understand," Paulina said, trembling with fear and anger.

Victor looked through Paulina as if she wasn't there. His gaze fixed on her face but not her eyes. "I'm not so sure you do."

"I do. I understand."

He caressed her cheek with the back of his hand. "I hope so, because if you try anything to disrupt the delivery of the boy tomorrow, I'll kill both of you."

CHAPTER 41

Costa Rican border with Nicaragua

Jason's hands trembled as he wiped the sweat off the back of his neck, his heart still racing with nervous energy. He exhaled loudly as the border crossing between Costa Rica and Nicaragua vanished behind the trees of the last curve, grateful for Shanna's presence in the passenger seat of the Jeep. Her exposed legs below the hemline of her dress had caught the attention of the young border guard. His focus was solely on her and away from the guns in the vehicle. Every second had felt like an eternity until they were cleared to pass into Nicaragua. Jason wasn't sure how much more his nerves could take and hoped this would be his last border crossing with illegal weapons.

"Is everything alright?" Shanna asked.

"Yeah, why?"

"You seemed nervous at the border checkpoint. Are you worried that your passport has been flagged or something?"

"No, that wasn't it."

"What was it?" Shanna inquired.

"I'll show you later."

Fifteen miles into Nicaragua, the narrow highway turned north, and Shanna and Jason were treated to expansive views of Lake Nicaragua. Tiny waves rippled across the steel-blue lake and formed whitecaps as they broke near the shore. A perfectly symmetrical triangle mountain rose a mile above the lake.

"Whoa, I saw the lake on the map a dozen times but didn't realize it was this big. It's huge," Jason bellowed. "Is that a volcano in the distance?"

Shanna turned to her phone and scrolled through several screens. "Yeah, that's Concepción, and it's one of the most active volcanos in the country. It's part of the island we're going to later today."

Jason swung his eyes back and forth from the breathtaking lake on his right to the oncoming traffic to avoid causing a head-on collision.

"The website I found says the oval-shaped lake is one hundred ten miles long and thirty-six miles wide, making it the largest freshwater lake in Central America. It also said Lake Nicaragua is home to several oceanic animals that thrive in fresh water, including tarpon, swordfish, and—

Jason turned to Shanna, who'd kept her eyes on her phone but stopped talking. "And what?"

"It has bull sharks in it."

"That's not uncommon," Jason offered to ease her concern.

"Bull sharks kill people!"

"All the more reason to make sure we stay in the boat."

The sun had moved over the Pacific Ocean in the west as Jason approached the town of Rivas. Their destination of San Jorge was just past Rivas, so Jason pulled into an old, deserted park surrounded by tropical trees. He exited the SUV and walked around the vehicle as if checking for a flat tire, but he was scanning the area for law enforcement. Jason moved into the second row of the Jeep and reached over the back seat.

"Is something wrong with the car?" Shanna asked.

"I will show you why I was nervous crossing the border."

He slid his hand under the folded-down third-row seat and presented a matte-black pistol to his wife in the front seat. Shanna recoiled as if he were holding a serpent.

"Jason, you can't have that down here. You'll get arrested!"

"I know. That's why I was nervous."

"They put you in prison for bringing guns into this country. Didn't you see all the signs?"

The sight of the Glock 17 pistol made Shanna uncomfortable, and Jason noticed. She had a habit of talking excessively when she was anxious.

"If they catch us with that, we could both go to prison."

He slid the pistol under the driver's seat to ease the tension.

"I assume you don't want to see the other weapon I picked up down here."

"You have two guns?"

Jason held the AK-47 high enough for Shanna to see and quickly hid it under the seat. He jumped out of the second row and returned to the driver's seat.

Shanna looked out the window in all directions several times. "We could get in a lot of trouble for those guns. You realize that, don't you?"

Jason pursed his lips. "Everything I plan to do to get JJ back could land me in prison if the local police catch me, but I don't care. I've seen how ruthless Victor Romero is, and I'm not about to step foot on that island without a weapon."

The statement seemed to ease Shanna's nerves. The SUV cabin was quiet for several beats as they peered through the windshield at the growing shadows.

"I'm giving you the handgun when we go to the island, so I want you to get comfortable with it before we get there," Jason said as he pulled the Glock out from under his seat. "Try it and see how it feels in your hand."

Shanna pulled her hands away. "Here?"

He humored his wife by looking around to confirm nobody else was around to see them and handed the Glock to her, keeping it out of view from any potential onlookers. She held it awkwardly at first, but then she wrapped her fingers around the grip like she'd learned with her gun.

"It's a Glock, similar to what you have at home. It has a longer barrel and two more rounds in the magazine."

She bounced it in her right hand several times as if calculating its weight. "It feels good. Where did you get it?"

Jason tilted his head wearing the *You know I can't tell you* look, and Shanna continued with her next question.

"If I have this, what are you going to use?"

"I'll take the Kalashnikov. I'll need to find a music shop in Rivas to buy a guitar case to get it from the Jeep to the boat."

Shanna returned the pistol to her husband, who slid it back under the seat. Jason turned to face his wife, and he could see her expression turn somber. Her eyes darted around the cab in search of something, although they couldn't seem to focus on anything in particular. He reached across the console and squeezed her hand.

"Are you worried about tonight?"

They'd discussed the plan multiple times during their four-hour journey, and Jason wondered if she was having second thoughts.

"A little bit. I just want JJ back."

"Me too."

Jason closed his eyes and leaned back into the headrest, going through each detail of the mission in his mind just as he did during his time as a PJ in the Air Force. He always imagined a successful outcome, which, in this mission, meant leaving the hacienda with JJ safely in his arms and a slow, agonizing death for Victor Romero.

He turned toward Shanna and caressed her cheek. "I'm ready to go."

Shanna held her husband's gaze for a beat and nodded. Jason started the engine and tightened his fingers around the steering wheel until his knuckles blanched white.

"Let's go get our son."

Chapter 42

Jason ducked into the back seat of the car as Shanna kept a lookout for anyone showing unusual curiosity toward their vehicle in the far corner of the parking lot. He had found a store similar to Walmart in Rivas, where he was able to purchase all the necessary items. After thirty minutes of shopping, Jason returned with flashlights, a guitar case, and supplies for their mission to infiltrate the hacienda. He even picked up a box of snacks for JJ once he was safely off the island.

"Clear," Shanna said from the front seat.

He opened the guitar case on the floor of the Jeep and carefully slid the AK-47 rifle inside. He covered it with packages of cheap T-shirts and underwear he purchased to prevent the rifle from rattling around while transporting it.

"That's everything we need here. Now we have to rent a boat in San Jorge."

As the sun dipped below the palm trees lining the west bank of Lake Nicaragua, Jason parked the Jeep. The harbor was more like an oversized boat launch, with a handful of charter vessels and boats available for rent. Most people were there to catch the vehicle ferry to Ometepe Island. Jason hurried inside the small rental shop before it closed for the evening. When he emerged, Shanna was waiting in the SUV as she looked at old pictures of JJ on her phone.

"Did you get a boat?" Shanna asked.

Jason nodded. "Yeah, but they didn't have many options left for tonight. It is a twenty-two-foot wooden-hull, open-air boat with a single outboard engine."

Shanna shrugged. "What does that mean to someone like me who has never manned a station on a battleship?"

"It means we will have a long, bumpy ride across the lake tonight. We should leave around midnight to ensure we get there before twilight."

Jason started the engine. "Let's get something to eat, and then we'll return here to load up the boat."

Before he left, Jason's phone buzzed. He saw it was Special Agent Woods, so he answered.

"Hey, Archie."

"Hi, Mulder. Do you have a minute?"

"Sure. Shoot."

"Where are you right now?"

"I'm sitting in the car with Shanna on the western shore of Lake Nicaragua."

"Your wife is with you?" Archie inquired with a hint of scrutiny, but Jason brushed it off.

"Yeah, what's up?"

"I spoke to some people at State, and they sent a team to Corinto to recover Ruben Zambrano's body. They found him in a shallow grave, and he's on his way home to his family now. I just thought you'd want to know that."

Hearing Zee's name brought back a wave of emotions that stung like a hundred wasps impaling his body. The reality still hadn't completely sunk in that Victor Romero had brutally murdered his teammate and friend. Jason's chin dropped to his chest in disbelief.

"Thank you. That means a lot to me."

A faint hiss of static was the only sound on the call.

"I appreciate the call, Archie. Is there anything else?"

Archie cleared his throat and sighed. "I heard from our friend Mike. He did some more digging on Victor Romero, and it's not good."

"I already know he's a murderous psychopath and a kidnapper. How much worse can it get than that?"

"JJ is not the first child he's abducted."

Jason's empty stomach lurched at Archie's statement. "What? I thought the kidnapping was likely personal to get back at me."

"It may be, but the Colombian Coast Guard intercepted a cargo ship headed for Venezuela, and they found fourteen kids aged three and under with a broker. He fingered the other parties for a lighter sentence, and two children came from Victor Romero. The Colombians have a warrant out for his arrest."

Jason pounded on the steering wheel. "So he is into trafficking children along with adults and drugs. I can't wait to get my hands on that piece of shit!"

"I understand the sentiment, Mulder, but be careful, especially with your beautiful bride down there with you. This Romero character is a bad man with connections all over Latin America, and nothing is off limits to him. Watch your back and trust no one down there, even the police."

Jason's pulse slowed after his earlier eruption. He was ready to assault Shadow Island.

"Thanks for the heads-up, Archie. We have to run now, so I'll check in when I get home."

Jason killed the engine and let the boat drift the final thirty yards to a rickety wooden dock. He moved to the bow and swung a leg over to inspect the condition of the dock, which didn't appear to have hosted a vessel in years. It groaned under his weight but held up, so Jason carefully disembarked from their rented boat. Jason scanned the narrow beach and noted the leafy trees lining the shoreline on Shadow Island, casting shadows in the moonlight that would provide the cover he needed to reach the hacienda.

Shanna stood at the helm of the boat, prepared to make a quick escape as soon as Jason returned with JJ.

"Thirty minutes," he whispered. "If I'm not back by—

"I'm not leaving," Shanna interrupted. "I'll meet you right here when you have our son."

Already in tactical mode, Jason spun and darted across the rocky beach with the AK-47 rifle slung across his back. He took a knee in the undergrowth out of range of the lapping waters of Lake Nicaragua. The former PJ retrieved his recently acquired binoculars from his pack and scanned the beach before him, focusing on the hacienda seventy-five yards away. The grounds were shrouded in darkness, except for two illuminated rooms on the second floor. Jason opened his phone and covered it with his gloved hand to prevent anyone in the hacienda from seeing the light from his screen. The tracker showed JJ was near the middle of the complex, but he couldn't tell if his son was on the first or second story.

"I'll have to check both," he whispered.

Jason adjusted the binoculars until the fine details of the hacienda's colonial architecture were clear through his optics. He scanned the structure until he located a promising entry point—an aged wooden door with a tall rectangular window. Just as he prepared to move, movement caught his eye. A sentry with a rifle patrolled the area near the north door. He carefully searched the grounds until he saw a second armed man outside the south door. Both entrances were well guarded, so Jason had to neutralize at least one of the sentries to get inside.

The guard at the south door was smoking near the entrance and appeared more interested in his phone than his surroundings. Jason crept behind him, using the man's exhale to mask the sound of his approach. As the man chuckled at the contents of a social media video, Jason's hand clamped over his mouth while his knife thrust into the soft spot beneath the guard's ear. He held the guard tight as his body heaved and seized. Once he fell limp, Jason lowered the body silently into the shadows. He scanned the grounds like a lion after a kill, searching for additional threats. Seeing none, Jason entered the hacienda.

Inside, the hacienda smelled of mold and wet carpet. Moonlight filtered through barred windows, casting striped shadows across the worn floor. The first floor appeared to contain a kitchen with Saltillo tile counters reflecting in dim light from the appliances. Jason crept past the kitchen and found several open doors to rooms that appeared to be offices for workers. He suspected the lights on the second floor were an indicator of where Victor held his victims, so Jason moved to the north end of the hacienda. The other sentry was visible through the slit of glass in the door. He sat on a low stone wall, staring aimlessly across the compound grounds engulfed in darkness. His rifle leaned against the wall.

The guard at the north door never saw Jason coming. In one quick motion, the door opened and Jason's blade was buried between the man's wide eyes. The guard succumbed to death in a matter of seconds and slumped against the wall.

Jason returned inside and found stairs to the second level. He pulled his gloves tight and took a deep breath. The wooden steps would give him away if he wasn't careful. He tested each step before committing weight, moving in stealth mode like a black panther in the night. At the top, he found himself in a long, hotel-like corridor lined with thick wooden doors.

Jason reached the first door with the AK-47 slung around his neck, resting on his chest, so it was accessible in a second if needed. He turned the handle slowly. It wasn't locked. He pushed it open and moved one hand to the rifle grip while the other sprayed the room with light. It contained four empty bunk beds that looked like they'd been vacant for an extended period. He quietly exited the room and moved further down the hall.

The sturdy slide lock on the next door drew Jason's attention. His heart rate increased at the thought of what lay behind it. It was the only door on the floor locked from the outside. He carefully slid the lock open and twisted the handle. It was unlocked.

This could be the jackpot.

During close-quarters-combat training in the Air Force and DEA academy, Jason was trained to enter a room with at least two people, but he'd have to improvise and cover all angles himself. Wanting to have both hands on the rifle to aim and shoot instantly—and accurately—he unfurled a bungee cord from his pack and affixed his flashlight under the barrel of the rifle.

Three, two, one, Jason counted down to himself.

He pushed through the door and swept the flashlight beam across the room. Jason had hoped and expected to see JJ, but he wasn't in the room. He froze, unable to believe what he saw.

CHAPTER 43

Shadow Island

Jason noticed the scent of sweat, body odor, and fear before the beam of his flashlight found a target. A pair of eyes stared back at Jason, blinking rapidly out of fear or confusion. He kept the AK-47 sights locked on the man sitting on a bottom bunk and, after determining he wasn't a threat, panned around the room. Six adult males in their forties and fifties glared back at him, their bruised faces showing various stages of beard growth and exhaustion. They all recoiled and raised their hands as if to deflect a punishing blow that never came when Jason stepped forward.

"Who are you?" Jason demanded in Spanish. He saw glances back and forth among the men, but nobody answered.

He gripped the rifle tighter and stepped toward the first man. "Are you with Victor Romero, or are you his victims?"

"Victims. We've all been abducted," a voice answered from the dark.

"Who are you? Where are you from?"

The men slid from their bunks and stood beside them like soldiers. A tall man with messy white hair spoke first. "We're all executives of companies they abducted for ransom. I'm the vice president of operations for a Mexican petroleum company, and they took me during a visit to one of our wells in Guatemala. I'm still waiting for my company to raise the ransom money."

The tall man waved to the others. Some of us work in the pharmaceutical, transportation, and tech industries. They treat us like cattle here. Sold to the highest bidder."

Jason was concerned his son was in the same predicament. He had to get more information from the men, but the tall man spoke again before he could ask his questions.

"Now it's your turn. Who are you?"

"Someone looking for his son."

Jason removed the flashlight from the barrel of his AK-47 and lowered his weapon. "Have any of you seen a little boy here?"

"We all had hoods over our heads when they brought us here. I haven't seen anybody else other than the guards and their leader. I don't even know where we are."

Jason looked around the room. They all had the thousand-mile stare of someone who had experienced life-changing trauma.

"You're in Shadow Island in Nicaragua," Jason shared. "Have you seen or heard anything that could help me find my son?"

The tech executive spoke next. "I heard the faint sounds of a child crying a day or two ago. It sounded far away. Maybe from a different floor."

"What else can you tell me? What direction?"

"I'm not sure. I don't think the sounds came from this floor. It may have come through the window."

A thick woven blanket was nailed to the wall, covering what Jason assumed was a window. He yanked on it, and the blanket fell to the floor. Jason squeezed between a bunk bed and the wall to look out the window. The room faced the rocky cutout from the mountain in the back of the hacienda. Directly below his feet was a small casita that seemed to be attached to the kitchen he had passed on the first floor. He realized this was the only part of the building he hadn't yet cleared.

"How many guards have you seen on this compound?"

"I've seen six different guards come into the room, so we have at least six men in this building we have to deal with if we want to escape," the pharmaceutical executive replied.

"Now you only have four," Jason replied.

"No. I've counted at least six," the executive responded.

"I've already killed two, so you only have four remaining."

Jason noticed six sets of eyes widen in surprise.

"Don't forget about Señor Romero's personal security with him in the building next door," the tech executive added.

Jason's blood ran cold. "Are you sure Victor Romero is here?"

"Positive. He came here yesterday to tell me he'd kill my family and hang me naked from a bridge if they didn't come up with the ransom by today."

"How many men came with him?"

"He had two additional men with him."

Jason ran his fingers through his hair. "Wait here. I'm going for my son."

"You're going just to leave us here?" the pharmaceutical executive whined.

"The police will be here soon. They'll get you off the island and back home."

The tech executive stepped forward, his face resolute in the light of Jason's flashlight. "I refuse to wait here and risk getting caught by the guards," he declared. "They'll have no mercy if they find us with the door open and unlocked. I'm going to make a break for it."

Echoes of "Me too" came from around the small room.

Jason unslung the AK-47 from his shoulder. "Anyone here know how to handle one of these?"

The men exchanged uncertain glances until the tech executive raised his hand. "I was in the infantry with the Colombian Army twenty-two years ago, so it's been a while."

"Take this." Jason extended the rifle and held it chest high until the tech executive took it into his possession. "You are as qualified as anyone. Just don't shoot me."

"Is that your only gun?" another executive asked.

"If you want more, you'll have to kill the guards and take their weapons. I think the gun belonging to the dead guard by the north entrance may still be there if you want it."

"This is enough," the tech executive roared. He sounded more like the infantry soldier he once was. "Follow me. I'm blasting any guards I see before they know what the hell hit them."

Jason waved to the hallway. "After you."

The six executives moved into the hallway, the Colombian Army veteran leading with the AK-47. Jason watched them disappear north before he moved south toward JJ. Each step brought him closer to his son but also a potential conflict with Victor.

Back on the first floor, Jason looked out the narrow window in the south door. Nobody had come to replace the deceased guard yet, so he exited the main building. He observed a corridor between a smaller, ranch-style residence and the hacienda that was about sixty feet long. It was the only way to reach the casita he saw from the room upstairs, but Jason didn't like the risky choke point. Once he entered the corridor, he would be exposed inside an ideal ambush zone. Jason held his knife tight and stepped into the dark corridor. His eyes strained to see movement in the twilight. Seeing none, he took a dozen quick steps and stopped to look and listen for anyone approaching from either end. He repeated this process until he reached the end of the corridor. Jason tilted his head back to alleviate the suffocating tension and watched bright turquoise bands of the sky appear on the eastern horizon. He took a few deep breaths to calm his racing heart before moving in the shadows along the casita.

Jason opened the tracker on his phone. The blue dot on the screen was inside JJ's bear, and the black dot identified the location of Jason's phone. The dots overlapped.

"He's in there!" Jason said with a small pump of his fist.

It took all his willpower not to rush into the building and scoop up his son, but Jason was thinking clearly. A tactical entry was the only way to ensure they both left that casita alive.

He reached for the handle, his hand trembling slightly. After weeks of searching, after all the pain and death, his son was just a couple of feet away. But Victor Romero could also be waiting for him, the man who'd survived their last encounter and taken everything from him.

The handle turned easily. That worried him more than a locked door.

Jason took a deep breath, steadying himself. He opened the door, ready to face whatever waited on the other side.

A soft-white light glinted off Jason's bloody blade as he padded into the room. He adjusted the grip on his knife, coiled to strike at the likely ambush at the end of the short hallway.

Jason cautiously peered around the corner, only exposing his left eye, and his stomach sank. He saw JJ for the first time in twenty-seven days. His son was less than five steps away but wasn't alone. A young woman in pajamas rocked JJ in her arms as she stood, whispering to his boy, who clung to the teddy bear with the tracker.

Upon seeing a stranger caring for his son when he expected to find the opposite, the rush of emotions was disorienting. Should he be angry, worried, or grateful?

Jason decided that anyone involved in the abduction of his son was the enemy and he'd treat the young girl as a hostile. He lunged into the light and landed an arm's length from the woman. His blade was high, so the crimson-stained tip was only inches from her face after she spun around.

"Give me back my son," Jason demanded in Spanish.

The young woman clung tighter to JJ and looked left and right as she expected to see someone else.

"The guards are not coming. Hand over my son before you meet the same fate as them."

The commotion woke JJ, and he began crying. The young woman cowered with him in the corner of the room.

"Don't hurt him," she cried.

Jason lowered the knife and returned it to his pocket. He raised both hands in an attempt to calm her down.

"I would never hurt JJ. He's my son."

Her expression softened as she appeared to see the relationship in Jason's eyes. She looked at the little boy in her arms. "This is your son?"

"Yes, Victor Romero took him from us, and I'm here to bring him back home."

Surprise replaced the fear in her face. "You know Victor?"

Jason nodded. "I fought Victor in Arizona. I thought he was dead until I learned he kidnapped my son."

The woman never took her eyes off JJ. She pursed her lips as his cries died down, and Jason could tell she was considering her next move.

"Who are you? Do you work for Victor?"

The woman finally met Jason's gaze. "My name is Paulina. Victor asked me to take care of the boy a few weeks ago."

Jason knew that he could eliminate Paulina in under two seconds, secure JJ, and return to Shanna waiting in the boat, but there was no need to harm the young woman. She appeared to take good care of JJ, and Jason preferred that Paulina hand him over to avoid further traumatizing his son.

"I need to go before someone else comes, so please give me my son."

Her eyes welled up in tears, and several escaped to run down her cheeks. Paulina kissed JJ on the forehead and handed JJ over to Jason's waiting arms.

Jason curled his son into his chest and squeezed him tight. He kissed his son on the forehead and smelled the shampoo Paulina used in his hair. A solo tear of joy streamed down his cheek as Jason whispered, "I missed you so much," into JJ's ear.

It was as if JJ had been born again, and Jason got to experience the euphoria of being a first-time father once more. He looked down into JJ's hazel eyes and saw the recognition. JJ's cries transformed into soft whimpers as his father held him.

The jubilation was short-lived. "Victor and his men are in the building next door. You better go now, or we'll both be killed."

"What will happen to you when they find JJ missing?"

"I don't know, but you must go now!"

Jason secured JJ in his left arm like a football and held the knife tight with his right hand. He scurried toward the door, stopped, and turned to Paulina.

"Thank you for taking care of my son."

She wiped tears from her cheeks. "Please hurry."

Jason returned the way he came. The only way to the beach and boat to take them from the island was through the corridor he'd crossed earlier. He didn't have time to go through the corridor tactically, so Jason sprinted as fast as possible.

The rippling water of Lake Nicaragua under the early morning sun came into view, and Jason knew he was almost in the clear. He turned the corner and expected to locate Shanna and the boat but lost his balance. A nanosecond later, he felt the excruciating pain on the back of his head and unconsciousness overcoming him like a flash flood. Jason dropped to his knees, gently placed JJ on the rocky soil, and the world went black.

Chapter 44

Lapping water against the shore and the warmth of the rising sun on Jason's face eased him back to consciousness. He struggled to open his heavy eyelids. Gradually, he could make out the sand and pebbles of a beach. Jason didn't recognize where he was; everything seemed to be rotated by ninety degrees. He was lying face down on the shore of a massive lake, and his head throbbed with pain. For a moment, Jason couldn't remember where he was or why he was there, but then everything came rushing back to him like a tidal wave.

"JJ?" Jason called out. He pushed himself up from the sand, lost his balance, and collapsed back to the beach. He spit out sand, rolled to his haunches, and turned toward the hacienda. The woman from the casita held JJ in her trembling arms.

Jason extended his arms. "Give me my son."

"Not so fast, Jason Mulder."

The voice came from behind him and was instantly recognizable. Victor Romero moved into Jason's view with a pistol aimed at his chest.

"Welcome to Shadow Island. It's a rather nice safe house for my captive guests, isn't it?" Victor asked in accented English.

Jason scanned the property. "Not bad for a pathetic drug dealer and spineless kidnapper. What happened to your fancy compound outside Corinto?"

Victor's lips twitched as if he might smile. "Well played, Jason Mulder. That compound was ideal for my narcotics distribution business flowing through the area, but this place is more comfortable for my guests. I own everything you see—and everyone."

The former PJ stumbled back to his feet, swaying unsteadily as he regained his balance. The pain from the blow to the back of his head left him reeling, and the world seemed to spin around him. Jason fought off waves of nausea, refusing to let it distract him from his mission to save JJ.

"I'm sure your guests appreciate the hospitality, but it's time for them to check out. I'm taking my son back!"

Victor shook his head. "You are in no position to make any demands. Soon, you will wish you never meddled with me in Arizona or let me slide over that waterfall."

"Is that what this is all about? You kidnapped a one-year-old little boy and held him here because you're butthurt that you lost to me in our fight in Arizona? That's petty, even for you."

A scowl washed over Victor's face as anger pinched his eyes and nose. "I lost everything because of you. El Jaguar cut me out of all the business I created at La Palma and tried to have me killed. Now you will also experience a pain that will haunt you forever."

Jason assumed the threat was directed at JJ and wanted to charge the kidnapper and rip his throat out. He couldn't believe that anyone, even a ruthless cartel member, would harm an innocent child.

Or was it directed at Shanna? Or does he intend to torture me?

He looked casually over his left shoulder and saw the boat they rented from the mainland still tied up at the dock. Shanna wasn't waiting at the helm as they had agreed.

Where is she? Did one of the guards find her? Is Victor holding her inside the hacienda?

Massaging the knot on the back of his head and stretching his neck, Jason pondered his next move. He had to know who Victor was targeting.

"How exactly are you going to inflict this pain?"

Victor's fingers went to his permanently disfigured face. "I'll make you feel the same excruciating pain I endured in Arizona."

Jason was relieved to hear Victor's ire was directed at him, not his wife and son. He was unarmed and would be severely outnumbered when the guards arrived, so he had to act soon or face the torture Victor had in store for him.

JJ wiggled and yelped in Paulina's arms. He'd heard his father's voice and struggled to free himself. Jason noticed and made a plea to Victor.

"Give me my son, and you'll never see or hear from me again. I'll tell the FBI and DEA to stop looking for you. You've proved your point; now let me have my son."

Wrinkles spread across Victor's forehead as if he were considering the proposal. The pistol aimed at his chest lowered several inches, and Jason took that as a sign to retrieve his son. Jason stepped toward Paulina and JJ, who were standing twenty feet away. When he had reduced the gap to fifteen feet, Jason extended his arms to take his son, but instead of JJ, he received a 9mm round in his arm.

A searing pain exploded in Jason's left biceps, accompanied by a deafening blast. The impact of the bullet pierced through him, spinning him around like a rag doll before sending him crashing to the ground. His right hand instinctively moved to the bleeding biceps on his left arm and applied pressure. Despite the temporary shock he'd experienced, the former PJ felt the entry and exit wound below the wetness in his shirt.

At first, Jason could only hear a high-pitched ringing in his ears until he heard JJ wailing in Paulina's arms. His son may not have understood what happened to his father, but the thunderous blast from the pistol surely scared him to death.

Jason got his knees under him and stumbled to his feet to face the man who had shot him.

"I thought you wanted a fair fight to show me how much pain a tough guy like you can inflict. You're nothing but a weak man. You're a coward."

His right hand turned crimson as Jason continued to hold his left arm and wobble toward the man who abducted his son.

Victor's eyes widened as Jason inched closer with each step. He adjusted his aim until the barrel pointed to Jason's chest.

"I'm not here to win a fair fight. I will make you pay for what you did to me."

Jason continued his march toward the former cartel lieutenant. Since he had no firearm, his only chance of neutralizing Victor would be to get close. That also increased the probability he'd get shot before he could get his hands on JJ's kidnapper, but it was his only option.

The barrel of Victor's 9mm pressed into Jason's chest, forcing him to stop. Jason was close enough to disarm Victor, but the kidnapper jumped back before he could use his training to secure the pistol.

"I remember what you did last time, and that won't happen again. Take another step, and it will be your last."

Jason stopped and glared at Victor, who took several additional steps back.

"Now, that's better. It's time for this back-and-forth to end."

Victor turned to Paulina. "Hand me the boy."

Paulina squeezed JJ tighter and twisted to put her body between Victor and the boy.

"I said give me the boy!" Victor growled.

The barrel was still pointed at his chest, but Jason saw Victor's attention focused on his disobedient girlfriend.

Can I cover the ten feet to Victor before he pulls the trigger?

Jason knew this might be his last opportunity to save JJ, so he lowered his head and charged toward Victor like an angry bull.

Boom!

The concussive report from the 9mm pistol five feet from Jason sent him to the ground. His hands reflexively moved to his chest to examine the severity of the entry wound—but it wasn't there. He didn't feel wetness or pain like his biceps. Jason looked up and saw Victor's gaping mouth as he stared at the expanding crimson circle on his abdomen. Victor collapsed against a wall and held his hands over his bleeding stomach like he was in silent prayer. The acrid smell of sulfur and gunpowder filled the air as Jason looked over his shoulder.

"Shanna?"

His wife stood twenty feet away in a perfect firing position with a waft of smoke rising from the barrel. Shanna kept the pistol aimed at Victor, her face focused and fearless, prepared to fire again.

Jason got to his feet and rushed to Shanna. She glared at Victor as if her eyes could burn a hole in him. He carefully removed the Glock from her fingers that were wrapped tightly around the grip. "I've got him. Get our son."

Shanna turned to see Paulina holding JJ, who was clinging tightly to the young woman after the gunshots. She turned back to Jason, and he immediately understood.

"She's okay. She took good care of JJ the whole time he was down here."

Shanna moved swiftly to Paulina and stopped before her. "Thank you for taking care of JJ."

"JJ?" Paulina asked in heavily accented English.

"Yes," Shanna smiled.

Paulina returned the smile, kissed the boy on the top of his head, and handed JJ to his mother. Shanna wrapped her arms around her son and squeezed him tight. Tears flowed as she stroked his thin hair. "You're back with Momma now."

Shanna started toward Jason to reunite the entire family.

"Get down," Jason yelled as two armed guards emerged from around the hacienda. The deafening roar of AK-47 gunfire erupted, shattering the lakeside tranquility. Jason rolled, aimed, and fired, obliterating both men with headshots that painted the walls of the hacienda in a crimson spray.

Jason remained in a firing position when he heard a gut-wrenching whine from a female voice behind him. "Shanna, are you okay?"

He spun around, looking for his wife and son. Jason spotted Shanna lying on top of JJ. "Are you hit?"

Shanna pushed herself up. "No, I'm okay."

Another cry came from further up the shore. Paulina's contorted body lay on the smooth pebbles, gasping for air. Jason rushed to her side and heard wheezing sounds coming from her bloodied chest. He ripped off a section of his shirt, wadded it into a ball, and pressed it against the gruesome wound. Shanna arrived moments later with JJ.

"Don't let him see this," Jason warned.

She put her body between JJ and Paulina. Shanna turned and asked over her shoulder, "Is there anything you can do? Is she going to survive?"

Jason subtly shook his head, so Shanna crouched next to the woman who cared for JJ for the past four weeks. Paulina turned to Shanna, her eyes fluttering as if they were too heavy to keep open.

"Thank you for taking care of our son."

"He-he's a good boy," Paulina croaked.

"I know he is," Shanna replied, choking back tears. "We'll never forget how you saved JJ."

Paulina's lips curled upward briefly, and then her eyes slammed shut as if waiting to hear those final words before she passed.

Jason stood and pulled Shanna and JJ into his arms. He squeezed harder and harder until JJ complained. "Dadda. No. Hurt."

The sound of JJ's voice nearly brought Jason to tears, but the sirens from the approaching police grabbed his attention. Jason nudged Shanna toward the boat.

"We're not out of the woods yet. They may be on Victor's payroll, so we need to go."

Shanna ran to the boat with JJ, but Jason stopped at Victor's feet. The kidnapper and drug dealer seemed to gain some strength and color in his face, indicating he might survive Shanna's blast. He leaned against the stone wall and glared at Jason through vengeful eyes. Jason knew that murderous look. He'd see it in himself now if he stood in front of a mirror.

"This isn't over. You-you will pay for this," Victor wheezed.

Jason shook his head. "No, this is our final showdown, Victor." He raised the Glock gifted by El Jaguar and aimed at Victor's chest.

"This ends now."

CHAPTER 45

Jason and Shanna sped away from Shadow Island as gunfire erupted behind them. Police cars with flashing lights raced along the coastal road until they stopped near an empty lot about a quarter mile past the hacienda. Jason wondered what drew the police to that location until he saw the six executives from the hacienda running for cover behind boulders and stone mounds. As soon as the police exited their vehicles, they immediately opened fire on the executives.

"Those police are definitely with Victor," Jason shouted over the boat engine. "We have to get out of here."

The tech executive fired back with his AK-47, and it sounded like the company executives had acquired one more rifle to fend off a half dozen local police officers. Jason had regretted giving up his powerful rifle to the abducted executives but now saw that it provided an unexpected benefit. By standing their ground, they drew Victor's crooked cops into the fight, and that was fewer police to chase after Jason and his family.

Within minutes, the popping sounds from the gun battle were drowned out by the boat engine and the rhythmic slap of the bow on the choppy waters. Jason opened the throttle to maximum speed to get them out of the area before additional law enforcement on Victor's payroll arrived.

Shanna sat beside Jason, holding her son in her arms. She appeared at peace for the first time in a month. Jason was committed to getting his wife and son back to their home in Arizona, but first, he had to get out of the country. They couldn't risk going back for the Jeep in San Jorge, so Jason guided the boat across the expanse of Lake Nicaragua to its south shore. They'd be within a few miles of Costa Rica, which opened up several opportunities to cross into a country with more friendly resources to help protect them from the reach of Victor's cartel. It wasn't ideal with Shanna's leg and Jason's arm injury, but it was the best choice among many bad options.

The landscape on the south shoreline over the bow drew closer, and Jason slowed several miles per hour to minimize the bumps jarring Shanna and JJ. A high-pitched sound caught his attention. Jason searched the boat for the source but couldn't find it until he looked behind him. Two police boats with lights and sirens were in his wake and rapidly approaching.

"Hold on," Jason shouted.

The boat lurched forward after Jason returned the throttle to maximum speed. They zoomed through the water, occasionally catching some air as they hit higher waves. Jason glanced at his son nestled in Shanna's arms to ensure he was okay with the turbulence from the speeding boat and saw a blank expression on his face. After all that had happened, it seemed like nothing could faze him, or maybe JJ was like his father and enjoyed the wild ride. It was an incredible feeling to have his son back by his side. The engine sputtered, slowed, and returned to full speed a mile from the south shore.

"What's wrong?" Shanna asked.

Jason checked the gas gauge and saw they still had a quarter of a tank. He spun around and noticed a large pool of water rising in the stern. "I think we're getting water in the engine with all the waves splashing inside. I need to slow down, or we'll never make it."

He slowed down and strained to identify the best place on the approaching beach to land their boat. Jason checked on the two police boats pursuing him, and they had almost caught up. They were less than a quarter mile behind him.

"Shit! They will catch up to us in a couple of minutes."

The former PJ began to work on Plan B when his phone rang. Jason planned to ignore it but saw it was Archie and thought it could be beneficial to answer his call.

"Hey, Archie, I'm getting chased by several local police on Victor Romero's payroll in boats. They'll be on me in a few minutes, arrest Shanna and me, and take JJ. I can't let that happen."

"What?" Archie asked. "What are you going to do?"

"I plan to drop Shanna and JJ off and go on the offensive. I have a pistol with a few rounds left, so I may get lucky and take them out before they kill me."

"Hold on, Mulder," Archie growled. "That may be the dumbest plan I've ever heard!"

"I'm running out of time, so you got anything better?"

"Yeah, I've got a million better ideas, and one of them is why I called. Our friend Mike called me when he got word from an asset in Central America of a shootout on Ometepe Island. I told him you were in the area, and he thought it might be related to you."

"Faster, Archie, I'm about to run out of lake," Jason shouted over the whining engine.

"Can you get into Costa Rica?"

"I think so."

"There are about three kilometers of jungle between the south shore of Lake Nicaragua and the border, so you better find a way to get your wife, son, and yourself across it."

"What's in Costa Rica if we can get there?"

The engine sputtered again, forcing Jason to ease up on the throttle again. The police were close enough for Jason to see the determined looks on their faces. They were also close enough to shoot Jason and his family with their rifles.

"If you can get to Saint Cecilia on Highway 4, two kilometers inside Costa Rica, Mike has an asset who can get you to safety."

Jason turned to the police boats fifty yards behind. "Tell Mike I'll be there, but we'll be traveling on foot, so I don't know how long it will take. Who should I ask for in Saint Cecilia?"

"Mike will let his asset know you're coming, so he'll find you."

A bullet whizzed past Jason's head a nanosecond before he heard the shot from the police boat. "Gotta go. They're shooting at us."

Jason hung up and pushed the throttle as far forward as possible, but instead of speeding up, the engine sputtered and died. He pulled the Glock from his waist and fired at each boat racing toward him. Neither round connected, but both vessels took defensive measures and sped away from Jason.

He'd learn in minutes if he and Shanna had enough left in them to elude the police and escape into Costa Rica. If they failed, Jason's family legacy would end on a rocky beach in Nicaragua.

CHAPTER 46

The boat drifted and halted thirty yards from shore, forcing them to wade through the shallows of Lake Nicaragua. Jason carried JJ while Shanna sloshed behind them, both parents scanning the tree line for the quickest escape route. Thick gray clouds allowed the morning sun to intermittently peak through, but the jungle remained dark and inviting for someone on the run.

Jason heard the roar of the boat engines getting closer, and both police boats slammed into the shore seconds after Shanna, Jason, and JJ slipped into the tree line.

"Police!" a voice shouted in Spanish. "Stop, or we'll shoot!"

Jason's heart hammered against his ribs as he moved swiftly with JJ and urged Shanna, limping with her injured leg, to catch up. The corrupt officers wouldn't hesitate to kill them and eliminate all the witnesses with knowledge of Victor's operation.

"I can't," Shanna cried. "I can't go that fast with my leg."

He slowed down so they could all stick together while they eluded the police. Two hundred yards into the jungle, Jason kneeled at the edge of a clearing with a view of the oncoming police from the beach.

"Take JJ," Jason whispered. He handed her their sleeping sixteen-month-old son, who must have been exhausted from the traumatic events over the past month. He stirred but didn't wake.

"Head southeast through the jungle. I'll draw them away and meet you at the border."

"No!" Shanna barked as she pushed back on the handoff. "We're not splitting up. We have to do this together."

The crack of a pistol echoed through the jungle, sending shards of wood raining down upon them from above. Reacting quickly, Jason grabbed Shanna and pulled her into the safety of the thick underbrush. More gunshots pierced through the air, but the darkness of the early morning and the dense foliage provided enough cover to keep them hidden from the corrupt officers on their tail.

"Down!" Jason said as he covered JJ's mouth with his hand. Two officers from one of the boats were under thirty yards from their location. A police officer swept the area where they'd been standing moments before with his flashlight.

"They went deeper into the jungle," one said in Spanish. "They are heading toward the border with Costa Rica. We have to catch them before they cross."

"Does Victor want them alive or dead?" the other officer asked.

"He's not answering his phone."

"I think he'd want them dead," one of the officers stated.

"This is a great place to kill them. No one will ever know."

The officers darted into the jungle, and Jason took a brief break from the calamity to check his weapon. Five rounds remained in the magazine, which wasn't enough to sustain a prolonged firefight, especially with JJ and Shanna to protect. He had to be efficient and deadly accurate with every shot.

Jason scanned the area, checked the wound on his arm, and turned to Shanna, resting on a downed tree.

"The Costa Rican border is a few clicks from here," Jason said as he chopped his hand toward the southwest. "Can you make it if we go a little slower?"

Shanna bit her lower lip and nodded. "Yeah, if we don't go too fast."

"You lead to set the pace, and I'll navigate behind you."

They moved deeper into the jungle, Shanna leading while Jason followed her exact footsteps to minimize noise. Their trek through the jungle continued until they reached a narrow stand of trees, barely twenty feet across, with cliffs dropping into tributaries that flowed into Lake Nicaragua. Remaining hidden would be difficult, and the only way to reach the Costa Rican border was through the narrow jungle passage.

"Stop," Jason whispered. Shanna halted and dropped to one knee, just as Jason had taught her. He moved even with his wife and examined the areas to their left and right. Four officers from the boats were on foot and trying to track them in the jungle. They were closing in, and Jason accepted the fact that they weren't going to outrun the pursuing police with Shanna, JJ, and his injured arm. He had to confront them without putting his wife and son at risk.

"Take JJ for a minute while I figure out how to get through here," Jason whispered to Shanna.

Once JJ was in his mom's arms, Jason raised his head above the undergrowth to look at the obstacles ahead. He was still forming a plan when a branch snapped behind them. Jason spun and pushed Shanna and JJ behind a fallen log. Two flashlight beams illuminated the shadows, accompanied by a conversation in Spanish.

"We know you're out here," one officer called out. "We'll find you, and you'll regret running from us."

Jason tightened his hand around the Glock's grip and slid his finger through the trigger guard. He could kill both dirty officers, but they needed stealth to escape, not a firefight.

JJ whimpered softly. Shanna pressed him closer, but the sound carried through the trees. The flashlight beams swung toward their position.

Jason's fingers dug in the dirt by his feet and found a palm-sized rock. He threw it far to their right, and the officers took the bait, rushing toward the sound. The moment their backs turned, Jason led his family through the narrows and deeper into the jungle.

Jason and Shanna moved slower through the dense brush as they both fought crippling fatigue after the adrenaline rush of recovering their son wore off. Neither Shanna nor Jason had slept in two days, and she'd been impaled on the boat, and he'd been shot. They needed to find the strength to continue if they ever wanted to return home with their son.

They pushed deeper into the jungle and closer to the border but not fast enough to lose the police as exhaustion took its toll. JJ whimpered softly against Shanna's shoulder as branches scratched at their faces. Suddenly, footsteps crashed through the undergrowth behind them. Jason spun and met the officer an arm's length away as he emerged from the darkness. His pistol pointed at Jason's chest, and his wide eyes showed surprise.

The officer should have immediately pulled the trigger, because his hesitation was a fatal mistake. Jason pushed the barrel away from him and his family while simultaneously driving his blade up under the man's ribs. They grappled for a moment; the officer groaned and grunted as Jason continued to twist and apply pressure on his knife. The man went limp, and Jason lowered him quietly to the ground.

It wasn't as stealthy as Jason had hoped. He heard the officer's partner thundering through the underbrush toward his dead partner. Jason took shelter behind a tree with his family when the second officer found the bloody body of his fellow officer. After a rage-filled, spartan yell, he raised his pistol and fired wildly in all directions until his slide locked.

Jason moved from behind the tree, assumed a firing stance, and sent three rounds into the officer's chest.

"Our stealthy escape is blown. We need to run," Jason shouted. He put his good arm around Shanna to help her escape the area that would soon be crawling with crooked cops.

Minutes later, Jason saw more sunlight penetrating the jungle as they neared a clearing, so they stopped thirty yards away.

"You and JJ rest here while I check it out and ensure everything is clear."

Jason moved tactically to the clearing and saw it was a dirt road that didn't look like it was used very often. He checked his GPS and confirmed that Costa Rica was on the other side of the dirt path. Reaching Costa Rica didn't guarantee their safety, but it did get them closer to Mike's asset in Saint Cecilia. He remained at the road's edge for several minutes, looking and listening for approaching footsteps. Jason knew from his time in the Air Force that roads were notorious for ambushes by the enemy.

Detecting no human activity, Jason darted across the road to ensure the remaining two officers weren't waiting at the border for them. He reached the shredded barbed-wire fence that identified the Nicaraguan border with Costa Rica. Jason took note of the well-trodden footpath, a clear sign that this area was popular among illegal crossers. After thoroughly searching the area, he did not detect any immediate danger or cause for concern. He turned back to guide Shanna and JJ across the road when suddenly, a loud noise shattered the calm of the jungle, sending a jolt of fear up his spine. The sound of an engine revving filled the air, followed by the approaching rumble of a vehicle on the road he had just crossed.

"Shit!"

Someone must have watched me cross the road. Was it border control? Or are they Victor's men?

Jason reached the tree line along the road seventy yards from where a police SUV stopped suddenly and kicked up a cloud of dust. Both front doors opened, and he saw the logo identifying that the vehicle belonged to the San Jorge police, just across the lake from Shadow Island.

"More of Victor's police," Jason said to the jungle.

The cops on the boat must have called their partners on the mainland and had them stake out possible spots to cross the border.

A tall and short officer vanished through the trees as the dust settled.

"They're going for Shanna and JJ."

Jason bolted across the road and stealthily through the undergrowth back to his wife and son. A scream cut through the jungle like a giant machete.

"Don't hurt him!" a female voice pleaded.

The recognition that the voice belonged to Shanna arrived at the same time as a tsunami-sized wave of adrenaline exploded in Jason's gut. He pushed through the trees at a full sprint before the echoes of the scream died out in the jungle. A nightmare exponentially worse than the one he'd already lived with JJ's abduction was about to become a reality for Jason if he couldn't save his wife and son from the dirty cops.

Chapter 47

"No! No! No!" Jason mumbled repeatedly as he jumped over logs and slid down shallow ravines in his mad dash to reach Shanna and JJ. Less than a minute after the scream, Jason arrived at the location where he'd left his wife and son to rest.

Why didn't I leave the Glock with Shanna?

It was a knee-jerk question to the stressful situation, but Jason's rational mind knew that Shanna and JJ would likely have been shot if she had been armed.

He did a quick rotation with his eyes focused on the soft soil and saw the grooves of feet dragging toward the road.

"I have to get them before they're in the back of that SUV."

Stealth was no longer a concern as Jason crashed through the jungle like a charging bull. Sixty yards of jungle felt like a mile until Jason broke from the foliage and emerged twenty-five feet behind the SUV on the dirt road.

One officer held the back door open while the other shoved Shanna toward the back seat of the SUV. She held on to her wailing son with one arm and fought off the officer with her free arm.

Jason ejected the magazine of his Glock to confirm he had enough ammo to eliminate both officers.

"Shit! Only two left."

It was terrible news, but two rounds would be all he would need if he were efficient and accurate. Jason sidestepped until an unobstructed view of the officer holding the door came into view. He aimed through the steel sights of the old Glock until the stubby post hoovered between the officer's eyes. Jason exhaled and began to apply pressure on the trigger when Shanna's head flashed in front of his aim.

He looked over his weapon and saw Shanna flailing wildly outside the SUV as one officer pushed her inside the vehicle as she resisted with all her might. Jason knew the strength of his wife and was confident one officer couldn't get Shanna in the vehicle by himself.

The officer holding the door must have come to the same conclusion, because he left his post and moved behind the other officer to help push Shanna, fighting back viciously, into the SUV. Jason saw Shanna losing the battle as parts of her body disappeared into the back seat. He knew only seconds remained before she was inside with the door shut.

Jason took three steps forward to increase his chances of a successful kill shot. He aimed at the shorter police officer who had been holding the door and intended to shoot him first before quickly moving to the taller officer shoving Shanna and JJ into the SUV. Jason lined up the shot just as his wife and son disappeared into the police vehicle. He fired as the shorter officer slammed the door shut, and one of his final two bullets whizzed within an inch of his nose.

"Dammit!" Jason roared. He couldn't lose his wife and son to Victor's men.

The shorter officer spun, unholstered his pistol, and aimed at Jason in one move. Before he pulled the trigger, Jason sent his final round toward the officer. As soon as the slug cleared the end of his barrel, he charged aggressively toward the second target. Jason felt for his knife when he saw both officers fall to the ground in a thud.

Jason stopped and scanned the area to see if someone else had fired a shot. The place was deserted, so Jason kept his Glock trained on the men despite the slide being locked to the rear as he cautiously approached them. He noted a gaping hole through the left eye of the short officer and a growing crimson circle over the chest of the taller officer behind him. Jason had killed two men with his last bullet.

"It's about time I had some damn luck."

Jason hurriedly opened the door and extended his hand to help Shanna out.

"Are you okay?"

Shanna handed JJ to Jason, then slid out of the SUV, pushing her long black hair back from her eyes and adjusting her disheveled clothes.

"I'm okay now. Where are we?"

"We're at the border, but we're still not in the clear. We need to get moving before their friends show up."

Shanna started up the road and turned into the jungle. "Okay, let's go."

Severe thirst gripped the Mulders as the sun moved overhead. Jason's muscles screamed with exhaustion, and each step required more effort than the last.

"Are we there yet?" Shanna asked.

"We have to be close."

Jason checked his GPS. "We should see signs of Saint Cecelia on the other side of this hill."

A small village with simple wooden houses, smoke rising from their chimneys, lined a paved road that carved its way through the jungle in the distance. They trudged toward the village, and Jason scanned for someone willing to provide water. A shadowy figure detached from a nearby building and moved toward Jason and his family.

A massive man stepped into their path, his wild beard and muscled frame marking him as someone who could end their escape with his bare hands. Jason moved in front of Shanna and JJ, knowing he had no ammo and little strength left for another fight, but he was willing to die to save his family. The protective father felt the knife in his pocket as the menacing man blocked their passage into the village.

The giant studied them momentarily then spoke in a distinct New York accent. "Are you the Mulders?"

Jason blinked, his tired mind struggling to process the question. "Who wants to know?"

A grin split the man's beard. "I'm Mike's friend. He called in a favor and said you need safe passage back to San José to get home."

Jason's knees nearly buckled with relief. Behind him, Shanna let out a sob that was half laugh, half cry. JJ, picking up on the change in mood, blurted out a string of unintelligible words that sounded musical to Jason.

"Come on," the asset said, already leading them out of the jungle. "Let's get you folks out of here."

Shanna stood next to Jason and wrapped her arm around his waist. "Is it really over?"

Jason kissed Shanna on top of her head before looking at his son, who returned a toothless grin to his father. "Yes, it's finally finished."

Chapter 48

Three Days Later in Whispering Pines, Arizona

Jason sipped his coffee on the back patio as the rising sun melted the frost from the pale-yellow grass in his backyard. He wore a jacket to remain comfortable in the brisk February air, but it was a refreshing change from the oppressive humidity he'd endured for weeks in Central America. Knowing that his wife and son were sleeping soundly inside his home only feet away from him brought Jason a sense of peace he'd never experienced, and he planned to savor it for as long as possible.

The solitude and serenity of his house nestled among the pines were a welcome relief from the whirlwind of visitors, hospital visits, FBI debriefs, and phone conversations over the past two days. He briefly spoke with Zee's girlfriend on the phone and had an extended conversation with Archie and Special Agent Holland to thank them for their support, which had led to JJ's recovery. Holland was appreciative, while Archie scolded Jason for asking Shanna to come to Central America to help.

After Shanna's mom and Jason's parents had reunited with their grandson, Jason spent most of his time with Special Agent Reddy from the FBI. Initially, she was hostile with her questions about how, and mainly why, Jason chose to keep her in the dark about JJ when she could have helped. Two hours into the debrief, she appeared to thaw and understand that Jason did the only thing he could have under the circumstances.

"JJ is lucky for the experience and skills you have from the Air Force and DEA. If you were an ordinary guy on the street, we'd be holding another vigil right now for both of you," Reddy admitted as she departed.

Jason finished his coffee and rose from his patio chair to refill his cup. He adjusted the sling on his left arm, stabilizing his biceps until his stitches were removed. The sound of gravel crackling under tires in his driveway caught his attention, so Jason moved to the railing and saw two black SUVs enter his driveway. He couldn't see through the dark-tinted windshield, but Jason wasn't concerned. His entire arsenal of weapons was just inside his back door, and he wouldn't hesitate to unleash a barrage of deadly force upon anyone who dared to harm his family.

Central, from his PSD team in Washington, DC, jumped out of the first SUV. He scanned the area and nodded to the second vehicle. Clay exited and opened the back door, which revealed Senator Conrad and Chief of Staff Crenshaw. Jason rushed down the patio steps and met the team in his driveway.

He shook Senator Conrad's hand and hugged Clay, Crenshaw, and Central with his good arm.

"What are you all doing here?" Jason asked.

"We're attending a summit at Lake Powell with all the states impacted by the POLAR ACT to review additional legislation," Crenshaw answered. "Thanks to you and this team, the POLAR Act may be even stronger by this summer."

"We arrived early and took this detour to check on you and your family," Senator Conrad added. "So, how are you all doing?"

Jason lifted his arm for everyone to see. "I'm doing well, and Shanna and JJ also seem okay, considering what everyone went through. Thank you for coming to check on us."

"You're a tough son of a bitch, Mulder, but you may be the weakest link in the family. That wife and son of yours are tough as nails," Senator Conrad said with a chuckle.

"Thank you, Senator. That means a lot to me."

"Sorry for the quick visit, but we have to get to Lake Powell soon," Crenshaw said.

The senator, Central, and Chief of Staff Crenshaw shuffled toward the SUVs, when Clay called out to them. "I need a minute with Mulder."

"Walk with me," Clay said, moving toward Jason's backyard. They stopped out of earshot from the SUVs and faced each other.

"I'm thrilled you and your family are back home and safe. I wasn't sure you were going to pull this one off."

Jason's eyes fell to his boots. "I still can't believe Zee is gone."

They both faced the woods behind Jason's house without speaking until Clay explained the real reason they had shown up unannounced.

"Are you going to come back to work with us?" Clay asked.

Jason knew the answer, but it was harder to tell Clay than he'd thought. Clay took the hesitation as indecision and tried to sell Jason on returning. "I know it was crazy before you left because of the CFO Act that got everyone on the Hill whipped up in a frenzy, but it died in committee. The bill will never see the light of day, so protecting Conrad won't be as challenging."

It was an appealing proposition with the CFO Act dead, but Jason had made up his mind. He was not going to live and work so far from his family.

"Clay, I love working with you, and I like Conrad and everyone else on his staff, but I can't work in Washington, DC, with my family here."

Clay removed the plastic straw that was like a permanent fixture from his mouth and smiled. "I figured you'd say that, but I had to give it one more try. What are you going to do now?"

"I haven't figured that out yet."

"We've already worked together a couple of times, so keep me posted when you finalize your plans," Clay said. "You don't know what's around the corner for either of us."

"You never know," Jason replied.

Clay gave Jason a side-hug and returned to the SUV. Jason watched them back out of his driveway, sad to see them go but resolute in his decision to stay home with his family instead of joining the caravan driving to Lake Powell.

After lunch, Shanna, Jason, and JJ were on the carpeted floor in the family room, playing with JJ's new toys from his grandparents. A knock drew their attention to the back door, where Jason saw his brother, Noah, and his girlfriend, Morgan, through the glass.

"Come in," Jason shouted.

Noah and Morgan entered and rushed into the living room. Jason's brother immediately picked up his nephew and spun him around, to JJ's delight.

"I'm sorry it took me so long to get here. I was at a conference in Philly and just got home late last night."

Shanna and Morgan visited while Noah played with JJ. Jason watched contently from his chair in the adjacent dining room. After the one-year-old was tired of playing with his uncle and returned to his new toys, Noah joined Jason at the table.

"What are you going to do now?" Noah asked.

Jason noticed Shanna turn her attention from Morgan to their conversation.

"I'm not sure yet."

"Are you going back to DC?"

"No. I'm definitely not heading back to DC."

"Are you resigning from the senator's security detail?"

Jason looked up at the wood beams on his ceiling and back at Noah. "No more military, law enforcement, or security teams for me. I'm done."

Shanna limped next to the table, still recovering from the new stitches in her leg. "So what are you going to do?"

Jason shrugged.

"We should team up and start a family search-and-rescue business with my drones and your pararescueman skills," Noah added.

JJ wobbled into the dining room, wedged himself between his father's knees, and held up his arms. Jason picked up his son and placed him on his lap.

"A family business?" Jason inquired. "Tell me more."

***

Robert Goluba writes adrenaline-fueled action thrillers with grit, wit, and heart.

He was born and raised in Central Illinois, where he attended college, served in the Army National Guard, and met his wife. At age thirty, after a self-diagnosed allergy to snow, he moved to sunny Arizona, where he now lives with his wonderful wife, two kids, and canine companion.

He's published four books in the Jason Mulder Action Thriller Series: **CARTEL HUNTER, REVERSE PURSUIT, STRIKE BACK, and FINAL SHOWDOWN.**

Robert loves hiking, spending time outdoors, watching football, and reading thrillers and mysteries.

Visit RobertGoluba.com to learn more.